REQUIEM OF THE SOUL

A SOVEREIGN SONS NOVEL

A. ZAVARELLI

NATASHA KNIGHT

PROLOGUE
IVY

The lace of my dress scratches my skin. I shiver. It's cold, a wet cold as soft mist turns to rain. Rain on your wedding day is good luck, right? Isn't that what they say?

Candles protected inside glass lanterns line the stairs leading up to the double front doors. I stare up at them, remembering the last time I stood here. It's been a while.

The doors are opened. Organ music and incense pour out.

I close my eyes, listening to the sound, and take a deep breath. The scent and sound combined are dizzying.

No, it's not those things that have me swaying on my feet. It's what's coming. What's waiting for me at the end of the aisle.

My brother wraps his hand around my arm. He mutters a curse as he rights me.

I grip my bouquet of blood-red roses. If I'm not careful, I'll crush them. They're striking. Beautiful. Like my dress. He has impeccable taste, my fiancé, and he likes things a certain way. He has rules. And he's used to getting exactly what he wants.

I'm slow as we ascend the stairs toward the entrance. It irritates my brother, I know, but everything irritates him. The toe of his shoe catches my long veil, tugging my head backward momentarily. A few steps more and we stand inside the vestibule, the organ louder, the incense stronger, combining with the smell of melting wax.

The doors close behind us, that final divide between what was and what will be. My past and my present. The voice inside my head urging me to run grows louder, but I don't run. It's no use.

Our guests rise to their feet, gazes blank as they turn back to look at me, their sacrificial bride. I don't see their faces, though. They're just shapes in my periphery. I only have eyes for one man. The stranger before the altar. The stranger in whose bed I'll sleep tonight.

I feel numb. Like it's not real. Like it's not me.

The room sways, and my brother's grip tightens. I'll have a bruise tomorrow. We take one step then another. I clutch my bouquet like it's my lifeline. My nails break the skin of my palms, the blood slippery, wet, the pain keeping me from giving in to the vertigo.

A thousand candles bathe the cathedral in a soft glow, the music more fitting for a Requiem Mass than a wedding march. I guess he chose that too. It goes with the dress at least. My fiancé's doing. I understand why.

My eyes lock on him. He's half-turned toward us, watching us.

My brother walks me past our guests. I only recognize one or two. All men. Only men. A dozen of them. My own mother is absent. I glance at my brother, see a dark smear of dirt or blood on his collar. I hadn't noticed it before, and I want to ask what it is but don't. His jaw is set, eyes hard. It should have been my father walking me down the aisle, but he can't do that.

Sadness washes over me, but I don't have time for it. Not here. Not now. Because we're almost there.

I look down at the polished marble floor cold against my bare feet, and I take my final steps to the altar where every sound is amplified in this strange dream that is somehow my reality.

My brother turns me to face him. He lifts the veil, then leans down to brush his cold cheek against mine. My eyes lock on my fiancé over his shoulder. His face is still in shadows, but he's watching us. Watching me. I see the glint of hazel eyes.

Santiago De La Rosa.

The man who has chosen me for his wife.

The man to whom I will belong.

My brother straightens. With a tug, he offers my hand to Santiago.

I swallow hard, my heart pounding against my chest, and when Santiago takes my wrist, the flowers slip from my grasp to scatter at our feet, blood-red against the stark, cold marble.

I barely notice because I am riveted.

Because that's when the candles flicker, sending light and shadows dancing across his face, and I get my first real glimpse of him. My breath catches in my throat, the gasp drowned out by the organ, by the sound of the priest telling the witnesses to be seated, and the creaking of the ancient pews as the ceremony begins.

TWO DAYS EARLIER

1

I keep my head ducked against the rain as I climb out of my car and tug my bag out from behind the seat. It's a worn messenger I'd found collecting dust in the attic before I left for school this past fall. I strap it over my shoulder and hurry toward the apartment building.

In my rush to get inside, I almost miss it. But some things you don't have to see to know they're there. Some things you feel.

And the instant I feel it, I come to a dead stop in the middle of the lot. Rain soaks through my thin coat, but I ignore it as I turn to look at the one car that doesn't belong here. That doesn't fit. A shiny black sedan with tinted windows. Rolls Royce. Their signature vehicle. Old-fashioned. Elegant. And screaming of money and power.

My heart races.

Through the windshield, I can see that no one's inside, so I walk a few steps closer, and if I had any doubt who it might belong to, it's wiped out in the next moment because there, embossed on the leather headrest, I see it. Even through the rain-skewed glass, even in this dark night and without the help of the busted streetlamp, I can make out the gold lettering in the familiar font.

I.V.I.

I shudder, cold and sweating at once.

I always knew they could come at any time, didn't I? That was part of the agreement.

"No." Shaking my head, I turn to the building's entrance and walk toward it, no longer hurrying through the rain.

It doesn't have to be something bad. Maybe my dad's come for a surprise visit.

Maybe it's the reason Evangeline hasn't answered her texts all night.

Once inside the building, I stop and take a deep breath in, then out.

It's nothing bad. The car could be Dad's.

Then where is Joseph, his trusted driver?

I climb the stairs to my second-floor apartment, looking around for Joseph or my father. I don't see either man.

My father has a key, so he's probably waiting inside my apartment.

But something's wrong. I've felt it all day.

And there's no avoiding whatever it is. I know that when I walk down the hall to see the door of my apartment is ajar. It's just slight, not left wide open, and there's a light on inside. Whoever it is doesn't want to surprise me.

I push the door open but don't quite enter. Instead, I stand on my own welcome mat looking into the living room of the small apartment.

The light is coming from my bedroom.

I take a deep breath in and step inside. I don't close the door behind me. On the counter lies a ring of keys, a pair of worn black leather gloves ominous beside them.

But it's when I smell the aftershave that my stomach sinks.

Not Dad.

As if he's been listening to my thoughts, my half brother, Abel, steps through the bedroom door and into the living room. Stopping, he cocks his head to the side and looks me over, his expression that of someone utterly unimpressed.

"Don't you own an umbrella?" he asks. They're the first words he's spoken to me in over a year.

I slide the messenger bag off my shoulder to ease it to the floor, then unbutton my coat as I try to keep calm. Or at least appear so on the outside.

"What are you doing here? How did you get a key?"

He steps into the light and smiles. He hasn't

changed. His smile is little more than a sneer, his eyes disapproving as I take off my soaked coat and drape it over the back of a chair.

"It's nice to see you, too, sis." He walks past me into the kitchen and picks up the bottle of whiskey I keep for when Dad comes. He opens it, sniffs, then takes a clean glass out of the drying rack and pours himself some. "Should you be drinking?" he asks, turning to me and leaning against the counter as he sips.

"It's not for me. It's Dad's. What are you doing here?"

"Can't I come visit my sister?"

I don't bother to answer that. Abel and I have a hate-hate relationship. He hates me, and I hate him. Have from day one. He's a jerk.

"Why are you so late?" he asks, tone ugly. Walking over to my desk, I see he's been through my calendar and my notes from various classes. I wonder what he thought he'd find.

"I had to work. Why are you here, Abel?" I close the calendar. There's nothing he'd uncover anyway so I'm not worried about it. I know the rules, and I know myself. As much as I'd like to say I don't care about them or the consequences, I do.

"The library closed an hour ago. You were still working?"

"It's called clean up. How do you know the library hours anyway? Are you having me followed? I'm here with Dad's blessing, and you know—"

"I hope you're not lying, Ivy. I hope you weren't on a date."

He swallows the last of his drink, sets his glass in the sink, and walks into the living room.

"Is that why you were going through my calendar?"

He grins. "I have some bad news." He shrugs his shoulders. "And some good news. Which do you want to hear first?"

That sinking feeling I've had all day is back. I put my hand on the back of the chair to steady myself.

Abel doesn't miss it. "Don't fucking pass out. Like I said, it's not all bad."

"What is it?"

"Dad's taken ill."

Abel's never been close to anyone in the family, but that's not exactly out of the ordinary. We're not so close-knit. But the way he says it is almost like he's gloating or happy.

"What do you mean?"

"I mean he's had some sort of attack—"

"Attack? Like a heart—"

"Let me finish," he says, taking a seat on the sofa and stretching one arm across the back of it. With the other hand, he touches the small hole in the cushion beside the one he's sitting on. A cigarette burn, I guess. "Are you smoking, Ivy?" he asks, sounding genuinely shocked.

"The furniture came with the apartment. It was already like that. What happened to dad?" I get my bag and dig around for my cell phone.

"That's not going to do any good," he says when he sees the phone in my hand. "Dad can't come to the phone right now," he mimics the typical recording, but his tone is strange, eerie.

"What is wrong with you?" I push the button to call Dad, and it goes right to voicemail. I try Evangeline and get the same thing. I even try my mother, and hers just rings and rings.

Abel's on his feet, taking my phone from me with his big hand. He ends the call and tucks the phone into his pocket.

I look up at my older half brother. Almost ten years my senior, he's the product of Dad's first marriage and ever hateful of my sisters and me, the products of his second, acknowledged marriage.

His face grows dark. "He's in a coma. They're running tests, but it's not looking good."

"What? How? When?"

"Two days ago."

"And you're just telling me now? Where is he?"

"At the hospital. Where do you think he'd be?"

"Which hospital?"

He looks at me like I'm stupid. I know which hospital. Members of The Society only go to one.

I turn and hurry into my bedroom to pack a few things. I'll be heading home. I have to. God. I never thought I'd go back of my own free will.

"Don't you want to hear the good news?" Abel asks me from the doorway.

I glance at him as he casually leans against the frame.

"No, I don't. Dad's in the hospital, and I need to go see him. Find out what's going on. It's not like you're telling me anything, is it?"

He steps into the bedroom. "I'll tell you what I think you need to know."

"Do you even care?"

He looks at me like he's confused by my question.

I shake my head. Stupid thing to ask. I rummage under my bed and pull out a duffel bag. Setting it on the bed, I unzip it. "I need to pack some things. Just get out, Abel." I open a drawer and take out a few sweaters.

"You won't be needing any of that," he says, walking toward me and catching my wrist. "Someone will clear out the apartment, but there's no time for that now."

I look down at where he's holding me. His grip isn't hard, but he's crossing a line. I shift my gaze up to his. His eyes are dark and empty. Ever since I was a little girl, the look of soullessness inside them has always scared me.

"Let go of me."

He doesn't. Instead, he checks the time on his other wrist. "We need to go."

"I'm not going with you. I have my own car. I can—"

"I said we need to go."

A feeling of dread comes over me. A familiar anxiety. And I process what he said a moment ago. That someone will come to clear out the apartment.

"Let go."

"You didn't hear the good news, Ivy," he says, his tone serious. "The time has come for you to fulfill your duty to the family."

I'm going to be sick.

"You've been chosen," he adds almost formally.

My heartbeat accelerates, a wave of nausea making me clutch my stomach.

Chosen.

It was always a possibility, if not a probability. But our family, we're not very high on The Society's social scale. Not as desirable as either my mother or father would have liked. And after what happened with Hazel, the chances of any of the Sovereign Sons choosing either my sister or me narrowed even more.

"What do you mean?" I ask him, my throat dry.

With an exhale, he releases my wrist and grips my jaw instead, turning my head so I have to look up at him. He brushes my hair back from my face, my right eye.

I lower my lashes and shift my gaze away. A cold, clammy sweat creeps along my skin. Abel squeezes my jaw. I know what he wants, so I do it. I force myself to look at him.

He focuses on my right eye. The one with what my mother considers a deformity. It's just pigment. It doesn't impact my vision. It would probably go unnoticed if my eyes were darker. There was actually a period when I was younger that my mother made me wear dark contact lenses to hide what looks like an elongated pupil, almost like a cat's eye. My great-grandmother on my father's side had it too, and I took after my dad's side of the family with olive skin and dark hair. Light green eyes are all I inherited from my mother, and they only amplify the flaw.

My brother makes a face of disgust. "God knows why, but he chose you."

He releases me, almost tossing me away like you'd toss out a used tissue. I get it. It's creepy. Hideous even. It's why I keep my bangs longer so people don't have to look at it.

I hug the sweater I'm still holding on to and try to focus on what matters. "I'm going to go see Dad. Then I'm coming back to school."

"No, you're not. That pipe dream is over. It should never have been allowed in the first place. Your selfishness has caused a lot of problems, Ivy."

Sweat runs down the back of my neck. I hold Abel's gaze as the room around him spins. "I won't," I mutter.

"I'm head of this household now. I'll say what you will and what you won't. And I'll tell you right now you will do as you're told, and you won't shame this family again."

Hazel. He means Hazel. He was so angry when she left, he wanted to go after her himself. Find her and drag her back, kicking and screaming.

"Abel—"

"Don't you even want to know who it is?" I can't tell if his smile is one of pride or spite.

"I don't care who. I won't do it. I'm not—"

"Yes, you will, sweet sister. If I have to drag you to the altar myself, you will." He takes my arm and starts to lead me out of the bedroom and through the apartment. "Now, there's a lot to do before the wedding and not much time. He's certainly anxious to get his hands on you."

I pull back, trying to free myself. "Stop. I'm not going with you, and I'm not getting married to a stranger!" I catch hold of the back of the couch. It's stupid, I know, but it's all I can do. "Let me go!"

Abel tugs, and my grip slips. "You're acting like a fucking baby, Ivy."

"Our father wouldn't allow this!"

He stops, then releases me. He tilts his head to study me, and the look on his face is enough to have me scrambling backward as he advances on me.

I put my arms up in defense, but he grabs my wrists to tug them out of the way. And when the back of his hand comes crashing across my face, and he simultaneously releases me, the impact sends me flying into the wall.

I'm stunned, both by the violence and the pain of the blow. For a moment, the room goes dark. I slip to the floor, my hand on my cheek. It stings, feels hot, and the back of my head throbs.

"Shit." He reaches down and hauls me up by my arms. "See what you made me do?" he asks through gritted teeth.

I feel a tear slide down my cheek as I try to focus my eyes. I don't want to cry. I don't want to be afraid. And I know this is it. I know he's right. I'll do what he says because I have to. I've always known it could come to this. But I'd thought my father had safeguarded me.

My father.

"I want to see Dad."

"I told you—"

"First. Let me see him first."

He considers. "Now you're being reasonable."

He lets me go, steps backward, and I can see from his face he's of two minds about what just happened. Not sorry—that's a stretch too far for my brother—but split. I wonder if it has to do with whoever *chose* me.

Chosen.

God. Does The Society realize we don't live in the Dark Ages anymore?

He checks his watch again. "We need to go."

"I just want to get a few things."

He grits his jaw, but then nods once. "Five minutes. I'll be downstairs."

I nod too.

"Don't try to run, Ivy. I'll send soldiers after you if you run."

"Where would I go, Abel?"

He studies me, eyes narrowed in hate, then walks to the door.

"Who?" I call out just as he gets there, my curiosity getting the better of me.

He stops and turns back to face me.

"Who is it?" I ask.

He smirks like he's won some strange secret victory. "Now you want to know who?"

"Just tell me."

That smirk vanishes. In fact, all emotion but hate vanishes. "It's fitting, actually."

I stare at him, not understanding. "What do you mean?"

"I'll let you see for yourself."

"Who, Abel?"

"Santiago De La Rosa."

2

I ease my body onto the marble pew in the De La Rosa family chapel as my gaze moves to the flickering candles up on the altar. The space remains unchanged since my father designed it. White marble columns, ornate gold embellishments, decadence in every fine point. This holy sanctuary is just one of many extravagances in this estate long established by my bloodline. For decades, the Da La Rosa lineage has flourished in this manor. There was never any question that I would possess it someday. I just hadn't expected it to be so soon. Now, I am the chosen descendant doomed to haunt these halls where memories remain etched into every surface.

My father used to bring me to this chapel as a boy when there was a lesson to be learned. Lorenzo De La Rosa was not a soft man. He was a direct heir to a founding father of *Imperium Valens Invictum*. A Sovereign Son. Our society is a well-established organization rooted in powerful dynasties around the world. Some call us thieves in the night. A criminal syndicate. Mafia. The truth is much more intricate than any of those simplistic terms.

Our ancestors learned long ago there was power in secrecy. The legacy handed down to us was much more evolved than that of the criminals waging war on each other in the streets. We have money. We have power. And we are much more sophisticated than your average knee-breaking Italian mob boss.

IVI holds its members in the highest regard. With that power comes expectation. Education. Professionalism. And above all, discretion. By day, we appear as any other well-bred member of society. They don't and never will know the way our organization operates.

From infancy, my father anointed me with this same great responsibility. He was a well-respected member of the upper echelon in our society, and he was determined that his children would be molded in his image, no matter the cost.

The cost won me many hard lessons over the years. Kneeling on hard marble flooring for hours. The bite of a leather strap against my skin. The sting of a wooden paddle. The repetition of prayers and the smothering guilt of repentance for never being quite...*enough.*

De La Rosas can't afford to be soft. My father's words still echo off the walls as my eyes drift over the photos of him and my brother Leandro hung on opposite sides of the altar. I have no doubt in my mind they would tell me the next steps are imminent and necessary. The only way to right the wrong of their deaths is to punish without mercy. Their blood is on Eli Moreno's hands, and that motherfucker just had to go and get sick before I could squeeze every last wisp of his soul from his body.

My head dips as the force of my rage rises within me and blackens my vision. For four years, I've been waiting for this. Four years of countless surgeries and physical therapy. Endless anguish and grief have been my only companions in the darkness while I searched for answers to the truth.

Eli can't take this away from me. His illness won't be the easy way out. While he lays in that hospital bed, shriveling up and withering to nothing, I will destroy everything he ever loved. And if he should wake again, it will be to a horror even worse than death.

Fate has decided for me. Time is a luxury I no longer have, so I must act now. That certainty is vibrating through my bones and rattling the rusted cage around my heart. Every last Moreno will pay in blood and misery so acute, they will know suffering more intimately than I ever could.

The passage door at the side of the chapel

crashes open, jarring me from my thoughts as my entire body reacts with a violent shudder. How fucking difficult is it to indulge my one simple request of complete silence in my own home?

The new maid spills into the room, unaware of my presence as she switches on the light. The brightness stings my eyes, and I watch her in disbelief as she begins to dust the pews, humming as she works. She hasn't noticed me yet because she's wearing earbuds, and her senses are duller than a mouse heading straight for a trap.

Slowly, I rise to my full height and pivot my head to look at her. She catches the movement from the corner of her eye and glances up at me. In a fraction of a second, her face morphs to horror as she witnesses me without the benefit of dim lighting. The duster she was using clatters to the floor, and she brings a trembling hand to her mouth, but not before a scream erupts from her throat.

Every fiber in my body knits together as I pierce her with an unrelenting gaze. I should be used to the revulsion by now. Yet on the rare occasion someone glimpses me in the light, I am reminded who I am. The monster lurking in the shadows. The scarred remains of the only De La Rosa male to crawl from the ashes of our destruction. This is what I have been reduced to. And this is why those responsible will pay in blood.

"What did I tell you about the lights?" I roar.

The maid shrinks into herself, bursting into a fit of hysterical tears as she shakes her head, scuttling away like I might devour her soul at any moment. In her hasty retreat, she manages to switch off the light and seal me back into the room, as if that would stop me should I decide to give chase. But she is not the prey my soul hungers for, and I doubt after tonight, I will ever see her again.

I WATCH THE SALES ASSISTANT IN THE FULL-LENGTH mirror as she wheels out a selection of dresses as requested. Her eyes are cast toward the floor, and she never looks at me once. At least she is capable of following directions. Or perhaps she is just terrified of me, as most women are.

The luxury clothing store squatting in the shopping district on Canal Street is owned by IVI, so it isn't a problem to wake someone in the middle of the night to meet me here. That's the power of the De La Rosa name. As a Sovereign Son, nobody challenges my whims. And if they are smart, they follow my demands without question.

This mousy little assistant has done so to my exact specifications. The shop is dimly lit, with only a few flickering candles casting a soft glow over the expensive fabrics hanging from the racks. There is no background noise, not even the gentle whirr of a fan. Silence and darkness. They are my two constant requirements in life.

"I'll return with a few more in just a moment, Mr. De La Rosa."

She exits to the back room with brisk footsteps, leaving me to study my reflection in the mirror. It isn't often I indulge in such an act, considering I had all but two of the shiny surfaces removed from my home. The grotesque sight of the face staring back at me is almost unrecognizable. Although improved from the surgeries, and somewhat hidden beneath the permanent half Calavera mask tattooed on my face, the reflection still feels like a stranger to me. A face more suited to Dia de Los Muertos, with shading around the eyes and jaw, creating a lifelike representation of a skull. One foot in the grave, some might say.

I added the markings to cover my scars, but they also serve as a reminder of all that was lost. A permanent memorial to my father, my brother, and the friends taken the day Eli Moreno betrayed me.

I'm not even aware of the soft clicking of the door until Mercedes is upon me, making her presence known with a smirk as she comes to a standstill beside me. My sister is tall and beautiful like our mother. She lures men in with a sweet smile, but she's as toxic as poison. Her hair is long, the same shade of black as mine, and she inherited my father's dark eyes, while I inherited my mother's hazel. She is the youngest, too intelligent for her own good, and too spoiled to do anything with it. When it came to our father, Mercedes did not escape his brutality, but she was often shielded by Leandro and myself. As much as we could, at least.

"Santi." She smooths her palms over my shoulders, examining the fabric of my blazer with a keen eye. "Is this new?"

She's referring to the bespoke Canali cream suit stitched around my frame with such mastery, I'd venture a guess there isn't another in the world like it. It was made to please me alone, but Mercedes has always had a taste for the finer things in life. A side effect of the family disease we call wealth. Wealthy doesn't even begin to touch on our lineage. We bleed gold.

"What are you doing here?" I ask her. "You should be offering your services where they are needed."

"Did you think I wouldn't come?" She pouts. "Oh, how you wound me, my dear brother. As soon as I received your message, I gave my notice and came straight back home."

"You should have stayed," I answer flatly. "Your presence isn't required."

Ignoring my sharp remark, she meets my gaze in the mirror. "Tell me the truth. Is it really happening now?"

"Yes. I have no choice. Eli has fallen ill, forcing my hand."

Mercedes releases a breath, and a slow smile bleeds across her crimson lips. "Finally."

"You have other things to occupy your time," I tell her. "Like finding some poor soul to marry you. This isn't your concern."

She steps in front of me, grabbing me by the lapels as she glares up at me. "I'm not leaving. This isn't just about you. You aren't the only one who lost them, and you aren't the only one who's been waiting years for revenge."

For a moment, a frisson of guilt moves through me. I know I'm not the only one who lost them. Our entire family is dead, and Mercedes has been leaving an unchecked wake of devastation in her path ever since. But she can't be levelheaded about this. If it were up to her, revenge would be bloody and swift, leaving a gaping hole of discontentment that could never be filled. She doesn't have the patience or the foresight to see the possibilities of drawing it out. A swift death is only preferable to those who are on the receiving end of it.

"You will have your revenge." I pry her hands off my suit. "But it will be done my way."

"Of course it will." She placates me with a soft tone. "All I'm asking for is a front row seat. I want to help. Whatever task you give me, no matter how small, I will savor it. Please, Santiago. Let me be a part of this."

"I will consider it."

The sales assistant returns with more dresses, hanging them up and asking if I require anything else at the moment before she disappears again. As I stalk toward them, Mercedes is right beside me, her eyes fixed on the side of my face.

I ignore her and begin to examine the pieces carefully, one by one. They are all black, as I requested. Lace and pearls and silk are too beautiful for the likes of Ivy Moreno. Yet she will have one regardless. No wife of mine will marry me in tatters, but I will surely take pleasure in seeing the destruction of her beautiful dress once the ceremony is over.

"You're actually buying her a gown?" Mercedes scoffs. "Why?"

"Because she will be my wife," I growl. "And I will not have her tarnish the De La Rosa name by wearing anything I don't approve of."

"She will be a De La Rosa in name only," she snarls. "Who cares what she wears when her blood will stain the floors of The Manor? If it were up to me, I would do it at the ceremony in front of her family for all to see. She should have to walk naked over fiery coals to deserve your hand in marriage."

"That's why it isn't up to you."

"I still don't understand why you have to marry her. Just torture her and be done with it."

"You don't have to understand." I dismiss her coldly.

The room falls silent, and I can feel Mercedes watching me as I pick apart each dress. There is still much to be done, and her presence is only delaying my efforts. But sending her away now would only add to the salt in her wound.

I reach for the finest dress in the selection and hang it on the end of the rack. After I call for the sales assistant and tell her to package it up, Mercedes mutters under her breath.

"She doesn't deserve to wear something so beautiful. Fucking Morenos."

"Perhaps not, but it's not your decision to make."

She watches me carefully as I roam the store, seeking out a pair of heels to match. The jeweler will be here soon with a selection of rings. The rest I can send my staff to pick up. Flowers. Candles. Hairpieces. I pause in front of a lingerie display, swallowing the knot in my throat.

"You must be kidding," Mercedes hisses. "Don't tell me you actually plan to bed that awful woman."

I finger the black lace and try to imagine what Ivy would look like in such a display. My enemy and my soon-to-be wife. The woman twelve years my junior. I have not seen her up close in years. Not since the explosion. But I have watched her. I know her curves, her softness, her impossibly girlish dreams of escaping this life. She will be mine to do with as I please. Mine to take. Touch. Torment.

And horrify.

As if I've been burned, I yank my hand away and reach for the pen in my pocket. Too late, I realize Mercedes continues to watch me like a relentless hawk, devouring my every move and silent thought for her own motives she will undoubtedly remind me of later.

"What is that?" Her eyes flick over the pen curiously.

I return it to my pocket and ignore her. A potentially dangerous move when it comes to my sister. She has a habit of unearthing information, and my reaction will only serve to intensify her curiosity. I know her well enough to understand this one universal truth about her. The woman is nothing if not determined.

She only discovered my suspicions about Eli's betrayal because she went rifling through my office herself when I wouldn't give her the answers she wanted. After she uncovered my files on the Moreno family, she was like a python chasing a rodent. Unstoppable. Even now, she's practically frothing at the mouth, and I know I will have to be vigilant about the rules when it comes to Ivy.

Mercedes might want her vengeance, but she also understands her place. I am the head of the De La Rosa household. It is me who controls her life.

Her destiny. And she knows better than to even blink without my approval first. It will be the same with Ivy.

Sweet, poisonous Ivy.

"When will you kill her?" Mercedes asks, her voice tinged with the need for reassurance.

I ignore her and pick out a pair of heels for my bride, much to my sister's annoyance.

"If I didn't know any better, I would think you actually want to marry this woman," she accuses.

I glance at her so there can be no misunderstandings between us. "What I want is to destroy her. Make no mistake about it. It will be done."

"Then tell me how?" she begs, her voice betraying a raw grief she rarely displays. "Tell me how you will kill her."

I have only one answer for her.

"Slowly."

3

IVY

A little after two in the morning, we turn onto the cul-de-sac where our home sits. Well, home is a stretch. It's the house I grew up in. I know Hazel felt the same way, and I suspect Evangeline does too.

At least I'll get to see her. My little sister is just thirteen years old. I'd been thirteen when things changed for me. That was the year The Society stepped into our lives in a way they hadn't before.

The Moreno family is pretty low in the hierarchy as far as desirability in what I've always considered as being about a step away from a cult. There's almost a sort of caste system, one upon which my father's side of the family didn't rank well.

My mother is a different story.

My father had a wife before her. He never mentioned her when we were growing up. I don't even know her name. In fact, I've only ever seen a photo of her once. That was when I was late one morning on the way to school and needed to grab lunch money, and Dad's wallet was the only one around.

I missed the bus that day because when the small thumbnail-sized photo had slipped out along with the dollar bills, I'd been surprised. My father had a picture of a stranger in his wallet. He didn't even carry photos of his kids.

She was beautiful, I remember, in a very different way than my mother. She had the same dark eyes my brother does, except that hers shone bright. Hers held a warm smile inside them. His? His are dead. Have been for as long as I can remember.

I'd quickly shoved the photo back into the flap of the wallet when I'd heard my mother's high heels rushing toward the kitchen as she yelled at me that I'd missed the bus. She'd made me walk the six miles to school in the pouring rain.

I hate my mother.

As we pull onto the long driveway of our house, the single light that's on in Evangeline's room goes out.

Abel mutters something about her not listening under his breath but drops it.

I look up at the house. It's the first time I've seen it in half a year. It's a sprawling, once beautiful home in a cul-de-sac on a quiet street just outside of the

French Quarter. And as I stare up at it, all those feelings I had growing up come churning back, leaving my stomach in knots and my hands growing clammy.

"Home sweet home," Abel says as he kills the engine of the Rolls Royce.

"Why didn't you have Joseph drive you?" I ask when he opens his door. I find it curious he drove himself since my brother is all about appearances and climbing that social ladder of a society that doesn't want him.

He has one leg out the door but stops and turns to me. "I'll hire my own driver. I don't need Dad's leftovers."

"He's not a leftover. He's a human being. What is he, seventy years old? Did you fire him?"

"Joseph isn't your problem, Ivy. Let's go. I'm tired, and we have a big day ahead of us."

He climbs out, and I follow, reaching into the back seat to grab my duffel and messenger bags. I brought some schoolbooks, as much as I could fit into the bags, as well as a few changes of clothes. Just a few. I guess some part of me is holding onto the dream that it wouldn't be as bad as Abel made it out to be with my dad, and I might even return to school.

But then his words play back. *You've been chosen.* And I know I'm not going back to school.

I follow my half brother to the front door and wait for him to unlock and open it, then step inside even as my legs grow leaden. It's like they know once I enter, it will be that much harder to get out.

The smell of the place washes over me, overwhelming my senses. My mother's candles. Vanilla and cinnamon. I know how much she pays for those candles. It's a ridiculous price for wax that will melt and disappear. It's not a bad smell, but it carries memories, and I set my hand on the table beside the door to steady myself as I take it in.

Was the dizzying nausea always this bad? Or is it worse now that I've been gone, free for more than half a year?

"I thought Dad said you had that under control," Abel says.

I take a deep breath in and turn my head to look at him as the fog around the edges of my vision clears even as sweat dampens my forehead.

"I'm just anxious. It's worse then." I have vestibular balance disorder. It's usually manageable, and I know how to keep it in check, but when I'm out of my element or stressed, it comes back with a vengeance.

I'm not complaining. So many people have it much worse than me. People who don't know me just think I'm clumsy. And a disorder where I lose my balance or knock into things is the least of my problems, considering.

"Well, get your shit together. Let's go," he says,

grabbing hold of my arm and taking my bags with his free hand.

"That's almost gentlemanly of you," I say as he marches me toward the stairs. "At least it would be if you weren't leaving a mark on my arm." I don't mention the tightness in my face where he slapped me. I'm pretty sure that's bruised, too. He's never hit me before. He's come close, but he's always known Dad wouldn't allow it. But now, I guess Dad's rules don't apply.

"Fuck you, Ivy," he says but lets go of my arm. I didn't expect him to, and again, like when he slapped me, I wonder if he's nervous about leaving a mark. Nervous the man who "chose" me will be pissed off. Because although technically, as head of household, Abel could choose to beat me to within an inch of my life, at least as far as The Society is concerned, he is mindful of leaving a mark.

My mind goes back to Santiago De La Rosa. My husband-to-be.

I know him. I even met him once. Actually, I've seen him on a few occasions. I only spoke with him once, though. I'm not sure he noticed me apart from the day in my father's study.

But that was before the accident.

No, not accident. Incident.

I wonder why a founding family member would choose me for his bride. Is it because his options have diminished, considering? I'm not privy to many details. All I know is he's become a sort of recluse and has remained holed up in his estate ever since that night.

I stop at the bottom of the stairs. The De La Rosa family is one of the original families who founded The Society. *Imperium Valens Invictum. Strong unconquered power.* It's a little arrogant if you ask me. Obnoxious even. But it's an organization that spans the world over, a secret society. Exclusive. Elusive. And dangerous.

The families that make up The Society are powerful. Heads of state, leaders in every sector of government. Medical experts. Scientists. Professors. Church leaders. And, of course, the lower castes, like my own family, who do their bidding.

The De La Rosa family is at the very top of the food chain. They're like royalty within The Society.

There are thirteen founding families. I remember it because when I'd studied the history, I'd thought how fitting the number thirteen. An unlucky number that seems to play again and again in my life.

I was thirteen when Hazel disappeared.

Thirteen when the society intervened, and I was forced to attend one of their schools.

Thirteen when I first met Santiago De La Rosa.

I remember that day. It was during my first week at the all-girls Catholic school I'd been forced to attend. It's not like I'd had a lot of friends at the public school I went to before, but at the new school, I was treated like the lowest of the low. All it took was one girl to spread the word of who I was. How and why I'd even been accepted into the exclusive school only daughters of the higher echelon attended.

I still wince at the memories of how mean the girls had been. At least at first. They'd taunted me about my eye. I'd had to wear my hair pulled back from my face, whereas before I used my bangs to hide it as much as possible, but the nuns had rules, and if you broke them, you were punished.

It's ironic how cruel nuns can be to the children of Christ whom they're supposed to protect. To cherish. Or maybe I'm reading too much into the teachings of the Bible.

I'd met Santiago after a particularly ugly day at school. The girls had been taunting me for days, and as much as I tried to act like I didn't care, the things they said about me, about my family, about my deformity, as they called it, hurt. I was lonely enough without needing to be singled out and it was like they felt that vulnerability, and one, in particular, Maria Chambers, went in for the kill.

That was the day I'd endured both their hate and Sister Mary Anthony's punishment at my response to the girls, and when I'd gotten home, I'd burst into my dad's study to tell him I was finished. I didn't care what he said. I wasn't ever going back to that place.

I hadn't realized he'd had company. In fact, I'd been so focused I hadn't seen Santiago sitting there until my dad pushed me away—something he did in front of others even though when it was just the two of us, he could be warm. I remember the look on his face. Like he'd been embarrassed by me. Ashamed of me.

And I remember how I'd pulled my hair out of its required bun to hide my eye before Santiago saw it.

That was the first time I'd seen the man who had stolen all my dad's attention and sometimes his affection too. I understood why, even at thirteen. The De La Rosa family could elevate us. And as much as it hurt, I knew even then this was the most important thing to my father, even over his children.

"Why would Santiago De La Rosa choose me? What aren't you telling me, Abel?"

Abel studies me. "Why would he lower himself, you mean? A high and mighty Sovereign Son taking a peasant for a wife?"

"You know that's a form of classism, don't you? This whole caste system you've got going. And if I'm a peasant in their eyes, then what does that make y—"

His hand wraps around my throat, and he has my back to the wall before I can finish my sentence. Rage burns inside his eyes as he cuts off my windpipe.

I clutch at his forearm, digging my nails into his flesh.

"Abel!"

My brother's head snaps to the top of the stairs. He loosens his hold enough that I can turn my head to look to where my mother is standing, tying her cream-colored silk robe around herself.

Her gaze flicks to me, then back to him. "She's not yours to punish. If you leave a mark, you don't know what he'll do."

Not don't hurt her. Only fear of the consequences of being found out.

I'm not sure what surprises me more—the fact she is intervening or the fact Abel seems to listen to her. He hates her. And even as she hides it, I know some part of her is afraid of him.

Abel returns his gaze to me. He squeezes his hand again and brings his face to within an inch of mine.

"You think you can get a rise out of me?" He releases me, then steps back just enough to look me over. "You'll be put in your place tomorrow. And I'll not only deliver you, but I'll happily stand by and watch."

I swallow hard, my hand around my throat. He hates me. I know this. But his tone, the look in his eyes, terrifies me.

Abel turns and climbs the stairs, leaving my bags

where they are. He passes my mother without a word and disappears into his room.

I remain where I am and look up at her. Still beautiful, even being woken up in the middle of the night. Still as cold as ever.

"You've been here two minutes, and already, you're causing trouble," she says.

"It's good to see you, too, Mom," I say, bending to pick up my bags. I'm anxious to get to my room now and away from her. I clutch the railing and climb the stairs as I try to steady my heart and the trembling of my hands.

She folds her arms across her chest and watches me as I make my way down the hall to my old room. I open the door and am about to step inside when she calls my name.

"Ivy."

Stopping, I turn with one hand on the doorknob.

"Do not shame us."

4

IVY

I drift in and out of sleep. My old bed feels foreign, too small tucked up against the wall, the deep pink gauze draping it too childish. I reach out a hand and touch it, remembering how I used to like it. Used to pretend I was a princess in a tower.

The wind whistles in from the window I opened to air out the room. The curtain billows, filtering the light coming in from the lamp in the garden. I watch the shadows that dance on the far wall and remember how I would do that when I was little too. I see ominous figures there, the branches of the tree outside making for an eerie gathering as my eyes close again.

I don't know if I drift off for a minute or an hour, but when I wake again, rain is hammering the window. I need to close it, or Mom will be angry. Water damage. Like she cares about the house.

I rub my face and untangle myself from the blankets to sit up. I'm momentarily dizzy, but that's always the case when I first sit up, so I just close my eyes until the wave passes. But then I hear an unfamiliar rustle, followed by the window giving way as it's pushed closed.

Confused, I open my eyes and almost jump out of my skin at the sight that greets me.

There at the window is a figure. Tall and dark and wearing a robe like the Grim Reaper.

But the Grim Reaper wouldn't be worried about a little rain getting into the house.

I almost scream as it—he—straightens and turns toward me. I push my back to the wall.

The figure is in a black cloak with a wide hood pulled up over his head so the little bit of light coming in from outside doesn't illuminate his face. The cloak reaches the floor, and he's tall. Well over six feet.

I want to scream. I want to open my mouth and scream for help, but when I do, nothing comes. No, a sound more pathetic than nothing.

Am I dreaming? Is this a dream, a nightmare I'm trapped in?

But some part of my brain remembers that it knows these robes. Ceremonial. My father had worn one once. I'd been terrified when I'd seen him too.

We remain like that—neither he nor I moving, me not even breathing. He has an advantage. He can see my face. See my terror. I can't see his.

Him.

It's a man. His height and build give that away. More reason to scream if only sound would come. Where is my brother now when I need him?

I stare wide-eyed as he takes a step toward me, and when he does, the light just touches his face. But it's even more terrifying then because he's wearing a black half-mask, and what I glimpse of his face is impossible.

"Wh...what—"

"Ivy Moreno."

Cold, bony fingers seem to crawl along my spine at the deep tenor of his voice, and I visibly shudder. The devil's touch. It's what Sister Mary Anthony used to say when that happened. I make the sign of the cross out of habit.

That makes him laugh. It's an ugly laugh. Short and unamused and hard.

I rub my eyes, wanting to wake up, but he's still there when I open them again. Closer even.

"How do you know my name?"

"You don't remember me, Ivy? I didn't make an impression? I'm offended."

"I...I don't—"

"You'll be my wife," he continues as if I hadn't stammered my feeble attempt at a response. "It would be strange if I didn't know your name, don't you think?"

His *wife*?

I peer closer. This is Santiago De La Rosa? Why is he wearing that cloak? The mask? It's for ceremonial purposes only. Worn by the male founding family members and only when tradition dictated it. They'd lent my father a similar cloak when he'd attended one such event. I still remember his excitement even when my sister and I had been terrified to see him in it.

But there's a more pressing question. What the hell is Santiago De La Rosa doing in my room in the middle of the night?

Then I remember hearing Abel out in the hallway at some point tonight. I remember being irritated that he was making so much noise he'd woken me.

Did Abel let him in here?

"What do you want?" I ask.

I can just make out how his eyes roam over me, and I look down at myself. I'm wearing a T-shirt and panties, one foot up on the bed, the other dangling off it. I pull both in and gather up the blankets.

"No need for that," he says, stepping closer still to take the edge of the blanket and tug it slightly off me. "I came to give you something."

I press harder against the wall when he steps to

the edge of the bed. He takes a moment to look at the ornate frame and all the pink.

"A bit childish, isn't it?"

"What do you want with me?"

He looks down at me, and I don't know if I see or imagine a grin. Don't know if I imagine the skeleton that peers closer as I back into the corner.

"Oh, that's no way to behave with your husband-to-be, sweet Ivy." He sits on the edge of the bed, inching closer.

"What do you want?" I scream it, thinking surely, Abel will come. Surely someone will help me.

But nothing. No one comes. I am alone with this man.

He exhales like he's disappointed, then reaches out, touching the tips of his fingers to my cheek before he slips them to my neck where my pulse beats wildly.

I keep the back of my head pressed to the wall.

I'm dreaming. I must be. But he feels so real.

"What do you want?" I ask, this time in a quieter voice, a frightened one.

"I already told you that," he starts, voice low and deep.

He takes my hand, his fingers like a vise around it, and pulls it toward him. His touch is ice-cold. Maybe it is the Grim Reaper after all.

"I have something for you."

He stretches out my hand, reaches into his

pocket and I watch in shocked silence as he forces a ring onto my finger.

"What—"

It's too tight, but he doesn't stop until he gets it past the knuckle.

"There." He releases me.

I pull my hand back and look at it. At the large teardrop-shaped dark stone on my finger. At the skeleton-like fingers that seem to hold the huge rock in place. Like bones. I glance at him, then instantly try to pry it off.

"It's no use," he says, watching me.

I still try. I don't want this. I don't want any of it. And when he moves to stand, I swear I see that smile again. A dead man's smile.

I feel the blood drain from my head, my vision fading as the room begins to spin.

"You belong to me now, Ivy Moreno, for better or for worse. Until death do us part."

5

IVY

I'm exhausted when I wake up. My head hurts as I look at the sliver of light coming in from the window.

Panicked, I check the time. I don't want to miss Evangeline before she goes to school. It's half-past seven. Today is Friday, which means she catches the school bus at eight.

I throw off the covers and hurry out of bed, but then stop. I look down at my hand and the foreign object there.

And I remember.

It wasn't a dream. Did I really think it was?

I sink onto the bed, my heart racing, my eyes locked on that ring. A huge teardrop-shaped rock. A salt and pepper diamond, I think. And clutching the stone are bony fingers. I peer closer. It's so detailed, such intricate work. I try to pull it off, turning my palm when I do, but it's impossible.

Something's written on the band. I'm not sure it's English: Aeternum.

Santiago De La Rosa had been in my room last night.

He'd come to give me his ring.

No, not give. He'd come to force it on my finger.

I remember how he'd looked. How he'd worn those robes and that hood over his face. He'd scared me half to death.

But maybe that was the point.

A glance at the clock tells me I need to hurry. I get up and go into the bathroom.

Between my visitor last night, thoughts of my father, and Abel's plans for me, my mind is racing. Dad's had health issues for a long time. He doesn't take care of himself like he should and overindulges in things he shouldn't. I remember the doctor telling him more than once that he needed to watch his diet as he prescribed pill after pill to manage his cholesterol and high blood pressure. And although I haven't seen him since being away at school, he told me he'd been more active and more careful with his diet. As careful as he could be while still enjoying life, he'd said. I'd laughed, but I'm worried.

He's in his fifties. Too young to die. I haven't had enough time with him. And Evangeline has only had thirteen years.

I hope it's not as bad as Abel made it out to be and I comfort myself with the knowledge that when I talk to the doctors I'll know more.

I switch on the water to take a shower and strip off my pajamas and underthings. I glimpse my reflection in the mirror when I turn to grab a bottle of shampoo and see the bruise around my neck. Abel's fingerprints. At least it's not too dark, and I can cover it up. But maybe I shouldn't.

The one on my cheekbone is worse. It's swollen and blue.

Looking at my stomach and thighs, I find bruises in various stages there too. They don't hurt. I'm used to them and try to make a joke of it when I knock into things.

When I told Abel it's worse with stress, I wasn't kidding. I'm not sure how I'll actually get through a wedding to a stranger.

But I push that thought out of my mind and step into the shower. I hurry to shampoo and condition my mass of thick dark hair and use the last of the body wash. After my shower, I dress in a pair of jeans, choosing something generic because it'll piss off Mom and Abel. Mom because she likes to keep up appearances, Abel because he told me to wear a dress. I twist my hair up into a clip and make sure some hangs down over my right eye, then step out into the hallway and go to my sister's room. I smile genuinely for the first time when I knock on her door and hear her squeal as she throws it open.

"Ivy!" She practically jumps into my arms, and I hug her hard, my smile widening.

"Eva! I missed you so much." I didn't even realize how much until just now.

"Me too. God. Me too."

I hear her sniffle, and when we draw apart, I see she's been crying. The delicate skin around her eyes is puffy.

"I wanted to call you, but they wouldn't let me. Mom took my phone," she starts, that smile morphing into a frown as tears spring from her eyes. "I wanted to tell you about Dad."

"Shh." I pull her in for another hug. "It's okay, sweetheart. You're not to blame. I'm here now." I want to reassure her somehow, but I don't know what my presence here will do for her.

We separate again, and I tuck a strand of hair back into a hairpin. The nuns won't excuse a hair out of place, even considering the situation.

"Are you okay?" I ask, looking her over. Given how Abel's been with me, I want to be sure he hasn't raised a hand to her.

"I'm scared for Dad. Mom and Abel won't tell me anything. I can go see him after school today, though."

"Abel's taking me to see him this morning, and

I'll talk to the doctors. I'll find out what's going on and tell you. I promise."

She nods, wipes her tears. "Ivy?" she asks hesitantly

"Yes?"

"Is it true? You'll have to marry that man?"

I don't know how to answer her.

"I've heard rumors, Ivy. He's deformed. A monster."

"You don't know that."

"Everyone knows about the explosion. Everyone knows he's hardly been seen in public since."

I know that much too.

"You can't do it. You have to find some way to get out of it."

"It's not as simple—"

"Evangeline!"

I exhale in relief at my mother's interruption because I've heard the same rumors. I know about the explosion where so many sons of The Society were lost. Where Santiago's own father and brother perished.

And although Santiago did survive, he didn't quite walk away uninjured. There are rumors about what happened to him and what he did to cover up his scars. Talk of how hard he's become, how bitter.

I remember my brief first encounter with him took place in my dad's study. I'd given him the gift dad had bought him, and as I'd dumped the box on his lap, I'd told him what I'd thought of him. I'd been just mad enough about everything to blurt out the truth, that I didn't like the school The Society made me go to because I knew it was him or his family who'd arranged for it as a thank-you gift to my father for tutoring Santiago. And I hadn't stopped there. I told him I didn't like him, either.

He'd just sort of smiled. I guess I remember because of my dad's reaction. He'd gotten angry with me. Told me I was being disrespectful. But I'd gotten the feeling Santiago had found it almost funny.

The truth was, I'd been jealous of him even though I didn't even know him. I'd been jealous because he'd had my father's affection.

Would I truly be forced to marry this stranger now? This deformed monster they only whisper about?

I shake my head, clearing the thought. One thing at a time. First, I need to see my father with my own eyes. I think about how Dad was supposed to go to that meeting, too. He'd gotten sick at the last minute, though.

"Evangeline, goddammit! Get down here!"

My sister stiffens at the sound of our mother's voice.

"You're going to miss your bus, and I can't drive you to school today."

Eva turns to me. "I'm sure she has a very important hair or nail appointment. Or maybe she's having her face lifted," she whispers. "Again."

We giggle, but it's strained.

"Evangeline!"

"I'd better go." She moves toward the door, then doubles back, opens a drawer in her desk, and shoves an extra-large Snickers bar into her backpack. "Breakfast will make me fat, according to Mom."

"You don't get breakfast?" Evangeline is like a twig already.

She shrugs her shoulder. "It's okay. I'm more worried about Dad and you than breakfast." She hugs me again. "I love you, sis. I'm glad you're here even though I know you don't want to be. I'm glad to have you close again."

For how long, though?

I follow her out the door and watch her fly down the stairs. Our mother stands at the front door with her arms folded disapprovingly. They don't say goodbye as my sister rushes out the door just as the bus turns onto our street.

My mother closes the front door, and Abel walks out of my father's study, holding his phone to his ear. Has he taken over Dad's office already? He meets my gaze and checks his watch, then disconnects the call.

"I told you to wear a dress," he says as I descend to the first floor.

"I didn't feel like it," I tell him and turn toward the kitchen to get myself a cup of coffee.

"You'll learn."

I have my back to him so I can't see his face, but something too self-assured in his tone gives me pause. But then my mother walks into the kitchen, and I turn my attention to her.

"Are you feeding Eva?"

"Of course I'm feeding her. But I'm also careful of her weight. Her metabolism isn't like mine, you know."

I look her over, raise my eyebrows. "I thought that was Dr. Abrams." Dr. Abrams is her plastic surgeon.

A few years ago, I overheard an argument between my parents that I almost remember word for word. Their marriage isn't one built on a foundation of love. For as far back as I can remember, my mother and father never really liked each other very much and have been pretty vocal about it behind closed doors. They only share one commonality as far as I can tell. They revere The Society and will do anything to remain in its good graces.

That night I understood why they stayed together. I learned that my mother had been a sort of present for my father. When The Society had realized he had a gift for numbers—one neither I nor any of my siblings inherited—my father had become valuable. And so, he'd gotten a prize. My mother.

Although she's no prize according to me and, I bet, according to my father. She's beautiful. And her genes carried on with Hazel and Evangeline. They mostly skipped me apart from the color of my eyes.

Beauty isn't everything, though. I wonder if there was a time when my father was blinded by hers. If there was a time he loved her. I doubt it. She's not the woman he had a photo of inside his wallet.

Although not a founding family, my mother's family is above my father's in The Society's hierarchy, so on a certain level, she had the upper hand in their marriage. And in a way, I think she hated my father for what happened to her—for having to marry beneath her station.

My mother opens her mouth, but Abel interrupts her. "Stop your bickering. Ivy, get your coffee, and let's go. We're late."

"Visiting hours don't start until ten."

"We have another appointment first."

I turn to him, suddenly chilled. "What appointment?"

"I'll tell you when we get there. Let's go."

I open a cabinet and grab a to-go cup. Filling it with coffee, I add a generous serving of cream even though I usually take it black. This is just to irritate my mother. I'm sure she doesn't want me getting fat before the big day. I twist the lid on, grab my coat, and follow Abel out into the chilly but sunny morning.

I climb into the passenger seat of the Rolls, and he starts the engine.

"Is there any change with Dad?"

"Not that I've heard," he says as we turn onto the road and head in the opposite direction of the hospital.

"What is this appointment you're taking me to?"

"We need to take care of a few things before the wedding."

"Speaking of, when is the big day?"

His phone rings, and he answers it rather than answering me. He's on the call for the next twenty minutes and only disconnects when we get to a neighborhood I'm not familiar with, one where the houses are about twice as big as ours and a guard asks your business before he opens the gate.

"Where are we?" I ask him anxiously, my stomach growing tense when we pull up in front of a large mansion where another Rolls is parked on the driveway.

We're here on Society business. I know it.

Abel parks the car behind the matching one and kills the engine.

"We're here at your fiancé's request."

"What?"

"Well, request isn't quite how I'd put it honestly. De La Rosa doesn't make requests. Even now, with his fucked-up face."

That last part he mutters, but I can hear the hate

in his words. He's still jealous of Santiago De La Rosa? Even after what happened to him, to his family? I knew he was jealous before back when Dad couldn't say enough about the child prodigy. Dad had been mentoring Santiago for years at The Society's request and teaching him what he knew. At one point, he'd mentioned how Santiago had surpassed him in knowledge, and he went on and on about Santiago's mind, how it was like a computer, how clever he was, and so on and so forth. In a way, I get how Abel felt. I felt it too. But Abel's jealousy is accompanied by something else. Hate.

"Have you seen him? Since the explosion," I can't help but ask. I want to know if it's true. If the reason he's become a recluse is his face.

He turns to look at me fully. "Would you, Ivy Moreno," he starts, taking my jaw in his hand and turning it, pushing the hair that hides my eye away before continuing. "With your own deformity, judge another on his outward appearance? That's a bit hypocritical, isn't it?"

"I wasn't judging...I just—"

"Sometimes, Ivy, I don't know what kind of person you are. The nuns would be so disappointed in you. I know dad was." He jerks his hand away roughly.

"That wasn't what I meant," I say quietly. His comment about my father cut, just as I'm sure he wanted it to.

"It doesn't matter."

He exhales, presses his lips together, and turns to look out at the house. He shakes his head like he wants to be sure I know exactly how disappointed he is, too. I don't care what he thinks, though. And the only hypocrite here is him.

I keep my thoughts to myself, though.

"I have a question for you." He turns to me again.

"What?"

"Do you want to see Father?"

The question takes me by surprise. "Of course I do. You said you'd take me."

"Then I need you to do as you're told now."

"Do as I'm told?" I feel my eyebrows creep up into my hairline.

"Exactly. Do as you're told. It'll be a good exercise for you."

The front door opens, drawing our attention to two men stepping outside. They remain standing in front of the open door, and it all feels wrong.

"What is this, Abel?"

"It's me looking out for our family. I will take you to see Father after we take care of this. If I feel you've behaved well enough."

I shift my gaze to the men again, then back to Abel, the coffee I drank turning bitter in my stomach.

But the hammer hasn't fallen yet.

"He's requested a purity test."

My mouth falls open, and I stare at him in disbelief. "What?"

"And I won't take a chance De La Rosa will humiliate our family so I've agreed."

I feel the blood drain from my face.

"It'll take a moment. No big deal."

"No big deal?"

"It's all very standard within The Society, especially the higher echelon. Your mother submitted to it, too."

"I don't care about The Society. I don't even care if my mother submitted. I'm not doing it!"

"You'll do it, or you won't see Dad."

"What? You can't do that."

"I can do anything I want. I'm going to greet those gentlemen. You have one minute to decide. If you agree to submit for the good of our family, then I'll see you at the house. If not, then you'll remain here, and once I've taken care of what I need to take care of, I'll be back to take you home, where you'll remain locked in your room until the wedding ceremony."

"I want to see Dad. You promised."

"I never promised. I simply told you that you were starting to be reasonable. Now I'm not so sure. If Evangeline weren't so young—"

"Evangeline?"

"She is the more desirable out of the two of you

but she is thirteen. If you force my hand, though, well, I'll do what I need to do."

Evangeline? He'd make her submit to something like this?

I give a shake of my head. He can't do that. "They won't let you do that. The Society won't allow something like that." No matter what I think of them, they're not that evil. I know that.

"I'm head of household."

"You go by the law of The Society, and they will never allow it, and you know it. Evangeline is thirteen," I say, shoulders squared.

His eyes narrow, and I know he knows what I'm saying is true. And I'm a little relieved.

"But you're not," he says, voice full of spite. "This is as much to protect our family as to satisfy your husband-to-be. I could drag you in kicking and screaming if I wanted to, but I'm leaving it up to you walk in. Giving you the chance to do this with some dignity."

Dignity. There will be no dignity in what's to come.

He opens the car door. "Decide if you will submit." He steps out.

I remain in the car watching as he walks to the entrance and shakes hands with the two older men. I notice one of the men has a heavy ring on his finger. They're otherwise indistinguishable from each other.

They want me to submit to a virginity test? I'd heard rumors of these. I hadn't given them much credence though. It's archaic. Will they check the bedsheets too?

But if there's one thing I believe it's that Abel will lock me in my room and not allow me to see our father. He won't care even if Dad were to die. And he could somehow punish Evangeline to punish me. These are the only things that matter. The only things I need to know.

I have no choice. I never did. I will submit to this just as I will submit to a wedding.

The men stop their conversation once I'm within earshot. The older ones shift their gazes to me first. My brother, who has his back to me, turns slowly to face me. The smile on his face is a victorious one.

"Ivy."

I look anxiously from him to the others. Their gazes appear almost lecherous. And they're old enough to be my grandfather. Will they really stand by and allow something like this to happen? Will they bear witness?

"Gentlemen, this is my sister Ivy."

I'm surprised he doesn't distinguish himself from me. We're half siblings and not full blood. Something he usually takes comfort in, if not pride.

The men nod. One of them sweeps his gaze over

me, and I wish I'd eaten something so I could throw it up on his thousand-dollar shoes.

"We're behind schedule," the one without the ring says.

My brother nods and, without introducing the men to me—not that I care—we walk inside, the men in front of me, Abel behind, me in the middle. A prisoner marched to her execution.

I barely notice the surroundings as I'm led through the large living space. An older woman sits reading a magazine. She only spares me a momentary glance. Across from her is a younger woman. She looks familiar, but half her face is hidden behind her magazine so I can only see her eyes. She tracks me as we cross the room, and a housekeeper enters, carrying coffee on a silver tray.

Do these women know what's about to happen?

"It's rude to stare," the older woman says to the younger one, her voice low.

I guess the younger one is her daughter because her face is now fully hidden behind the magazine.

I'm led from the main room to a corridor lined with doors. When we reach the last door, the man without the ring opens it, and the scent of antiseptic assaults my senses. This must be his office. Is he a real doctor? Or some freak employed by The Society to run these "tests"?

He gestures for us to enter.

When I hesitate, Abel places a hand at my back and urges me inside.

The man closes the door. There's no lock, I notice. I guess I'm free to go. But if I do, will they bring Evangeline here in my place? The thought is sickening, but looking at these men, the fat one with the ring who takes a seat on the couch across from the examining table looks far too eager, and I'm pretty sure he'd have no problem with the idea.

The room is average size and more brightly lit than the living space which was cozier. This has more functional lighting. A large desk is centered against the far wall. A sitting area against another and an examining table opposite it. There's a privacy screen in the corner of the sitting area.

"Ivy," the man without the ring says. He gestures to the single, simple wooden chair facing his desk. "Have a seat."

I do, and Abel stands behind me, hands on my shoulders as if he'd keep me down if I tried to run.

"I'm Dr. Chambers."

Chambers?

As in Maria Chambers' father? I think back to the girl who used to torment me. And I realize why the one in the living room seemed familiar. It was the gleam in her otherwise unremarkable eyes. The wickedness inside them.

She was staring because she knew exactly what would happen here. What they would do to me.

I swallow, feeling hot. I'm glad I'm sitting down because I think I'd fall otherwise.

"Your brother has explained the requirement, I'm sure, but I'd like to go through it to be sure you are here of your own choice."

"My choice?"

Abel squeezes my shoulders.

Dr. Chambers clears his throat, ignoring me. This is a sham, and everyone in this room knows it. And they're all taking pleasure in my torment. Am I surprised? Maria Chambers was a bully at thirteen. She must have learned it somewhere.

"Mr. De La Rosa is a member of one of our founding families. As such, we, of course, hold him in the highest regard, as I'm sure you do."

The man on the couch snorts in the middle of that sentence.

I glance over but only momentarily.

"I'm sure she does," Abel answers the doctor.

"You're a very lucky girl," Dr. Chambers continues.

I doubt that, I think, but don't say.

"But as The Society does not force anyone to submit to anything they don't want to, I want to be certain you've asked your brother, as a good and upstanding member, to bring you here so that your purity will be certified, and you will be declared fit for marriage to a man of such stature."

"Are you serious?"

"Ivy," Abel says. He'd have more to say, but the doctor holds up his hand.

"This is difficult for our younger ladies. I have a daughter your sister's age, Abel. I understand, believe me." He turns his attention to me. "But we should get on with it and not waste anyone's time. Will you submit to my examination, Ivy?"

"I don't have a choice."

Abel fingers dig into my shoulders. "Sister." There's a long, weighted pause. "If you prefer, I can take you home now. We have alternatives," he threatens.

"No," I say, standing up. "I submit. Let's get it over with."

"Very good. There is to be one witness, and Mr. Holton has generously given up his morning to be here in that capacity."

"How selfless of him."

The doctor stands. "You can undress behind the privacy curtain, then make yourself comfortable on the examining table. Everything off."

My legs wobble as I walk toward the privacy screen, and I knock into the coffee table, spilling coffee out of the cup there.

"Please excuse my sister. She's quite nervous," Abel says. I get the feeling he's kept my disorder a secret.

"It's natural," the doctor says.

Once I'm behind the privacy screen, I slump

against the wall and exhale a deep breath. I feel dizzy, and my skin is clammy. I close my eyes and force myself to breathe, counting to five on an inhale, holding, exhaling to five. Repeating.

I imagine myself at the swimming pool on campus swimming my laps. I do it every morning. It's one of the things that helps, that keeps me level and steady. It'll be over quickly, then I can get out of here. Then I can see Dad and maybe go for a swim in the afternoon before Eva gets home.

I undress and put on the robe, grateful there is one. Beyond the curtain, I hear the men speak in low murmurs while stirring sugar and cream into their coffee. I hear Santiago's name and strain to listen, but they seem to quiet even more when mentioning him. From their tone, I get the feeling they don't like him.

I know I'm taking too long when one of the men clears his throat, and my brother calls my name.

"Are you ready, Ivy? I'm sure these gentlemen have better things to do than wait on you."

Those gentlemen can go to hell.

I tie the robe tighter around myself and walk around the privacy curtain, not looking at them as I make my way to the examining table, which has been adjusted. The stirrups have been pulled out, and I realize to my horror that they'll have a perfect view right between my legs.

I hesitate, and Dr. Chambers, who has donned a

white robe, moves to the table and smiles at me. It's not a warm smile. In fact, I wonder if he's got an erection under that robe just thinking about what he's about to do. At how he's about to humiliate me.

"Up on the table, Ivy. You've done this before, I'm sure. You should have been having these checks annually. It is a father's duty."

"My father could be quite soft on his daughters," Abel says.

"That's too bad. I keep a tight leash on Maria. That girl has a wild streak, but I believe I keep her in check."

Wow. I actually feel sorry for Maria suddenly. I don't want to think about her having to submit to anything like this. I don't want to think about anyone having to.

My face burns as I tug the knot at my waist tighter and make my way to the table. I climb on, sit facing the door as I take a deep breath in, then lie back.

Get this done.

Get it over with.

That's all I have to do.

I set my feet in the stirrups and make the mistake of looking across the room at where Abel and the other asshole are sitting back, watching as if I were a show on a stage. Which I guess in a way I am.

"Very good," Dr. Chambers says, coming over to me.

I shift my gaze up to the ceiling as he moves my hands from the knot of my belt and sets them on either side of the table. I clutch the padded edges as he undoes the knot and opens the robe, exposing me wholly as he widens the stirrups.

Dr. Chambers clears his throat, and I feel his fingers low on my belly. "Not a promising sign," he says. "When they shave all the hair, you have to wonder for whom."

"I swim," I say. Not that it's any of their business if I want to shave every hair off my body.

"Quiet," Abel snaps.

Dr. Chambers touches two of the bruises on my belly but doesn't comment. I wonder if he thinks Abel beat me and that it's perfectly fine.

He moves to stand between my legs and pulls the table on wheels closer.

Holton gets to his feet and comes to stand just to my side, eyes glued between my legs. I make the mistake of letting my gaze drop to his crotch, and from under his protruding belly, I see the pressing of his small dick against his slacks.

Pervert.

"I need to bear witness," he tells me, patting my hand, which I pull away instantly. "I can't very well see from there, can I?"

I barely breathe as I listen to them talk about the weather, about Dr. Chambers' daughter, then about my vagina as the doctor lubricates his finger.

"You'll feel pressure, but it won't be painful, Ivy."

I grit my teeth to prepare for the intrusion, but there's no preparing for it as his cold finger slides inside me. It takes all I have not to scream. Not to fight. Because when I do try to bring my knees together, Holton pulls them apart.

"I must witness," he says. "You're not the first woman I've seen naked, I assure you."

Is he bragging? I dig my nails into the sides of the table as the doctor prods, turning his finger this way and that.

"She's very tight."

I feel a tear slide down the side of my face.

"Almost done," he says. "Just a moment longer."

I'm pretty sure he's felt my hymen, if that's even a thing, and this is simply for my humiliation and a visual aid for when they jerk off later.

"There." The doctor pulls his finger away and wipes it off on a paper towel.

I let my knees drop closed and exhale.

My brother is on his feet, anxious.

"Virgin," Dr. Chambers says.

I could have told them that.

"Well, not that I had any doubt," Abel says.

I start to get up.

"Not yet," Holton says, holding me down, pulling my robe wide to expose my breasts again when I try to close it.

I look at him, and his eyes are nowhere near my face.

"She is spectacular," he says. "Too bad she'll go to that bastard."

"Can I go?" I ask, my voice sounding strange.

"Just one more thing," Dr. Chambers says. He looks at my brother who simply nods. He picks up the needle lying beside the open tube of lubricant.

"What is that?"

"Vitamins," my brother answers before the doctor can.

I don't even argue as the needle comes to my arm. I want to get off this table. Out of here. I want to get away from these men, and I'm not sure how much longer I can keep from crying.

"There." Dr. Chambers closes my robe. "You're finished. I'll certify the document, and your brother can take you home."

I slip off the table as fast as I can, the floor chilly on my bare feet, but before I can get behind the privacy screen, Able catches my arm and stops me.

"Aren't you forgetting something?" he asks.

"What?" I ask, just barely holding back my tears.

"Thank the doctor and Mr. Holton."

"Thank them?" I wipe at my face, the first of the tears spilling, and I swear I can still feel that man's touch on me, the other's eyes.

"Yes, Ivy. Thank them for taking time out of their day for us."

I turn around, and I look at them. I make myself do it. I want to remember their faces. I want to know who they are, and one day, I swear to myself, I will make them pay.

"Thank you," I say through gritted teeth.

Abel releases me, and I disappear behind the privacy curtain and wonder if my husband-to-be has demanded this humiliation of me without even being present, what will he demand of me when I am his?

7

IVY

Neither Abel nor I speak as he pulls off the driveway. I feel humiliated. Mortified. What just happened in that house is only now fully dawning on me, and all I can do is sit here in the passenger seat with my knees drawn up under my chin and my face turned out the window so he won't see my tears.

"Take your boots off the seat."

"Fuck you."

He drops it. I'm surprised when he doesn't retort or reach over and make me take my boots off his precious seat, but he doesn't. Maybe on some level, he's been impacted too?

I wipe my face with the sleeve of my over-sized sweater, glad I wore it, glad to have the protection of it. It's when we're pulling into the parking lot of the hospital that I turn to study his face in profile, mouth tight, forehead creased.

His hate has aged him. Made him ugly.

"Why did you make me do that?"

"It was his request."

"You could have said no."

He pulls into the circular drive and stops before the sliding glass front doors, then turns to face me.

"It needed to happen. If you weren't a virgin, or even if De La Rosa claimed you weren't after the wedding night, we'd have no recourse. The entire family would be punished."

"Do you have any human emotion in there, Abel? Anything at all resembling empathy?"

"Empathy is for the weak, Ivy." He checks his watch like I'm holding him up. "If you want to see Dad, you'd better head in."

I narrow my eyes. "You're not coming to guard me? Make sure I don't run away?"

Shaking his head, he shifts his gaze to the street, absently watching traffic.

"What is it? Are you upset by what you did?"

"Don't be stupid," he says, looking at me again. Eyes dead again.

"No, you're right. That was stupid. I'm going to warn you now, though, if you ever raise a hand to our sister or try anything like that with her, I will kill you. I will murder you with my own hands. Do you understand me, Abel?"

He laughs. Well, sort of. It's more of a snort. "Once Dad dies, I'll take over guardianship of her. And do you know what I will do with her? I'll sell her to the highest bidder."

"You ca—"

"Don't worry, I'll wait until she's of age. And when I do, there won't be a damn thing you can do about it. So, go visit Dad. Hurry. Maybe your words will bring him back."

"I'm going to kill you."

"Only if your husband doesn't kill you first."

His words take me by surprise, and I waver.

Someone knocks on the window, startling me. I turn to look and find a tall man in a dark long coat and blond hair standing outside. He nods to Abel.

"That's James. He'll take you home when you're finished. You have one hour.'"

"One hour?"

"I would have given you all day, but you're not being very nice, are you?"

I open my mouth, but he puts up a hand.

"Don't, Ivy. Just don't. Go before I change my mind altogether."

Is he going to steal this from me too? "Please, Abel." I feel my eyes fill up again.

"Please, Abel," he mimics, making his voice higher than it is.

I give him the finger and push my door open. I have one foot out the door when he calls my name.

"Ivy."

I turn.

"It's tomorrow tonight."

"What's tomorrow tonight?"

"The big day."

"What?"

"At midnight."

"Tomorrow?" Cold washes over me.

He checks his watch. "Fifty-seven minutes."

"I hate you," I tell him and step out of the car, then pass James, who follows me through the sliding glass doors into the hospital.

8

SANTIAGO

"Dominus et Deus." Abel utters the forced show of respect for my rank as he bows before me in greeting.

My study at De La Rosa Manor is dark, all the monitors on the wall turned off for the day. But even so, I can tell as I glance down at Abel Moreno, he is not a man who likes to bow to anyone. He feels he deserves better, and I'm certain his ego insists on it. I've always detected a hint of his resentment, even as he offers his respect.

For all intents and purposes, Abel may as well be a bastard. His connection to IVI is weak at best. He was Eli's first and only son, but he was not born to the woman The Society chose for him. Therefore, he will never truly be of importance in our world. It's a simple concept to grasp, even for someone like him, but accepting it is another matter.

He has always been too smug for my liking. Too eager for approval. I don't like the way he carries himself, and I am even less pleased with how readily he agreed to offer his sister to me. He might not have a choice in the matter, but his lack of regard for his own blood does nothing to win my approval.

I expected a fight, and admittedly, I am disappointed that I did not get one. I've been watching his family for four years now, and I have found a weakness for all but him. Eli and his wife crave the power that comes with The Society. Ivy craves to escape through naïve dreams of school and a life she'll never have. Much like her older sister, who did escape, I wouldn't be surprised if she tried. The youngest Moreno, Evangeline, isn't old enough to have an opinion either way. But Abel does not seem to be cursed with affection for any of his family members, and if he loves anything other than himself, I have not yet discovered it.

Marrying Ivy off to me should have been torturous to all of them. But not once since I declared my intentions has anyone come to beg me to spare her. Not even her own mother. I'm beginning to think the only Moreno who might care is the one who's lying helpless in a coma, too cowardly to face the injustices he deserves himself.

"I wanted to offer you an assurance." Abel's eyes flick to the empty chair opposite my desk. He's waiting for me to tell him to sit down and make himself comfortable. I don't.

"What assurance?" My eyes narrow in on the folded paper in his hands.

"That your bride is pure. There can be no doubt now."

I consider his words carefully. Surely, he cannot mean what I think he does. But as I examine the tilt of his lips and an expression that can only indicate he is rather pleased with himself, my temples begin to throb violently.

I reach out and snatch the paper from his hands, unfolding it near the soft glow of the flickering candle on my desk. My eyes move rapidly over the report, collecting the details as my knuckles grow rigid at the confirmation of his statement. An image of Ivy comes to mind, filling in the gaps between my imagination and Abel's stupidity. It isn't difficult to envision her lying there on her back, legs spread as a stranger dares to touch what should only ever belong to me. How could Abel ever believe this would be a smart move?

When I return my hollow gaze to his, the gratified expression on his face falls away. I stalk around the desk, whipping my fingers out to latch onto his jaw, wrenching it upward in the deadly grip of my whitened knuckles.

"Who the fuck gave you the authority?"

My fingers bite into his skin with a force he's not

accustomed to, and he squirms in my grasp as red blooms across his face. His barely concealed disdain is simmering inside him, close to blowing the lid off his feigned civility. I'd like to see him try to test me right now. It would give me great pleasure to cave his skull in and paint my walls with his blood.

"I thought you would want it," he grits out.

Darkness swirls in the pits of his beady eyes, an undercurrent of rage thrumming beneath his pinched features. He wants to put me in my place. He wants more than anything to believe he is even a fraction of my equal.

"Let me be perfectly clear," I clip out succinctly. "She belongs to me. Nobody will ever touch her again without my permission, including you. If I find one goddamn hair out of place on her head, it will be you who pays the price. Do you understand?"

"Yes." He jerks his chin back, clearly revulsed by my face so close to his.

He wants me to know what he thinks of me, whether he can say it plainly or not. It's tempting to beat him within an inch of his life right now. I could, and nobody would ever question me for it. But I have to remind myself that he will pay for his father's sins in time. And there will be more satisfaction in watching him slowly stripped of his pride and supe-riority. When I'm through with him, he will wish his face was only half as damaged as mine. Abel

Moreno will come to understand intimately what it means to be truly ugly.

"Well, what do we have here?" Mercedes startles me as she speaks from the doorway to my study, peering in at the scene before her curiously. But when her eyes shoot to mine, her unspoken message is clear.

Not yet. I shake my head in silent answer.

I promised I'd let her toy with at least one Moreno before they die, and she's had her eyes set on Abel since I uttered the words. Between the two of us, I'm not sure which is worse. Mercedes is just as bloodthirsty but only half as patient. In her mind, she's probably already devised a scheme of torture more wicked than I even want to know. There will be no pity for him from me.

I release him with a sneer and retreat to my desk, sitting in my chair while Abel dares to let his greedy eyes roam the length of my sister's body. She sees his want and encourages his ignorance by offering him a feline smile. He isn't even remotely aware of how much she wants to destroy him.

"Let it be known," I speak, forcing his attention back to me. "Any decisions about my bride are to go through me. I want an update every hour from now until the wedding. Where she is. Who she's with. What she's doing. Is that simplistic enough for your comprehension?"

"Of course." He nods with narrowed eyes.

"And I will be at the Moreno's house to help her get ready tomorrow," Mercedes interjects.

I shoot her an irritated glance. She knows better than to suggest such an idea without speaking to me first. But given that I can't trust Abel, and I know Mercedes will follow through with my commands, I agree.

Abel bows his head toward her and then smirks. "Nothing would please me more than to see you again, Miss De La Rosa."

———

ANOTHER LONG, SLEEPLESS NIGHT PASSES AS I ROAM the halls of The Manor. The mansion is vast and often drafty with so much space to heat. When my father was alive, he would instruct the staff to heat the rooms we occupied and nothing more during the colder months. I haven't changed his directives in that regard since I've taken over as head of the household.

The Manor is a Victorian gothic behemoth in the Lakewood District of New Orleans. Nestled into the trees just past the cemeteries, the rare, sprawling eight acres of gardens affords more privacy than most estates in the city. The property has belonged to my family for generations, and though there have been many generous offers over the years, it will never belong to anyone who does not bear the De La Rosa name.

It is up to me to carry on our family's lineage now, and that is where Ivy will prove her worth. The mere thought of impregnating her both sickens and fascinates me. She is my enemy's daughter, and therefore, she can only ever repulse me, just as I will certainly repulse her. It is not the ideal situation, but given the circumstances, if anyone must bear my sons, I should think it would be torturous for her to do so. And God as my witness, she will.

The only remaining question is how long will she survive under my rule? How long can she bear the punishments of her father's sins before it becomes too much? And will she decide to put herself out of her misery, or will it be me?

Tomorrow, she will be mine to touch. Mine to take. Mine to do with as I please. She will know what it feels like to be well and truly owned. My brand on her skin. Her virgin blood on my cock. The first of a thousand tears she will shed drying on her cheeks by the time I'm through with her.

When I close my eyes, I can imagine it so vividly. But the vision wavers between rough and soft against my will. I have not been with a woman since before the explosion. Though many would do my bidding should I request it, I have not desired to expose them to the horrors of my scarred flesh. Ivy will have no choice but to subject herself to me, should I want her to. She will bear it every time she looks at me. I want her to feel what I feel inside. The Moreno blood running through her veins has destroyed me, and it should destroy her too.

Perhaps one day, I will let her see the landscape of terror her father left behind on my body. For now, I should use her only as a vessel. Her affection is not required to do what's necessary. To open her body to mine and accept my cock until her belly is round and swollen with my child.

My fingers move over the ornate gothic mask on my desk. It is not difficult to imagine her kneeling before me, naked with my fresh mark etched into her skin. The mask blinding her vision as she sucks in a breath, waiting for me to draw near. What a beautiful, terrifying sight it will be.

The clock on the mantel ticks down the seconds, the hours dwindling away and sealing her fate. Tonight, at the stroke of midnight, Ivy Moreno will be my wife.

I'm in my room sitting on my bed, and no matter how many blankets I wrap around my body, I can't seem to get warm.

Seeing my father yesterday was harder than I expected. He'd lost a lot of weight, and he didn't look good. He looked small and weak, cheeks hollowed out and so pale like he was fighting for every breath.

Or he would be if he weren't on a machine that was doing the breathing for him.

I talked to one of the doctors who said he'd gone into cardiac arrest. And he didn't have to tell me the outcome didn't look good. I could see that. So I sat beside him and held his hand and tried not to sob.

My dad and I, we're as close as you can get when you're a daughter of a Society family. The females are considered second-class citizens, and daughters are marriage material to, ideally, better your standing within the organization or birth the sons of the next generation. Sons hold more value. Although not Abel because he was a product of a marriage not sanctified by The Society.

But when we were alone, Dad was different. He was never unkind. My mother was the one always ready to smack you with the back of her hand or burn you with the tip of a cigarette she swore she didn't smoke. My dad was gentle. And at times, affectionate even.

No. He *is* gentle. He's still here. And as long as he's still here, there's still a chance.

He let me go away to college. That doesn't happen to most girls within The Society. Girls live at home. They study but only under the watchful eyes of their parents.

I think back to Dr. Chambers, shuddering at the thought of what it must have been like having him for a father. It actually makes me understand Maria a little more.

My dad is different. And I want to believe that some part of him hoped I would somehow get away from the clutches of The Society. At least on some subconscious level.

I try to remember those things as I sit here now. Not how small he looked in that hospital bed. Not the ongoing sounds of the machines he was hooked up to.

I stare at the garment bag hanging on my closet

door. It's clear. I can see through it to my wedding dress. It's beautiful. Black. It fits my mood. And it fits for a Society wedding to a stranger.

There must be yards of lace and too many satin buttons to count. The veil is in its own bag, and it's even longer than the dress. The shoes, though, as gorgeous as they are, will be staying in their box. Maybe he can return them and get his money back. Because if I wear those, I will surely break my neck.

I glance at the clock. A little after nine o'clock. Three hours to go.

Evangeline and my mother are gone. I haven't seen either of them since my visit with Dad. I wonder if my mother picked up Evangeline from school and is keeping her away on Abel's orders. Or Santiago's. The only other person in the house with me is James. I guess Abel isn't taking a chance that I'll make a run for it.

Twenty more minutes pass like this with me sitting on the bed numb and wondering how I'm going to do it. How I'm going to get up and get dressed and go to the church and get married.

Married

To a stranger.

Abel was smart to use Evangeline to trap me. His words before I got out of the Rolls replay in my mind of what he'll do once he has guardianship of Evangeline. Which he will get because our mother will give that to him as per the rules of The Society. The head of household must be male, and if Dad dies, he's it.

I'm thinking.

Santiago De La Rosa will be my husband in a matter of hours.

Santiago is a powerful man. Can he do something? Would he? Would he help me if I asked him to?

He can't be worse than Abel. I just can't believe anyone could be more hateful than Abel.

Pushing the blankets off, I get out of bed. I change into an old swimsuit and pull on a robe, then walk out of my room. I head down the stairs and, still barefoot, out the back door. James is on my heels, but I don't bother with him.

It's misty, the grass wet and cold beneath my bare feet as I make my way to the pool at the back of the dark garden. My mother keeps it heated throughout the winter to swim her laps. She wanted an indoor pool, and I remember the fight she'd had with my father when he'd outright told her we couldn't afford that. So outdoor it is.

James stands back and watches as I drop my robe. Shuddering in the cool night, I make my way to the stairs that lead down into the pool. The water is cold. Colder than I expect for a heated pool. Wasn't she heating it anymore? Although the house isn't maintained like it used to be. I don't stop. I keep going until I'm in as deep as my chest, then submerge myself entirely and swim.

I swim short laps back and forth and back and forth. It's not a very big pool. I don't know how long I keep going only opening my eyes when I come up for air. I just swim, staying under as long as possible, the sound and weight of the water drowning out my thoughts. Drowning out the world.

Maybe something good will come out of this marriage.

Maybe I can save my little sister.

Even if I have to sleep with a monster to do it.

I'm so wrapped up in the swimming that I don't even register the two people beside James. I swim another lap, then another before I hear a woman laugh, and then Abel hissing my name.

I stop when I get to the deep end of the pool only because Abel reaches down to grab my hand and keep me there.

Abel claims not to like swimming. I'm pretty sure he can't do it. If you ask me, he's afraid of the water. But he'd never admit to either of those things because both would be considered weaknesses. So instead of pulling away, I grip his hand just as hard, my eyes locked on his.

If I pulled him in, would he drown?

Would I save him? Or would I hold him under, maybe? It's an entertaining thought.

I tug.

"Let go, Ivy," he hisses and glances at the woman.

I follow his gaze and see why he's trying to be the big man here. She's beautiful. I've never seen her before and have no idea who she is, but she is striking. And about a thousand times out of Abel's league.

"Mercedes De La Rosa has come to prepare you for her brother."

The woman walks over and stops at the edge of the pool even while I'm still processing the way Abel just said that.

I let go of Abel, and he straightens, wiping water off his suit and apologizing to her. Looking ridiculous as he kisses her ass.

He wants her. It's so obvious.

It's also obvious she wouldn't let him lick the bottom of her snakeskin Jimmy Choos.

She only has eyes for me anyway. She's staring so intently all I can do is hold her gaze. "Hello, Ivy," she says, her tone haughty, her smile the opposite of warm.

I know instantly she and I will not be friends.

10

Sacred Trinity Cathedral is in the Garden District of New Orleans, less than a mile from the IVI compound. Though The Society has a chapel on their grounds, this church is one of many under our control. Weddings and baptisms are often held in this space because it is large enough to accommodate the local members of our faction. But this evening, there will be only fifteen of the upper-echelon members here to witness the ceremony, along with Ivy's brother. As for my side, I will be the only De La Rosa present.

The cathedral is built in the early gothic architectural style, with a tower and spires looming over the street below. Inside, the space is filled with rich, polished wood, ornate tapestries, and stained glass. It is dark without natural lighting, and tonight, it is only illuminated by the flickering candles lining the entryway and the aisle.

While the church's designated members finish making their preparations for the ceremony, I find solitude in the small chapel attached to the choir on the eastern side of the cathedral. I have grown so accustomed to being alone with my thoughts that this last week has completely taken me out of my element.

I am in need of silence, and I locate it in the shadows of the confessional reserved for more private occasions. Finding sanctuary on the wooden bench inside, I shut the door and close my eyes. The space smells of wood polish and incense, a scent that often pervaded my childhood memories. It would be fair to say I was raised within the confines of Catholic institutions, with only my summers spent at home. At least until I reached an age when it was appropriate for my father to begin molding me into the man he wanted me to be. He was not pleased to discover that my real talent was in mathematics. It seemed like such a waste to him. Though the upper-echelon members of IVI all agreed it would be a useful skill that could be well-honed, I have never been able to forget the hollow disappointment in my father's eyes.

From the beginning, his expectations for me were heavy. I did not act as children should. There was no mischievous innocence to be found in his firstborn son. I was always serious, always studious. I respected his wishes and followed them to his exacting standards. By all accounts, even my own mother's, it should have pleased him. But he found fault in the strange emptiness within my eyes, even as he demanded the very same. I had heard him observe more than once how cold I was, and it was the only thing that seemed to bring even a hint of agreement to his hard features. If ever I did feel a flicker of emotion, a glimpse of my own humanity, I would swiftly dispose of it and forget the event had ever occurred.

In the end, even after all my study and efforts to prove my worth, they did nothing to sway my father's opinion of me. Perhaps that was why it was so easy for me to succumb to Eli Moreno's poisonous praise. While my father never ceased to be disappointed in me, Eli never stopped being in awe of the way my brain worked. He told me more than once he'd never seen anything else like it. We pored over numbers together for days, weeks, months. It was the commonality that forged a bond stronger than steel. And somewhere during that time, I allowed the icy exterior around me to thaw, so he could see parts of me I'd never allowed to exist anywhere else. There were moments I smiled with him. Even moments I laughed. Those events felt so foreign at the time, yet they came naturally with him.

I began to see him as a father figure, and that

mistake cost me more than words can say. How foolish I felt when the seed of his betrayal planted itself in my mind. When I woke in the hospital, disfigured and deformed, I was the only surviving member of my family to walk away from that explosion. Eli had asked me to go in his place with my father and brother who were obligated to accompany me. How easily he swayed me with such a simple request.

I had heard countless times from The Society and my own father that trust was a fickle beast. We had an oath to protect and look after our brothers in the organization, but that didn't mean there weren't defectors or traitors among us. When it did happen, the consequences were often devastating, and the price was always high. I was taught to question the motives of others, and on every other occasion, I had. But Eli had blinded me with his false admiration. His approval was a balm to the weakness inside me, and I fell for it.

I failed my father, my brother, and everyone else who died that night. The opportunity to prove my worth to him is gone, but I can do one last thing. I can dole out the sentence for the man who sent him to the grave.

Eli may never wake again. But whether it is in life or death, he will know the suffering he has caused. He will feel the wrath of vengeance when his daughter pledges herself to me this evening, and for every day she remains in my clutches.

I am unfamiliar with true pleasure. The meaning behind it has always been lost to me. But I suspect it feels like this. The warmth that fills my icy heart when I consider all the ways Ivy will pay for her father's sins. Under my rule, she will be banished to eternal darkness. She will be owned but never loved. And when she looks at herself in the mirror after tonight, she will understand true shame. I will settle for nothing less.

From the shadows of the confessional, I run my fingers over the rosary necklace that will soon collar my wife. The ceremony is set to begin in thirty minutes when Mercedes texts me to let me know she has returned home after her preparations with Ivy. She informs me that my bride's face will be the perfect canvas for the blade of my knife. A strange sort of envy materializes in me as I realize how closely Mercedes was able to study my captive. Since I met her in her father's office many years ago, I have only seen her close up once. The night I gave her the ring was dark and shadowed, and it did not afford me so much detail. And though I have studied the photographs in her file for countless hours, it is not the same as breathing the same air as she does.

I return my sister's message with instructions to gather some things and stay at the compound tonight. After the phone is returned to my pocket, I lean my head back against the wooden partition and close my eyes, only to be interrupted by the bustling sound of someone entering the chapel.

"Just give me five minutes to myself. Please, Abel."

I recognize the lilting melody of Ivy's softness, followed by the growl of her brother.

"I'll be watching," he warns her. "Don't think about doing anything stupid."

There's a rustling of fabric, and the soft slap of feet against the stone flooring. She isn't wearing the heels I bought her. Silly, foolish girl.

For several minutes, I listen to her walk around the chapel. I can't see her, but I can imagine her seeking out sanctuary for herself. Somewhere to hide and never come out.

When the door to the other side of the confessional opens, I suck in a breath and ease my body back into the darkness as Ivy steps inside. She lowers herself onto the kneeler, mere inches away from me, the thin mesh panel the only thing that separates us.

Her scent fills the space as she shifts and sighs, murmuring the Lord's name in prayer. She smells clean and natural with a faint lingering hint of what I think is lotion or shampoo. It is a refreshing change from the cloying sweetness of expensive perfume I am often surrounded by in The Society.

Through the mesh, I can just make out glimpses of the dress I bought her. Black lace clings to her figure like it was made for her. My fingers itch to feel her flesh beneath that fabric. To grab and squeeze and claim her untouched beauty. The small taste of what my eyes can reach isn't enough, and I catch myself leaning forward with a craving for more. Abruptly, I stop myself, coming back to my senses.

What a dangerous game she could be.

This menacing thirst coursing through my blood feels unfamiliar, and I try to justify it away. Four years is a long time to go without feeling the warmth of a woman's body beneath me. It should only be natural that I want to taste what belongs to me. That would make sense, except I don't just want to taste Ivy. I want to devour her completely. She can never know the power of this desire. I must keep it under control.

She doesn't seem to be aware of my presence on the other side as she bows her head and makes a whispered plea. A request that her God, no matter how powerful, won't be able to grant her. I can only imagine what she must think I am.

Has she considered what it will feel like when my fingers fall upon her skin? Is she haunted by visions of me spreading her thighs apart and laying claim to the sweetness of her flesh?

I think not. If she were smart, she would not even entertain the idea of what a monster like me might do to her. Her fate is best left to be experienced without the stain of whatever horrors her own imagination has conjured, as she is well aware worrying cannot save her now.

I believe she has already accepted the future that's been written for her. She's staring at the wood panel, blank. So still, so emotionless, it almost feels like I'm looking into a mirror. And then, without warning, she draws in a ragged breath and brings a trembling hand to her lips. Her shoulders shake under the weight of her sudden despair, but she refuses to shed a single tear. She is stronger than I gave her credit for. And I think I could find eternal fascination in her suffering. I make a silent vow to myself that before the night is through, she will cry for me.

Several minutes pass, and she uses them to steel her faith. I wonder if she will pray to her God when I lay hands on her tonight. She does not yet bear my mark, but there is nothing to stop me from sliding open the window between us and forcing my cock down her throat. A taste of things to come. My fingers dig into the edge of the wooden bench beneath me as I close my eyes to imagine it, and the wood groans under the weight of my frustrations.

When my gaze jolts back to the window, I find her wild, startled eyes peering back at me. Only a sliver of light pours in through the narrow gaps in the wood on my side, keeping me hidden within the shadows. I don't believe she can actually see me, but she can sense me. The predator in the darkness.

She leans closer to the mesh divider, calling out for the priest she thinks I am, and my breath gets caught in my throat. But before she can open it, Abel's shrill voice interrupts the silence. An angry fist rattles her side of the door, making her jump.

The moment is over too soon, and before Ivy can discover me, he yanks open the door and hauls her out.

11

IVY

"Five minutes," Abel says and turns to walk out of the small chapel to the side of the cathedral. It dates back a century before the cathedral was built, and they preserved it during the construction of the cathedral itself.

My classmates and I took first Communion here years ago. As I look down the aisle, I remember walking toward the altar in our pretty white dresses with hands bound by our rosaries. Before the ceremony, we'd made our first confessions. There had been eight of us, and I remember shifting uncomfortably in the pew as I nervously waited my turn.

I remember the creaking door of the confessional, the smell of it as I knelt on the hard wooden kneeler—no cushion for the sinner—and spoke my sins aloud.

The priest's face was just a profile, barely that in

the darkness behind the mesh. I hadn't had much to confess, so I'd made things up. I thought if I didn't, he'd think I was lying.

Afterward, I joined the others at the foot of the altar and say my requisite number of Hail Marys and a few more than Father had prescribed because I'd lied to him.

Being in here after all this time takes me back. I shudder and wrap my arms around myself. It's cold, but it's not just the cold that has me shivering.

I walk around the room barefoot, the engravings on the tombs so old they're just scratches in the icy stone beneath my feet. I take in each of the twelve Stations of the Cross. Witness Christ's crucifixion. But when I get to the altar and look up at him, I think about how he could let this happen. How, if God were real, could he let this happen to me? To my dad?

And Hazel.

She'd run away days before her wedding.

How could he let it happen to her?

Or maybe this is his plan. Maybe The Society is right, and God is behind them, and God wants one of the Moreno sisters.

I walk to the back of the church playing with the edge of the lace veil. The confessional is in the same place, and I go to it, touching the rickety old wooden door. Its grooves are dusty. No one uses this confessional anymore, I guess.

Pushing it aside, I enter the little space I'd entered one time before. It's smaller than I remember. The mesh is metal now, the design a thousand crosses. I always wondered if the priests hearing the confessions knew who we were. If they remembered our sins.

I kneel on that kneeler now, then sit back on the small bench.

"God."

I wipe my face, then instinctively pull my bangs down over my eye. I remember the look on Mercedes's face when she'd seen it. Like she's never seen anything so terrible. *Bitch.*

I take a deep breath in. The smell in here is different than I expect. A hint of cologne beneath the incense and wood polish. Maybe I'm wrong. Maybe they do still use the confessional.

Sighing, I let my breath out, then close my eyes and place my knees back on that kneeler, bringing my hands together in prayer.

"If you're there...if you're real..." A sob breaks into my words, and I use the heels of my hands to wipe my eyes, careful of the mascara and black liner Mercedes applied.

I want to ask him not to let this happen. But that's stupid. It's happening. So, I ask a different favor.

I bow my head. "Don't let him be a monster," I whisper.

Something creaks.

I gasp, my eyes flying open, and I swear I see movement on the other side of the mesh separating confessor from sinner.

"Father?" I ask, peering closer when he doesn't answer. "Is someone there?"

I hear the chapel door open, then my brother's footsteps. It can only be him. "Ivy," he bellows when he doesn't see me. "For fuck's sake, where are you?"

I look from the closed door of the confessional to the mesh behind which the priest would sit and back as my brother roughly yanks the rickety door open, making it rattle on its hinges. He then grabs my arm.

"You're hurting me!" I cry out.

"Why are you hiding? You think I'm so stupid I won't find you?"

"I wasn't hiding, you jerk!"

"Christ. You're a fucking mess." He wipes what I guess is mascara from under my eye, then takes a breath in. He pulls the veil down over my face and seems to collect himself.

It's almost time.

12

I n The Society, weddings are typically a large affair. Members of the upper echelon are held to higher standards, and it is often a competitive sport between the women to see who can outdo each other at these events. They will commission ice sculptures and designer gowns and custom-cut diamonds because they have the wealth and power to do so.

There will be none of that fanfare at my wedding. The only men here to witness the event are those who are required by IVI as witnesses. If it were completely at my discretion, it would just be the two of us with the priest, but we must all abide by the rules, and this is one of them.

A strange undercurrent of tension runs through my veins as I study my reflection in the mirror. My leather oxfords are polished. The custom black

Brioni tux is flawlessly pressed with a crisp white dress shirt underneath. Ink on my arm peeks out from beneath the cuff. But it's the ink on my face that has my attention. Ivy is probably aware of my scars, but she hasn't seen me with the half skull yet. I can only imagine her reaction as she reaches the end of the aisle. What will she do? Will she try to run? Will her brother have to drag her back up to the altar and force her to quiet her grievous sobs so she can choke out her vows to the likes of me?

The thought leaves a bitter taste in my mouth.

Once upon a time, women in The Society were falling at their feet to marry me. Now, I can't be certain my bride won't just impale herself with a candlestick rather than give herself to me.

How Ivy feels about it doesn't matter. She is a means to an end. I won't tolerate her disrespect, no matter how disgusted she may be. The same can be said for her brother. And it isn't but a moment later that he appears in the doorway with my guard behind him.

"You called for me?" Abel asks.

With a nod, I gesture him into the room I've taken over in the rectory. The guests can wait. After what just happened, I have a pressing need to deal with Abel first.

His gaze moves over me in swift and cunning appraisal. He thinks he is quite clever. So certain he has me fooled with his respectful façade.

I take a sip of my smoked scotch and set the glass on the table before returning his gaze. "Did I fail to make you aware of how I felt about Ivy being touched by anyone other than myself?"

He shifts his weight as his face pales in the dim room. I can see his mind working, wondering how I could possibly know how he just grabbed Ivy in the chapel. I could tell him, but that would ruin the illusion that I have eyes everywhere, and I want him to feel it.

"I'm not sure I understand—"

I take two steps toward him, my face a mask of serenity. He isn't anticipating it when I slam my fist into his gut, and he doubles over, coughing and sputtering like he's never taken a punch in his life. His ignorance and weakness only serve to fuel my infuriation. I hit him twice more in the gut before he collapses to his knees and curls into a fetal position, choking out his repentance.

"I thought you wanted me to keep her in line."

"It's my job to keep her in line." I ease my leather oxford against his throat, pressing until he's clawing at me with wide, panicked eyes.

From the doorway, my best man and close friend Judge watches with a bored expression. There is nobody who would stop me from draining the life from Abel even at this very moment.

"Repeat after me." I dig my heel into his throat so hard his eyes bulge from his face. "After you walk her down the aisle and give me what is mine, you will never touch Ivy again."

"I won't," he croaks, digging his nails into the tops of my shoes, destroying a perfectly good pair of Italian leather.

For that offense, I release the pressure on his throat and force the tip of my shoe between his teeth so hard, I can hear them cracking as he gags and gasps for air. Once I am satisfied that he has tasted the dirt he is worthy of, I smear his bloody spit across his chin and leave him lying there as he stares up at me in disbelief.

"Fucking Moreno." I spit the words out and retrieve my drink, choking it down in two more swallows. "Get out of my sight. Now."

He drags himself upright, unable to look at me as he heads for the door with his fists clenched. Judge steps aside, and Abel disappears down the hall as I turn back to the mirror to adjust my clothing.

"I see you haven't lost your touch."

A familiar voice echoes from behind me, and when I turn to find my oldest friend, I am stunned by his presence. Angelo Augustine was a classmate back in our Catholic school days. He's also a Sovereign Son of IVI, hailing from Seattle. We have kept in close contact over the years, but I have not seen him in the flesh for at least six. Letters and phone calls were our only method of contact, given that visiting him in prison was too risky for The Society.

"Should I expect a SWAT team to arrive as witnesses too?" I ask dryly.

He chuckles, but the expression fades to darkness soon after. "I have been released early."

"How?" I tilt my head to study him. He hasn't changed much since the last time we met. His features are much like my own. Dark hair. Arctic eyes. He could have passed for my brother and often did when we were younger. Before the explosion.

"Details for another time." He steps inside the room. "Tonight is about you."

"You'll be staying then?" I inquire as I pour him a glass of scotch.

From my periphery, I see Judge nod to indicate he's going to give us a minute before he disappears down the hall. I wasn't expecting a visitor, but I'm not about to leave him here without understanding the reason for his return.

Angelo takes the glass and swirls it in his hand, inhaling the scent. It's a natural inclination amongst the Sovereign Sons. You never know what might be poisoned. But I attribute his actions to memories of times past rather than distrust. If there is anyone in this world Angelo knows he can trust, it is me.

"I wish I could." He takes a sip and closes his eyes, savoring it. "I can't be seen by other members yet. The time is not right to reveal my freedom. But I couldn't let the occasion pass without coming to see you."

I nod at him. There is an understanding between us that doesn't need words. Angelo knows betrayal as well as I do, and he is busy making his own plans. As much as it would please me to have him at the altar tonight, I won't ask that of him if it interferes with his revenge. In some ways, I often think his betrayal was worse than mine. I have Ivy's father to thank for the destruction in my life, but Angelo's was his own flesh and blood. He's spent the last six years of his life caged like an animal for a crime he didn't commit, and he won't suffer that slight gently.

He finishes his glass and pours another as he examines me. Angelo is aware of everything that transpired, but he never saw the damage firsthand. I can appreciate that he did not wince when he laid eyes upon me, as it has become a natural reaction from most.

"Nice ink," he remarks. "It suits you."

"It serves a purpose." I reach for a tissue and use it to wipe Abel's blood off my shoe.

"So, you are really going through with this." His tone is neutral, but he can't hide the wariness in his eyes. Angelo knows everything regarding my plans for the Moreno family. While I was recovering, we spent many hours going over the details in code over the phone.

I suspect my friend is concerned for me, but he should know me better by now.

"I am," I answer his question.

He opens the small wooden box resting on the table beside me, inspecting the rings. "It has all been decided."

"Yes."

"And what if it doesn't go to plan?" His gaze drifts back to me.

I toss away the tissue and wipe my hands. "What do you mean?"

"Forever is a long time to exact your revenge. I should think you'd want an end in sight."

I turn to study him. "Forever is only as long as it requires to give me sons."

He plucks out Ivy's ring and studies it. "So, you will bed her for as long as it takes to produce your heirs. Watch her bear those heirs. Care for them as only a mother can. And then either torment her for eternity or bleed the life from her body?"

His tone is uncertain, and it irritates me. "Do you doubt my intentions?"

"Your intentions, no." He replaces the ring and shuts the box. "The outcome, perhaps."

"What little faith you have in me," I mutter.

"Actually, I envy you."

The emptiness in Angelo's voice catches me off guard, but his words make me grimace.

"Why would you envy me?"

"Everything has always been so certain to you. I've never met anyone who calculates every decision and executes it without a second thought or regret. I can't imagine what it's like to live without the weight of indecision or emotions weighing you down."

I blink at him, frowning. He makes it sound like I'm a robot, although, I suppose it shouldn't surprise me. That's what most people think of me. The members in IVI call me the human computer. My talent lies in calculations, projections, and complex problems. They can all be easily solved by working it out on paper. But human psychology and the complexity of the emotional spectrum are not in my realm of understanding. There are too many variables, and there is no hard and fast answer.

However, it's not as if I don't have emotions. I just choose not to feel or express them.

Angelo chuckles softly as something seems to occur to him. "Remember how Sister Margaret would accuse you of being a sociopath?"

"Yes, well..." I shrug. "Perhaps she was correct."

Angelo leans against the table and dips his head. "That would be the easiest thing to believe, but I know it isn't true. I worry that you don't fully understand what you're getting yourself into here."

"Will you question your own intentions when the time comes to exact your revenge?" I pin him with my gaze.

"No." He stands up and stuffs his hands into his pockets.

I think we are finally finished with this topic, but Angelo proves otherwise.

"I know you've fucked women, Santiago, but it isn't the same as living with one. Facing her presence every day is an inescapable situation. So, please, heed my advice. If you are determined to do this, never forget who she is. Don't underestimate the power of proximity. Even if she's sleeping in your bed every night, she is still the enemy."

I smooth my hands over the lapels of my suit and nod in concession. "There is no need to worry. She will never sleep in my bed."

13

SANTIAGO

After Angelo's quiet exit, Judge takes his place beside me to the right of the altar. Before us, the rest of the witnesses are already seated in the church pews. The building is dimly lit with only a soft glow, and though I'd still prefer not to be standing here in front of everyone, it is made easier by the fact that they can only see faint glimpses of me.

Within a few moments, the organist begins to play the music chosen for the ceremony. Ivy appears in the doorway with Abel at her side. I glance at him long enough to see the stone set of his jaw as he meets my gaze, but already, my eyes are drifting to my bride. A silhouette of black lace and roses. She is a haunting thing of beauty, and I almost expect her to disappear like an apparition, never to be seen again.

Abel guides her down the aisle, not exactly dragging her but urging her forward with a firm grip on her arm that continues to provoke my last nerve. His mouth is clearly swollen, and dark bruises are starting to form beneath the tight muscles in his throat. And still, he chooses to deliver his sister to me so willingly.

My heart beats in time to the music, and I don't draw in a single breath until Ivy stands before me. Abel releases her, and she sways a little on her feet. Annoyance festers inside me as I consider the reason. Is it nerves, or has she been drinking?

When she has settled into her place, she tilts her chin up to look at me, and it's impossible to miss the startled gasp that falls from her lips. The glow of the candles dances over us, highlighting my features in distorted shapes. Almost immediately, her eyes are drawn to the half-skull, and the roses slip from her hands to scatter around our feet. She looks startled, slightly embarrassed, and morbidly fascinated as she continues to study me.

I regret not allowing her to see me until now because more than anything, I wish we were alone for this moment. In my mind, I had played out this scenario so many times. I imagined all the ways it might unfold. Fear. Anger. Terror. I could easily see her running from me. Throwing herself in front of a car on the street rather than go through with this. I never imagined she might look at me the way she is right now. That she would want to study me. That she would find me so... *intriguing.*

I'm not certain how long we stand there like that. I don't even realize I've reached for her wrist, anchoring her to me, until my thumb grazes over the warm pulse beating wildly there. Perhaps that is why she hasn't moved. Her eyes drift to the large fingers wrapped around her, examining them as if they are a weapon. It's tempting to release her, to see if she might still consider running, but I find that I don't want to.

Regardless, there isn't time to consider it. The music draws to an end, and we are both forced to focus on the priest. He instructs us to sit in the designated chairs on the platform, and so begins the traditional ceremony.

We open with a hymn, followed by readings from the Old Testament and the New. The priest speaks at length about marriage, gospel, and reflection, but I hear very little of it. When Ivy and I are united in front of the altar and asked to join hands, she offers them to me stiffly.

My fingers wrap around hers, noting she has grown cold and pale as if her reality is finally settling over her. She swallows and looks up at me from beneath her lashes, and I catch a glimpse of her oddly shaped pupil. Something she often tries to hide with her hair. That pupil was the source of much torment when she was a child, and the humiliation from her school days still lingers with her. When she is my wife, she will come to understand that I will not permit her to hide it from me or anyone else.

The priest begins the vow ceremony as I requested, opting to skip the formalities about coming into this marriage free of coercion and promising to love each other until we turn to dust. I don't miss the uncomfortable glance he casts in my direction, but I choose to focus on my bride instead of whatever opinions he may have on the subject.

Ivy and I start by declaring our intent, and then I repeat the sacred words that include the only promise I can keep. I will take her as my wife. I will be faithful to her in good times and bad, in sickness and in health, until death do us part. The intensity in my declaration burns my voice and heats my gaze, seeming to unnerve my bride as she casts her eyes to the floor several times before returning them to me.

Her voice is a mere whisper when she repeats the same vows, yet she promises herself to me with a resignation I find equally frustrating and fascinating.

The priest acknowledges our consent and proceeds to bless us before we move onto the ring ceremony. Ivy receives my ring with my repeated promise of fidelity in the name of the Father, the Son, and the Holy Ghost. When I slide the matching band to her salt and pepper diamond ring onto her trembling finger, I feel a sick sense of satisfaction.

That feeling only amplifies when she does the same to me.

Following my requests, the priest does not direct me to kiss her before he pronounces her as mine. That is something to be saved for the privacy of another time, where her disgust cannot be so visible to all my brethren.

We are united in prayer and then greet the witnesses to exchange a sign of peace, followed by communion. After our last nuptial blessing, we are dismissed with the intentions of meeting our guests back at the compound.

When I reach for Ivy's arm, wrapping my cold fingers around her skin again, she shivers. She keeps her gaze forward, but it is impossible not to notice how slight she feels in my grasp. As we walk down the aisle and out to the street where a driver is waiting with a car for us, I can feel the unsteadiness in her gait once more. It is only when she climbs into the car that I see she is still barefoot.

Marco shuts the door after I'm securely seated next to my bride. The privacy divider is already up, sealing us into a tomb-like silence.

Ivy wrings her hands together in her lap as the car lurches forward. She appears nervous, as she should be, but her fear does not satisfy me quite as much as I'd hoped.

"Where are the shoes I bought you?" My voice booms through the space between us.

She peeks up at me from beneath her lashes and begins to study the artwork on my face again. I watch her carefully for signs of her true feelings, but I only see her curiosity. It perplexes me beyond measure, and it irritates me more than I could have anticipated. She is supposed to be disgusted by me. She is supposed to hate me. This is the natural order of things.

"It was you, wasn't it?" she asks quietly. "In the confessional. Your cologne—"

The muscles in my spine turn rigid at her observation. I did not expect her to be so... perceptive. She should know better than to ask me such a question.

"Do you mean when you begged God not to let you marry a monster?" I sneer.

"That isn't what I meant—" She sucks in a breath and shakes her head. "You're twisting my words around."

I turn my gaze toward the window, stewing in my aggravation. What a disobedient little surprise she has turned out to be. Challenging me already. Refusing to wear the shoes I bought her. Questioning me as if she has a right to do so. As if a Moreno could ever possess the authority equal to a Sovereign Son. In her mind, she is probably glad for the match. This is, after all, what her family wants. Elevation. Money. Power. Attaching herself to me will give her all those things. And at her core, I have no doubt Ivy is just the same as her mother. She may have toyed with the notion of a different life, but she chose to marry me just the same. It would be foolish of me not to believe she has her own motivations, and whatever they may be, she will never have my trust.

I am relieved for her reminder of our respective roles. It is up to me to let her know this behavior will not be tolerated, and there is no reason it should wait. Ivy may have readily attached herself to me, but she will come to understand the only wedded bliss she is to receive are the punishments I dole out.

The ride is over after a few brief moments, and when Marco turns off the ignition, I tap on the glass and instruct him to leave us. He does.

The street is dark outside, only the lamplight filtering into the car. But it does little to hide the tremor in my bride's body as I turn to her and reach for her face. I'm determined to put her in her place at once, but when she tries to hide her strange eye from me, my intentions are momentarily displaced.

"Don't," I warn her as she tries to adjust her hair. "I want to see it."

She freezes, and our gazes collide. And for the first time, I realize that perhaps Angelo was right. It is difficult to hold onto my anger in the face of her beauty. As my fingers drift down to the beating pulse in her throat, I can't decide if I want to kiss her or strangle her.

"Never hide your defects from me," I tell her. "They are mine to enjoy now."

"But... I hate it." Her voice wavers.

A hollow laugh echoes from my chest. "Perhaps I quite like it."

She seems taken aback by my strange response, as am I. My grip tightens, and then I release her. I don't understand what she's doing to me.

"Please," she begs, her hand hovering near her hair.

"You seem to be under the impression that you can do as you like," I answer coldly. "Do I need to remind you of the basic rules of The Society? The rules you swore an oath to?"

She sucks in a sharp breath and unconsciously curls into herself. She understands the meaning of my words quite clearly.

"I don't need a reminder," she answers softly.

"Yet, you will receive one regardless."

Outside, I can hear the footsteps of members passing into the courtyard. The marking ceremony is set to begin momentarily. But I have a promise to keep, so it will have to wait. I open the door and gesture for Ivy.

She steps out of the car and lets out a small shriek when I hoist her up over my shoulder, her bare feet dangling beneath the fabric of her dress. We receive a few curious glances as I enter the courtyard and veer away from the chair and table waiting for her in the center. My footsteps are swift and certain as they echo down the corridor to the small, private chapel for members only.

The door creaks shut as I step inside and stalk toward the altar, where I deposit my disobedient wife onto her feet. A warm red glow from the glass votives illuminates her face as she dares a glance up at me. Frustration breeds my dark desires, blood coursing violently toward my cock and hardening it to the point of pain.

I have thought about punishing her since the temptation of marrying her sowed itself in my mind. Patience has been the only virtue I've possessed since the explosion. The notion that someday, every Moreno would suffer as I have. So it is difficult for me to reconcile that more than anything, right now, I want to feel her.

Once will not be enough to satiate my needs tonight. Her scent intoxicates me. The warmth of her flesh beckons me in the strangest way. I need... something from her, but I can't even be sure what it is.

The intensity of her gaze feels like a violation, so I spin her in my arms, making her gasp. One arm hooks around her waist and bends her over the wooden altar while the other comes to rest on the delicate lace covering her back. The veil is obscuring all that I want to see, so I rip it off and discard it onto the floor. She falls into complete stillness as I trace over the black satin buttons adorning the curve of her spine, pausing to appreciate the beauty of her form cinched up so elegantly in this dress.

"You should know if I give you something, I expect you to wear it," I tell her roughly.

"I couldn't," she whispers.

My hand falls away from her back, and I gather up handfuls of the fabric skimming over the wooden floor. When I tug it up to reveal her bare thighs, her body goes rigid beneath me.

"What are you doing?" She peeks over her shoulder, daring a glance at my face.

"Punishing you."

The moment the words leave my lips, she tries to jerk away, but I press her down firmly with my palm in the center of her back. Her face is mere inches from the heat of the candles, her chest heaving as she glances around for an invisible savior. There are none to be found for her here.

I shove the fabric up around her waist, revealing the perfect curves of her hips and ass on display in a tiny scrap of black lace. My eyes roam over the untouched landscape of her body, and I stifle the agony building in my throat, forcing myself to remember why we are here.

I reach for a candle, and Ivy's breathing escalates as she tries to crane her head back.

"Santiago."

The plea in her voice rips through me with

surprising efficacy. My fingers are wrapped around the candle, frozen. I blink at her, stunned by my reaction, and then shake it away.

Dragging the glass across the wood, I savor the way her body trembles beneath my palm. When I am satisfied that I have sufficiently drawn out the anticipation, I slip my fingers beneath the delicate band of her panties and tear it into two pieces. Repeating the process on the other side, I let the scrap of fabric fall to the floor until she is bare for me.

My palm curves over her ass, and I silently shudder as my fingers knead into the warmth of her flesh. I could take her now, but it wouldn't be enough. I need so much time for the things I want to do with her.

I dip my palms down to her inner thighs and force them farther apart until I have a beautiful view of her pink pussy glistening in the candlelight. The sight of her undeniable arousal makes my breath hiss between my teeth. I know it must be a fear response, but I'm aching to touch her there, to see it for myself, and I almost do. But first, I have a promise to keep.

I drag the glass votive over the curve of her spine and into the dip of her lower back. The warmth against her delicate skin makes her arch for me, and she sucks in a breath and begins to plead with me in earnest.

"You don't have to do this, Santiago."

"Yes. I do."

I hold her firmly in place with one hand and tilt the jar with the other. The first drop of wax splatters against her ass, making her hiss. I watch in fascination as it drips all the way down to her thigh, hardening within seconds. She jerks beneath my palm, and I press more of my weight into her, tilting the candle again on the other side. Another river of wax bleeds down her flesh, and I find that I could do this all night.

Ivy's breathing gradually begins to settle as I pour another drop. She stops fighting me altogether when my free hand snakes up her back to settle on the nape of her neck. Warm fingers caress her there as I paint the lower half of her body like a canvas. Scarlet blooms across her ass as I repeat the process over and over again, creating long meandering streams all the way down to her calves.

She is obedient and still, nails digging into the wood when I finally set the candle aside and admire my work. I have no doubt it stings, but she did not shed a single tear. I drag my palms over her ass, brushing the hard wax away, and in the process, it exposes her pussy to me again. When the cold air hits between her thighs, she squirms in my grasp and then nearly jumps out of her skin as I slide my fingers over the moisture gathered there.

"How strange it must feel to like such a punishment," I murmur.

Her voice is strangely absent as I slide my fingers back and forth through her wetness, toying with her clit with torturous slowness. After a few passes, she begins to melt onto the table, her body going slack as her eyes shut. She is no longer arching to pull away but arching into my touch instead. I press my body against her, playing with her pussy as I drag my fingertips through her hair, gathering a fistful and tugging until her head bows back. My lips hover over the skin of her neck, inhaling her. A shiver moves through her and my teeth graze down over the length of her shoulder before I bite into her skin, marking her. She whimpers as I press my hardness against the soft flesh of her ass and dip a finger inside her.

"Never forget who this belongs to," I growl into her ear.

She moans as I tease her so slowly it must feel as agonizing for her as it does for me.

"Say the words." I tighten my grip on her hair, disregarding the unrecognizable roughness in my voice.

"Santiago," she pants. "Santiago De La Rosa."

I groan into the sweetness of her skin, my fingers working without mercy as I bring her to the edge of sanity. It would not take much to make her come. Already, she is biting her lip, trying to contain the strangled noises in her throat. I bring her so close she can taste it. Every muscle in her body is tensing. A few more strokes and she could be free.

Right before she falls, I stop and pull away, leaving her aching and swollen for me. Agony is the only gift she deserves. When she opens her eyes and glances over her shoulder, she looks confused and frustrated by her own response. I'd be lying if I said I wasn't too.

I drag the fabric back over her hips and cover her. Slowly, she brings her body upright, and I pull her toward me. My fingers come to rest on her jaw, our breaths only an inch apart.

"Close your eyes."

She does as I request, and I tilt my head down to meet hers. She does not recoil as I'd expect when my lips graze hers. It is only a second and nothing more, but it's enough to feel what it's like before she truly learns to hate me. She opens her eyes and peers up at me, studying me too intently for my liking.

"Now, thank me for being so lenient," I tell her.

"Thank you," she answers bitterly.

The torment in her eyes unsettles me, and I'm not sure why it compels me to stroke her cheek, showing her a softness she doesn't deserve, at least for a moment.

"Prepare yourself," I order. "The time has come for you to bear my mark."

"*T*he time has come for you to bear my mark."

I step on the ruined veil as Santiago closes his hand around my arm and walks me to the chapel door.

I watch his back as I stumble along behind him. I smell him still, his cologne of wood and leather and money. I will forever associate this scent with him. It will forever make my stomach feel like the bottom has dropped out.

He had been there, sitting silent in the confessional as if he were my confessor. And if he didn't hate me before, he surely does after hearing what I asked.

Don't let him be a monster.

I hadn't meant physically, but how do I explain that to him?

Santiago chooses that moment to glance back at

me, and I shudder. Maybe I'm a hypocrite after all. It's the skull side of his face. The tattoo that makes my breath catch, that makes me unable to look away. It's grotesque and captivating at once.

I see the scars beneath if I look closely. I wish I could take my time and study them, but he doesn't allow for that. They're on the other side of his face too, the beautiful side, but not nearly as bad as what I see hints of beneath that ink.

Did he do it to hide them? The scars?

Why a skull? It's like he's already dead.

Or did he do it out of shame?

We reach the door, and he grins as he reaches for the doorknob, and I think no, not out of shame. It's a dare. A challenge. *Look at me if you can stand it.*

Or a big fuck you to anyone who would otherwise stare at the damage.

The oddest thing is that although I know it's meant to terrify, that he means to terrify me, I don't feel that. Not only that, at least. Because I know if I wake in the middle of the night to be greeted by the inked side of his face, he will succeed. I will be terrified.

But there's more there. I glimpse it in his eyes, too, when it edges out the rage. The hate.

I see pain.

"Keep up," he commands as he pulls the door open, and I wonder why he married me. Why he chose me when it's apparent he hates me. So why choose to tie yourself to someone you hate?

Or does he think no one else would have him with his deformity? He's a Sovereign Son. No matter what he looks like, any father would hand over his daughter should he demand it.

Demand.

That is what he's done with me. Demanded me. And here I am. Married to the beast.

We step into the dark corridor, and I stumble as I try to keep up. The air grows cooler as we head toward the courtyard.

The Society's seat in New Orleans is in the French Quarter, the main building a massive and ancient mansion three floors tall with a huge courtyard at the heart open to the sky. A fountain stands off-center. The building was expanded over time, but at one point, it must have been the centerpiece. Water trickles softly, the sound almost lost beneath the haunting melody playing over speakers hidden throughout the property inside and out. Something dark and gothic and modern. I recognize it, but I can't name the artist. I'm too distracted.

I hear voices too, a low hum of men talking. The clanking of glasses and the smell of whiskey and melting wax again, like at church. Because the place is lit by a thousand candles. The only electric lights are those antique lampposts that only cast the softest yellow light set here and there in patches of trees, near the half dozen sitting areas.

I have an idea of what will happen next although the ceremony is secret. Only founding family members and, of those, only men are invited to be present. But there were always rumors at school. Girls who would claim to have seen the mark on their mother or on a new bride. The stories were always grotesque, and I guessed them to be dramatized. But when I smell the burning wood of fire, all those stories come crashing back in vivid detail, and I instinctively pull back.

He wouldn't do that to me, would he?

Santiago turns to me, clearly annoyed. I take another step, trying to pull free, but he holds fast.

"What's going to happen?" My voice is a broken whisper. I'm scared, and I can't hide the fact.

He comes closer maybe to better study me in the dim light. He pushes the hair back from my face to make a point of looking at my strange eye. Maybe we have something in common. He is not repulsed by me as I am not repulsed by him.

I lick my lips, remembering his kiss. His lips on mine. His taste. Lace scratches my hardened nipples. My dress did not come with a bra. With each small movement, I feel the remnants of hardened wax on my skin, and I take a deep breath in at the memory of his punishment.

And of my arousal.

I swallow, goose bumps covering every inch of exposed skin.

Santiago steps to within an inch of me, the toes of his shoes against my bare ones.

I have to crane my neck to meet his eyes. I wonder if others look or if they cringe away? What is he used to?

"What's going to happen is you will do as you're told," he says.

"Will it hurt?" I ask stupidly. It's what I'm afraid of. Not that I'll bear his mark, that will come later, but the method of putting that mark upon me.

He cocks his head, one corner of his mouth curving upward. "Are you afraid of a little pain?"

I see the scars beneath the ink again and wonder how much those hurt.

"Are you?" he prods.

"Just tell me."

His mouth moves into a smirk as his gaze moves over my face, hovering at my lips before returning to my eyes. "Your answer is written all over your face, Ivy. So easy to read." He shakes his head like he's disappointed, but a moment later, that smirk is gone. "I like you scared, actually. You're very pretty when you're scared." He wipes his thumb across my cheekbone, and we both look down at the smear of black. Mascara. I must look a mess. "I like your tears too, and I'll have more of those."

He wraps his hand around the back of my neck.

The intricate twist his sister forced my hair into is tight enough to give me the beginnings of a headache.

I gasp when he jerks me to him, fingers rough on the bare skin there like he's testing it. They mark the back of a woman's neck. It's how the stories went at school, at least. I imagine a barcode there so male members can scan to see who they can touch and who they can't.

I hate everything about The Society from what it's done to our family to what it requires of women. What it requires of me.

"You're mine. And tonight, you'll bear a mark for all to know exactly that," Santiago says.

Abruptly he lets go of the back of my neck and turns, fingers digging into my arm as he pulls me forward. I stub my toe on a stone, stumble and hear a woman's gasp. I look in the direction of the sound and see a flash of color, a rustle of leaves, and behind the half-faced sculpture I can't name, I see a woman. She's young, my age, I'd guess. It's just for a moment that I see her, but when I meet her wide eyes, she quickly puts a finger to her lips, urging me not to give her away.

She's not supposed to be here. The women, if they're on the property, would be cloistered inside. Is she afraid I'll tell?

Santiago stops, turns in the direction of the sound. He heard her too.

I mean to take a step away from the sculpture to distract him but he tugs my arm and I end up bumping into his chest. I bounce off and he looks down at me.

"Are you always so clumsy?"

"I—"

"There they are, the bride and groom," someone calls out from the courtyard. "You've kept us waiting, Santiago."

Men laugh.

I see my husband's face morph and his expression shift. Something akin to an almost physical discomfort. Jaw tight, he closes his eyes and draws a slow, deep breath in. If I didn't know better, I'd say he's steeling himself. But I do know better. What reason would this man need for steeling himself? He is a king here.

When he opens them again, they're empty. It's like he's just slipped a mask on, another one.

We take the last few steps and we're in the courtyard.

I gasp when I see the gathering. I remember that night Santiago first came into my bedroom and put his ring on my finger. Because the sight that greets me is a terrifying one. All those men wearing those black robes with the hoods pulled up, white and black masks gleaming underneath.

"I don't want to," I say stupidly, sounding like a child.

Santiago laughs. "You think you have a choice?"

I shift my gaze from them to him.

"Besides, it's not those men you have to worry about," he adds.

I swallow.

He turns to them, and I understand all those candles. People are curious. I wonder if any have seen him fully. Santiago is careful. I get the feeling only those he allows actually see his face.

"I needed a moment with my new bride," Santiago says casually to a slew of nods and chuckles. He nudges me ahead of him.

The men shift their attention to me. I shrink back but behind me is the wall of Santiago's chest.

"Where are you going, sweet Ivy? We haven't yet begun," he whispers, arm wrapping around me from behind, fingers on my jaw lifting my face, making me look at all those men. A little more than a dozen. No women. Like at the church.

At least my brother isn't here to witness this next humiliation. Or is he one of them?

No, only the upper echelon wear the robes. They wouldn't allow Abel in even if they did allow my father.

Santiago keeps hold of me as we cross the courtyard. The rain has cleared, but the sky remains cloudy. The stone is cold and hard beneath my bare feet with the debris of dried, fallen leaves from the trees.

I have only been here once before. My father brought me when I was little, and he had business here. The babysitter had canceled at the last minute. I remember being awed by it then. I'm as awed now.

Two sets of staircases lead to the upper floors where any glass door or window has been shuttered against curious eyes. Green cascades from the railings, growing lush in the damp Louisiana climate. Even the air in this place is that of money. Of power.

The men fall quiet as Santiago walks me toward them, our steps slowed, him not so much dragging me anymore. No, not toward them. We're walking toward the ornately carved wooden canopy that looks to be centuries old. It's draped thickly with cascading red roses woven into vibrant green ivy. The floor beneath the canopy is littered with the flowers too. I can almost smell them there are so many.

The men's expressions grow more serious as they begin to take their seats in the chairs lined up across from this makeshift stage.

Beneath the canopy are a small table with golden legs and a single chair, large and golden to match the table, the pattern on the upholstered cushions too worn to make out from here.

As we near the table, I see equipment on top. Some of which I can't place, but others, like the leather restraints, have my stomach falling away. I stumble, catching my toe on a slightly raised stone as my gaze shifts to the firepits scattered throughout the courtyard and to the one closest to the canopy with the iron pressed into the fire.

That's the one that scares me.

I don't back up consciously. I don't realize I've done it until both of Santiago's hands come to my arms and turn me to face him.

"Wife," he says, and I drag my gaze from that iron up to him.

"You can't—"

He leans down toward me, his cheek brushing mine, igniting a spark. "I can," he whispers against my ear. He holds me like that for a moment, then licks the shell of it, making me shudder as he draws backward and nearly lifts me off my feet to take me to the center of the canopy. He crushes the roses beneath his shoes, and the smell and roar of the fires overwhelm all of my senses. Once I'm standing before the chair and table, he turns me to face the men, and keeping his hands on my shoulders, he gives me a single-word command.

"Kneel."

I swallow hard. I look up at him, and he looks down at me. Behind him, a sea of faces watches curiously, intently. Will I obey? Will I submit? And what happens if I don't?

"Please don't," I start, but no more words come. *Please don't hurt me.* It's pointless. He enjoys hurting me. Didn't I just learn that?

His hands tighten on my shoulders, and I go down, the lace of the dress rough between my naked knees and the cold stone. I kneel up, staring at him. My husband. I feel the first tear slide down my cheek. Is this what he wants? He hasn't even touched me yet, and I'm already giving him my tears.

But if it is, he doesn't acknowledge it. His expression is unreadable as he walks behind me.

I don't move, concentrating on keeping my gaze from roaming to that fire. To the branding iron in the flames. My heart races, a cold sweat covering me as my vision blurs around the edges. I'm not sure I can take that kind of pain. No, I'm sure I can't.

Santiago draws my wrists behind my back, and I feel cool leather cuff first my right wrist, then my left.

I still don't move.

Next come the cuffs at my upper arms. These force me to sit up, making my breasts jut out toward the watching men.

I swallow hard as he tightens the bonds, immobilizing me. I can still run, I think. I'd be clumsier than usual bound as I am, but I can still run. Although I know I won't get far.

Something cold wraps around my neck and I gasp, wanting to reach up but unable to. It's thin, whatever it is, and it fastens with a click.

I feel him stand and hear him as he walks

around me again. I look up at him. At the two sides of his face.

He watches me for a long minute. Only when I drop my gaze does he crouch down to take my face into his hand. His touch is gentle as he studies me, studies the few tears that drop from my eyes.

I want to tell him not to hurt me. I want to beg him not to brand me. But I can't form words. Can't make sound.

He lets something drop from his other hand. It makes a clinking noise when it hits the stone, and I shift my gaze to it. It's a long, thin chain. He lifts my chin higher and hooks it onto the choker he just placed around my neck and runs the other end through a small ring attached to the stone floor that I hadn't even noticed.

My gaze slides to the fire again, and the only sound I can make is a choked sob.

He tugs the chain, making me bow my head, but holds my gaze as he leans toward me, his cheek against my cheek again, the rough stubble on his jaw scratching my skin.

"Move and I'll use the branding iron, do you understand?"

He draws back to look at me.

I'm trembling, shaking. It's a good thing I'm already on the floor, or I'd have fallen by now.

"Do you understand me, Ivy?"

I nod frantically, tears falling wildly, feeling just a hint of relief as I see that iron in my periphery.

He nods once, then continues to shorten the chain, and when my head is bowed far enough forward, he locks it.

One of those tears drops on the stone floor. Then another.

He stands, the space he vacated empty and cold, and I find as he walks behind me that I want him close again. A warm body. Even if he will be my tormentor. Because behind him sit more vultures come to pick at the kill.

I try to move my arms, my head, but I can't, not even a little, unless I want to set my forehead on the dirty ground. He's immobilized me. Whatever he chooses to do to me now, I will submit. He has made sure of that. The chair behind me creaks. He sets his feet on either side of my hips. I can just see the tip of his shoe if I shift my gaze.

I gasp when I feel the tips of his fingers brush the back of my neck. The rumors were true, then. I realize this is why his sister twisted my hair so tightly. Did she know? Would she herself be submitted to such a degradation one day? Has she already?

But all thoughts vanish as he caresses my skin. He's gentle as though he's getting to know the texture of the canvas. Then, abruptly, he grips the already-torn lace top of my gown and rips it farther, making me gasp. The men, our audience, make an appreciative sound as Santiago bares my back, the dress falling to the tops of my breasts, exposing one nipple. I'm hunched over enough that I don't think the men can see it.

I wonder what a sight we make, the half-monster husband at his kneeling bride's back, her dress torn, a supplicant to him.

I wonder if he's aroused.

I close my eyes when I feel something cold and wet touch the back of my neck. I smell alcohol. He's cleaning the area.

This is really happening. I'm being marked like cattle.

The chair creaks as he drags it forward on the stone bringing his knees to hug my arms tightly, securing me even more before I hear the buzzing of a machine and feel the first prick of the needle.

He'll tattoo me.

It hurts, and I whimper. But it doesn't deter him.

It takes about five minutes before the men lose interest, some standing, some talking, only a few remain watching. I fist my hands at my back as the pain intensifies. A branding iron would hurt more, I tell myself. I can manage this.

I know he'll tattoo the initials of The Society onto my skin. I'm their property as much as I am his. Alongside it, I'll wear his mark. I don't know what it is, I realize. Not that it matters. All I can think about is the buzzing of the machine, all I can feel is the warmth of his thighs at my arms. Does he realize it gives me comfort? I'm sure he's only ensuring I remain in position.

I don't know how much time passes. The buzzing lulls me, the pricks of the needles somehow grounding me. And all the while Santiago works quietly at my back, thighs strong on either side of me, breath warm on the back of my neck when he leans close to inspect his work. I think about the chapel. About what happened there. How merciless he was.

I think about his hands on me, his fingers inside me. I think about his lips at my neck. His teeth.

My belly flips.

He'll take me tonight. Consummate our marriage. And there is a part of me that is curious. That wants it. Even knowing he will be as merciless when I lie in his bed.

The buzzing stops abruptly. The back of my neck throbs. It takes me a minute to realize it's over. I almost panic with the realization.

The bonds at my wrists are first to go. He works without ceremony, freeing me of those and the ones on my upper arms. I bring my hands to the floor on either side of me, my head still down, the chain at my throat still fastening me to the stone. I look at the rings on my finger. The salt and pepper diamond.

Strange and beautiful. Another symbol of his owner-ship of me.

"It's finished," he says, voice deep and low and still commanding the attention of everyone in the place.

I exhale. Finished. No branding iron for me. I would count myself lucky, but I know this thing between us has only just begun.

A few of the men come to look at his handiwork and compliment it. No one touches me, but Santiago remains close. I get the feeling no one would dare incur his wrath.

When I next feel his touch, I gasp, muscles tight-ening with anxiety.

"Don't move," he commands.

I still. I don't expect him to touch me. Not like he is, at least. But then I realize what he must be doing. Applying a salve.

I close my eyes, my breath leveling, my body relaxing at least a little. He's being careful. Gentle. When he's finished, I feel something cover the tattoo. I open my eyes and berate myself because he's not being gentle or careful with me or for me. He's protecting his work. It wouldn't do if it got infected.

Santiago stands and walks around me. I remain in position, head still bowed by the chain, back of my neck feeling warm, my arms and shoulders sore. He takes his time as someone brings him a drink. It's somehow more humiliating when they mingle among themselves. When they ignore me altogether, the collared bride kneeling head bowed at their feet.

But I don't care. Let them ignore me. Let them forget me.

Because what comes next will be more humiliating than any of it. And again, I know it is only the beginning.

I wonder once more why he chose me. Why he wanted *me*.

As if my thought reminds him it's not finished yet, not until I speak the words, he returns to me, crouches down to unlock the chain, then straightens to his full height. At well over six feet tall, he towers over my five-and-a-half-foot frame when I'm standing, so when I'm on my knees, he's a giant.

Chairs creak as the men take their seats to witness this next scene. I wonder if they go home to fuck their wives with the image of me submitting to my husband on their minds.

But when Santiago touches the underside of my chin to raise me to kneel up, I stare up at him standing in the shadowy, dim light of the candles. I feel more his, strangely. More so than after the wedding.

And I realize I've given him more of what he wants when he wipes his thumb across my cheek. He closes his hand over the top of my head, that same thumb coming to my forehead, tracing a symbol there with my own tear as if blessing me. As if he's some god. His lips move, and I think he's saying a silent prayer, and again, I wonder what we look like, me kneeling at his feet, his mark fresh on my bloodied neck.

He closes his eyes, bows his head momentarily, then opens them again, and the look inside them is dark.

"Say the words," he tells me with his hand still on the top of my head.

I know this part. The words. The act. I know exactly what I must do. Every daughter of The Society knows because every one of us will be made to submit no matter how high ranking.

And I know there's no way around it. There never was, even when I believed for those short six months that I'd somehow escaped and was in charge of my own destiny. I never was.

I hold his gaze a moment longer than is proper or than he's used to. I see a flicker of anger. Good.

He thinks I'll be easy to break. He thinks I'm weak. He thinks my tears are weak. I see it. But I'm stronger than he knows. I almost got away. And I'll survive him. I have to.

I empty my eyes of any emotion. I lock myself off from him, and I tell myself the words mean nothing. This is not an oath I choose.

"Dominus et Deus."

But when I say them, it's as if the act is sealed, and again, I wonder if God truly is on their side.

Dominus et Deus. My lord and my god.

I take his offered hand with both of mine, the one with which he marked me, and I press my lips to it. Raising my gaze to his, I watch him from beneath my lashes.

I think of my little sister. I think of what I have to do. How I have to play this game to which I don't even know the rules. Because even if I could run away and I managed to do it, like Hazel did, what would happen to Evangeline? I won't abandon her like Hazel abandoned us.

My lips pressed to his cool hand, I keep my eyes locked on his as the beginnings of a plan form in my mind.

When Santiago swallows, I watch his Adam's apple work. He's impacted. I'm not sure if it's me kneeling for him or the act of the marking itself. It has to be heady stuff. I get it. But he is affected.

I'll use that.

And I keep my eyes on his as long as I can as I bend, bringing my forehead to his shoe. I am to kiss it, but I won't do that. The men won't see. If my husband knows, he will punish me for it. It's a small rebellion, but it's mine, and it's something, and I'll submit to his punishment. At least he'll know where I stand.

When he grips my arm and hauls me to my feet, I know he hasn't missed my deviation from the rules. My dress slips as I fall into him, then stumble backward. He looks down at me, and I follow his gaze to my exposed breast. He roughly tugs the lace up, and the look in his eyes is darker than I've yet seen.

And for a moment, the weaker part of me, the scared part thinks maybe I should have kissed his shoe.

But then he's reined himself in, and I think this side of my husband is more frightening than the outwardly angry side. This quiet is more terrifying.

Because his eyes hold a promise inside them.

I'll deal with you later.

"Close your eyes," he says, voice low, not a whisper but simply quiet.

I do.

He pulls me close, and I gasp when he kisses me hard on the mouth, my hands coming to his chest as his fingers claw painfully into the ruined twist of my hair, his hard body against mine as I bend over backward to take his kiss. A small taste of what he'll do tonight.

De La Rosa Manor is quiet and dark when Marco drops us off at the front entrance. My wife peers up at the mansion with what I can only guess are equal parts apprehension and curiosity. The exterior is constructed from stone in a gothic revival architectural style. Carved buttresses, Palladian windows, ornate gables, and rambling vines of ivy lavish the historic structure she will come to know as her own personal prison.

An almost ever-present fog seems to lurk around the property, lending to the mystery of the area. Small groups of terrified tourists often peer through the gates outside while their guides whisper hushed rumors of the hauntings that occur here. But the only ghosts Ivy will need to concern herself with are those of my father and brother, calling out from beyond the grave for her Moreno blood.

She swallows and clutches the torn shreds of her dress to her body as her toes dig into the earth. It's these tiny signs of protest I study with interest. Though the air is sticky tonight, there's a noticeable chill moving through her as goose bumps break out along her skin.

Some traditions have no merit in The Society, but it is a selfish need that leads me to scoop her up into my arms and carry her across the lawn. She is still without shoes, and I want her soft for me. The scars I leave will be with careful deliberation, and it would be careless of me to let her injure her feet already. There is still much to be done tonight, and I won't waste my time tending to wounds so easily prevented.

She glances up at me with wide, confused eyes as I carry her up the stairs and across the threshold. Uncertainty clouds her features as the heavy door slams shut behind us, sealing her in with the monster she didn't want me to be.

"I'm capable of walking," she says, but her voice lacks the conviction to fight.

She is tired after the day's events, a fact made obvious by the heaviness of her eyes. It's already past three in the morning. But I have no doubt she will revive when a cascade of adrenaline and cortisol flood her body. Fear has a way of waking up even those near death.

I continue up the grand stairs to the second level,

carrying her down the corridor with an efficiency she doesn't seem to appreciate. From my arms, she's craning her neck, trying to take in the details of her surroundings. An opportunity I steal from her without regret.

When I enter the guest suite, I finally deposit her onto her feet. She takes a moment to glance around the space, examining the antique furnishings, ornamental rugs, and rich shades of plum and black. Everything is bathed in the soft glow of candlelight, a detail Ivy doesn't miss as her eyes flick to the light switch.

"Is this your room?" she asks.

"Let go of your dress," I command.

She glances up at me, renewed defiance in the set of her jaw. Her obstinance isn't doing her any favors, as she couldn't possibly know how much I love the thought of breaking her. I step closer, my fingertips moving to her throat. Already, her pulse is escalating, and she can't hide the nerves in her eyes.

I reach down to the torn dress she's clutching to her body and yank it out of her grasp. The remaining seams of fabric give way with a splitting groan before falling into shreds at her feet. She slaps her hands over her breasts, and my dark laughter pierces the space between us.

"There's no place for your modesty here." I lean in to whisper the words against the shell of her ear. "I will own every inch of you, dear wife."

A shudder moves through her as I forcefully pry her hands away and pull them back to her sides. She is completely naked and completely mine. A beautiful, shivering feminine form of gently sloping curves and valleys my palms are burning to explore.

But first, control.

"Kneel."

She hesitates, her eyes darting to the door behind me.

I slide my fingers into her hair and fist a handful, forcing her to arch back until she has no choice but to let her knees buckle and do as I request. Once she is on her knees, I release her, leaving her face only a few inches from the heat of my throbbing cock. Her eyes dart to the bulge in my trousers, and she licks her dry lips as her nerves bleed into every muscle fiber of her body.

I nudge my leather shoe between her knees and force them apart until just a hint of her pussy peeks through. From my trouser pocket, I produce the rosary necklace I've been carrying all day. An ornate design with a white gold cross flanked by sturdy obsidian and shungite beads. It's lengthy enough that when I drape it over her shoulders, it dangles between her breasts. I could wrap it around her neck twice and still have room to play.

Ivy glances down to examine the jewelry as I curl the beads in my fist. She may understand the significance of religion and punishment, as it is deeply ingrained in our society, but she could never know the extent of it like I do. I want this necklace to feel heavy on her soul, always. A constant burden she must carry around like the weight of her sins. A permanent reminder of who she is and who she belongs to.

"Never take this off," I tell her. "Do you understand?"

When she doesn't answer, I tighten my grip and increase the pressure around her throat. Her hands come up to mine, panic blotting out the light in her eyes.

"I understand." She winces. "Please."

I relax my grip, and without thinking, my free hand comes to rest on her head, petting her hair until her eyes flutter shut. It wasn't my intention to calm her, but it appears that's exactly what I'm doing, and I can't understand it. How can she possibly find any solace in my presence? Doesn't she realize what she's signed her life over to?

"You defied me." My voice is unusually gruff. "Again."

She opens her eyes, and she does not need an explanation. She understands exactly what I'm referring to.

"It's demeaning," she clips out.

"It's the life you agreed to. You knew the rules when you pledged yourself to The Society."

"As if I had a choice." Her voice wavers, and

moisture clings to the edges of her eyes, but she's trying desperately not to let it fall.

"We always have a choice." I tilt her chin up and stare into her eyes. "You still have a choice. You could choose to run at any moment, but you should know it would be a wasted effort. I would track you like a bloodhound, and I would always find you and bring you back to me. This is a promise I can make you. But it is only one of many. I think you understand there is no limit to my power over your life. There will be much bigger battles to come, so why choose defiance over something so small?"

Her shoulders tremble as she forces the words between clenched teeth. "After everything you made me do already... I just couldn't. Not that."

"I think you will discover the lengths you are willing to go in order to please me will surprise you over time." I smile down at her coldly. "But for now, you may repent by giving me three Hail Marys."

She seems disoriented by my request but follows through regardless. Bringing her hands together in a prayer position, she watches with curious eyes as I weave the rosary beads between her palms. She bows her head before me and recites the words in Latin with a mastered perfection.

"Good girl." I praise her as I step closer. So close, her cheek brushes against the aching throb pressing the fabric of my trousers.

When Ivy feels it, her eyes fly open, and everything else seems to disappear. I'm lost and bewildered as I stare into her strange eyes, and she seems to be aware of this as she sucks in a breath.

Abruptly, I sever the odd connection by turning away and stalking to the nightstand, where I have left the items required for tonight's ritual. When I return with the blind mask I ordered especially for her, Ivy gives the tiniest shake of her head, but she should know her pleas are useless.

I secure the heavy silver mask over her face, obscuring her vision from the world around her. Her chest heaves as she draws in a breath, her nipples crying out as they poke upward. For a moment, I can't do anything else but stand there and admire her. She can't see me now, and I have been waiting all night to indulge.

Her body has all the qualities I admire in a woman's flesh. Soft skin. Perfectly rounded breasts. Curved hips. They are not anything I haven't seen before, yet those features look more enticing on her than any other woman I have ever had the pleasure to look upon.

Perhaps, it is simply because I know she will only ever be mine.

I lean down and help her to her feet again. Her fingers wrap around my arm, clinging to me as her guide when I lead her toward the bed. It's the strangest sign of trust I don't expect, and I find that disarms me too. But her trust wavers when I pull her arms up over her head to secure them to the rope around the bedpost.

"Santiago." Her voice is pleading.

The undercurrent of fear in her tone hardens me like nothing else ever has. I have to take a moment, closing my eyes to resume control of the situation before I give in to my baser desires and ravage her without forethought.

I resume the task of securing her wrists and then step back to admire the art of her body. She's arched at the hips, slightly bent forward, arms straining upward. Her nerves are a powerful aphrodisiac, and already, I can smell the arousal between her thighs. She thinks she knows what comes next, but the uncertainty makes her shiver.

When my fingers caress the length of her spine, she curves into me like a cat arches into its master's palm. I don't even think she's consciously aware of the fact that she's doing it. And it's a shame that she should hope to find a protector in me when I can only ever be her tormentor.

I grab a handful of the soft flesh around her hip and squeeze, and her back bows even farther, thighs parted so enticingly. She's aching for something she doesn't even understand.

Taking my time, I dispense of my jacket and waistcoat and then slowly unbutton my dress shirt. Despite the fact she can't see, my wife is turning toward me, her ornate mask staring down the scars on my torso as my shirt drifts to the floor. It's unnerving, and it isn't logical, but I feel her gaze on me regardless. As if she possesses the ability to see through the layers of metal. As if she can see me for who I really am.

"Turn around," I command.

She jumps at the harshness of my voice but then settles back into her position once my hands are upon her again. This time, I'm stroking, caressing the length of her body. Getting a feel for my most interesting acquisition. She makes a soft sound of pleasure as my palms come around her waist and skate up over her tits. Her nipples are so hard she whimpers when they scrape against my skin, and I would bet all the money in my bank account her pussy is swollen for me too.

"Do you like this?" My lips hover over her ear, nipping at the lobe before they trail down her throat.

She makes a sound of protest that gets caught in her throat, but it ejects when I remove one of my hands and smack her ass so hard my fingers are imprinted on it.

"Santi—" My name dies on her lips as I repeat the action, slapping her ass again.

She tries to arch away as she shrieks, but my arm curves around her waist, forcing her to stay still and bear it.

Three. Four. Five. Six times I slap her, and her skin glows cherry red as the blood rushes to the surface. She's panting, heaving, twisting in my grasp when I slide my fingers down between her thighs to feel her soaking want.

"Please," she starts to beg as I stroke her. "I need... I can't..."

I'm not in the business of giving my enemies what they want. But her voice sounds so sweet. So full of loathing for her own request, I can only reason that she will hate me all the more for being able to control her this way.

I dip two fingertips inside her and then swirl them around her clit. She widens her legs for me without realizing it, opening her body as if to welcome me inside. I stifle the groan building in my throat by biting her shoulder, and Ivy screams at the same time her body releases, a gush of warmth sliding over my fingers. Spasms rock her core as her breath hisses between her teeth. She's still coming back down from her high when I smear the evidence of her own body's betrayal over her lips.

She jerks in my arms, and I breathe against her skin, relaxing the grip on her waist as I resume the long, exacting strokes over the expanse of her body. I'm studying her. Taking in all the details of this unfamiliar landscape. The freckles on her shoulder. The dip in her lower spine. The way her ribs press against my fingers when she leans into my touch. I want to memorize them all, filing them away like the data on my computer. I don't understand why, and I don't want to examine the reasons too carefully just yet.

Before I can give it much more thought, I notice some bruising on her arm. I investigate it thoroughly, pressing my fingertips into the purple ovals as undiluted rage boils inside me.

"Who did this to you?" I demand.

She sucks in a breath but doesn't answer. I'm tempted to shake her. Choke her. Force the words from her lips. But my eyes are already roaming the rest of her, scanning every inch for an injustice that hasn't quite formed in my mind.

There are additional bruises on her thigh, knee, and calf. And I know they must be from someone because she has stiffened in my arms. She's hiding something from me, and I won't accept it.

"Who did this?" I repeat.

When she doesn't answer, I wrap the length of the rosary around her neck until it bites into her skin. She strains against the rope to lean back into me, fighting the tightening of my fist.

"Who, Ivy?"

"Perhaps it was your doctor," she snarls at me with such vehemence, it shocks me into loosening my grip.

The beads cascade back over her breasts, settling between the mounds.

"Doctor," I echo, my mind coming back to Abel's hand-delivered purity test.

"The nightmare of a doctor you sent me to!" She hurls the words out with a bitterness that catches me off guard.

"Who told you I sent you to him?"

She falls quiet again, chest heaving in anger. There is a fire in her I didn't expect, and I find that I like it.

"Answer me."

I slip my fingers back between her legs, and she tries to squeeze them together. Slapping her inner thighs jolts her back into submission, and her head falls back against my shoulder as I begin to toy with her all over again.

"Santiago." She sniffles. "Please."

Her arms are growing tired. She can barely hold herself upright. But she must learn the true nature of endurance, for she will need plenty of it with me.

Discussing the doctor will have to wait. The night is escaping me, and I am yet to claim her. I let her know as much when I unzip my trousers and free my throbbing cock.

Ivy falls completely still, even as I stroke her sensitive clit and mold my body against hers. When she feels the hard steel of my flesh pressing against the softness of her body, she turns her head again, as if to see me.

"Don't make me keep punishing you," I warn her gruffly. "Unless you truly want to feel my roughness."

She forces her head forward again, and I slide my cock between her thighs, soaking the length in her messy arousal. She's so warm and soft, I don't know that I have it in me to be anything other than rough with her. It's been too long since I've felt a woman. I can't think of anything else now.

I grip her hips and rub the head of my cock against her entrance, slowly exerting pressure until it starts to sink inside her. Her hands clench, legs quivering, and I have to hold her up by the waist as I tease just the head in and out of her in a torturous rhythm. I keep stroking her clit, building and building that pressure inside her. I feel her squeezing around me, and it isn't enough. I need to feel everything.

With a sharp thrust, I tear through her virginity and seat my cock as deep as her body can take me. She cries out in surprise and then shatters as my fingers push her over the edge with frantic, unrelenting movements.

Her body squeezes me over and over again as the aftershocks roll through her, and I have to grit my teeth to repress the shudder of pleasure I feel from her tight pussy milking my dick.

"Fuck." The word hisses through my lips, and there's no holding back now.

I'm more animal than man when I hoist her ass up and pivot my hips back, slamming into her without mercy. Ivy wails, and the bedpost groans as the tautness of the rope and my body pull her in opposite directions. I close my eyes and get lost in the feeling of her warmth, her sounds, her sanctuary.

It wasn't supposed to be this way. Somewhere in the back of my mind, logic is screaming for my attention. But I'm too lost to her to consider the reasons I'm petting her hair and kissing my way down her spine as I fuck her into oblivion.

She looks like a rag doll in my arms. So small. So easy to toss around and use as I please. I don't know how this is going to work. I don't know how to rein in my control, but right now, all I can think about is burying myself balls deep and filling her womb with my seed.

The rope around her wrists begins to chafe as Ivy's weight sinks forward. She can't hold her head up anymore, and I can't stop. I hold her up with one arm as I yank the rope from the bedpost, leaving her wrists tangled in the remnants. I drop her torso onto the bed and roll my hips deeper and harder, thrusting without restraint until my balls draw up and I can't hold off any longer.

My fingers dig into her hips with a bruising grip, and agony explodes out of me as my cock jerks wildly, emptying four years of frustration into my wife.

My wife.

I blink open my eyes and look down at her, too

exhausted to move, breathing like she can't get enough oxygen. Neither can I for that matter.

I really did this. I married my enemy, and soon, she will be carrying my child.

The world tilts, and I collapse beside her with a grunt.

16

I can't lift my head. This headpiece he's put on me is too heavy. I feel him pull out, feel his come—no, our come. I came too. I came. And I feel it gush out of me.

My legs dangle off the edge of the bed. I'm lying facedown, unable to move. Barely able to breathe.

He doesn't speak, but I hear his breathing. It's ragged like mine. He's spent. Having my sight taken away makes my other senses work harder. They have to pick up the slack, and I need to remain on my guard with this man.

This man.

He is your husband.

As if I didn't know.

I think he's getting dressed. I hear a zipper. I still don't move. My eyes are open, but all I see is black, and all I feel is a throbbing pain between my legs.

He took me violently.

And you came.

Violently.

He shifts my weight, lifting me to lie farther up on the bed. My head lolls as I try to manage the weight of this thing. I put my hands to it, but he takes my raw wrists and untangles the rope, freeing me of it before setting my arms on either side of me with a single-word command. "No."

"Please."

"Don't make me bind you again."

"I can't breathe."

"You can breathe. Just relax."

He tugs something out from under me, then pulls one leg open.

I gasp, try to scoot away, but his fingers dig into that thigh as he wipes between my legs.

"I wonder if Eli will be pleased to see how I bled his daughter," he says.

"What?" I ask, not sure I heard right.

Is he satisfied with the blood? I wonder. I know there's much of it. He'd be happy to see my tears too, I'm sure, and I'd happily give them to him if he'd only take this damn thing off me.

"Stay," he says like he'd command a dog. I guess he's finished cleaning me.

I stay. I can't move anyway. And as my body settles, I become aware of every ache. I hear him walk, hear a door open, water run. He's back a moment later, his hands around my arms lifting me. I hold onto his biceps, feel his strength beneath my hands, my forehead almost falling into his shoulder.

"You'll learn to carry it when you're on your knees." He deposits me on the floor, carpet rough beneath my knees. I sit back on my heels and place one hand on the floor to support myself.

What more does he want from me?

"Close your eyes."

I do. I don't even know why. It's not like he can see. But I'm tired. I'm so tired. This day and this night have drained me.

He lifts the thing off me, and I reach up to touch my face, dry my cheeks with the backs of my hands.

"I've seen your face," I say and when I feel him move away, I open my eyes and watch him. His shirt is undone. I see his jacket strewn over a chair.

I watch as he puts the ornate mask into a glass case like it's something sacred and it takes me a moment to realize he's watching me in the tarnished mirror. Our eyes meet but it's so dark with just the candles and the black walls that I can't see him clearly.

"And you'd like to see it again?" he asks. "I doubt that. Bow your head and lower your eyes. Now."

"You don't know me," I tell him but do as he says.

"Don't I?" He crosses the room to the door. I

watch him from behind my lashes. "This will be your room. You'll stay in it until I come for you."

"When will that be? When you need another fuck?"

He puts his hand to the doorknob, and I see him cock his head. He turns a little. It's the skull side.

I lift my head. I can't not look at the shadows of the flickering candles playing across his face.

"You should be more careful, Ivy."

"Or what? You'll put that thing on me again? Tattoo me again? Brand me this time? Make me marry you all over again? You've taken everything. Done everything there is to do."

"I've only just begun."

I snort.

He walks back into the room, back toward me and I find myself leaning away. Watching him come to me, his face uncovered, a half-living-half-dead man, it's a little terrifying.

"Lower your gaze. I won't say it again."

"No." My heart pounds against my chest like it wants out before the attack that is surely coming.

"No?"

I shake my head.

He raises his eyebrows. "I'm not sure if that's bravery or stupidity."

"I'm not scared of your face if that's what you mean."

He laughs outright. "You think I'm worried you

won't like my face?" He crouches down and it takes all I have to keep my eyes on his, but he must see me lean away and he leans closer. "You want to see me, Ivy?"

I just swallow as I take him in, trying to focus on his eyes, just his eyes. But it's too much and I blink, turning away.

"Didn't think so," he says, standing, crossing the room again.

"It's not...I don't..." I trail off, not sure what I want to say. He was beautiful once. I can see that. Now he's something else. Something most would sneer at. Run from.

"You'll remain in your room until I come for you." He opens the door.

"I won't."

He stops. "No?" he asks, turning. "You'll rebel?" He waits for me to answer but I don't. "Look at you. Still on your knees before me, my mark etched into your skin, my come leaking out of your pussy. I think you'll do exactly as you're told. But you're welcome to try to prove me wrong. I will enjoy punishing you." He walks out into the hallway.

"Why?" I call out. "Why did you choose me if you hate me so much?" I have to wipe my eyes again.

He stops. It's quiet for a long moment and I realize how silent this house is. How still. Does anyone else even live here? He studies me, eyes sharp and intent on me. He has an agenda. A purpose. And I am so far out of my league.

"Your tears won't move me. I thought you knew that."

"Just at least tell me why."

"Do you love your father?"

"What?"

"Do you love him?"

"Yes. Of course."

"And he loves you." It's not a question.

"My father has nothing to do with this."

"No?"

My tears turn into sobs as everything becomes too much, too heavy, like this rosary around my neck. Like his hands are still around it.

"Christ, get a grip," he snaps.

"Fuck you," I tell him but it doesn't have the force I want, not when said through the sobs. But I think for a minute I shouldn't have said that. I think he'll come back in here. Punish me again. I don't think my body can take any more. Not tonight.

But he doesn't. Instead, his lips just curve upward, a skull on one side the monster on the other and I feel my shoulders slump, my body curl in around itself as I cringe away a little.

"You belong to me."

"I don't." He's right though. In our world, I do belong to him.

"Do you understand what that means for you?" he asks as if I haven't said anything.

I don't reply. I don't know how.

He shakes his head, gives a little snort like he's bored. "You're weak, Ivy. And you'd better toughen up because you're going to need all your strength to survive me."

17

"Miss."

I groan as I start to wake up, every inch of my body sore, the worst of it between my legs.

A woman clears her throat. "Miss."

I open my eyes. The room slowly comes into view. Black walls. No, not black. Dark, carved wood. A small square of light high up.

"Miss, I'm sorry to wake you."

I turn, look at the older woman in a uniform standing on the other side of the bed. There's another one, a younger one, standing just inside the door. I take in the bed, the bloodied sheet half pulled off one corner of the mattress. The thick blanket heavy as I draw it up to cover myself and sit up a little, wincing and very aware of the fact that I'm still naked.

"I need the sheets, Miss. It'll just take us a minute to put clean ones on."

I clear my throat, wipe my face and glance around for a clock. "What time is it?"

"Nine o'clock, Miss."

I look back at the woman. She must think me an idiot. "Where is the bathroom?"

She points. I notice the other girl trying to act like she's not looking at me.

"I just need one minute," I say, hoping they'll get the hint and leave so I can make it to the bathroom without having to run across the room naked.

"That's fine, Miss," the older one says and turns. She waves the other girl out.

I take a minute to sit up, still too tired from last night. I try to remember the last time I ate something but can't.

"Are you all right?" the older woman asks.

I smile, hold the blanket to me as I swing my legs off but when I try to stand, the room begins to spin, and my knees give out. I throw my arm out to catch the nightstand but end up knocking a heavy brass lamp over, catching the edge of it on my forehead before it and I go tumbling to the floor.

The woman gasps and is at my side in an instant.

I sit up, still holding the blanket, and lean my back against the bed, very aware of the ache between my legs, the rawness there.

"It's okay. I'm fine." This happens all the time, I don't say. "I just need to eat something. I'll be fine."

She bends over me, worry creasing her face. She nods, calls to the girl she just shooed into the hallway. "Go get some toast and juice. Bring it upstairs."

"But the master said—"

"I'll worry about the master. You do as I say. Quickly." She disappears into the bathroom and comes back with a glass of water.

I take it, drink a sip. "Thank you." I touch my forehead.

"You've hurt yourself."

My fingers come away bloody. "It's fine. It's just a cut." I look at my wrists at the same time her eyes fall to them. What does she make of me, I wonder? A new bride with rope burns on her wrists, those ropes on the floor between us. Blood on the sheets.

I feel my face get hot.

She clears her throat and helps me back on the bed, and I try not to look at the blood smeared on it. Try not to think about how he used those sheets to clean me.

The girl returns then. I hear her coming. She must be hurrying because whatever is on the tray is clattering loudly.

"Here we are," the older woman says as she takes the tray and sets it on the nightstand. I glance at the lamp that fell over, realizing there's no bulb in it. I look around the grim room at the remnants of all the candles. Does he use only candles throughout the house? It's a behemoth. I saw that much last night.

The woman hands me a cup of freshly squeezed orange juice, and I happily take it, drinking it all.

"Better," I say, feeling the sugar do its work. "Thank you."

She pours more into my cup from the small pitcher and I sip that one and eye the toast.

"Go on and eat something. We'll start in another room and come back."

"But ma'am," the other girl starts.

"You hush," she tells her and hustles her out.

Once they close the door, I put my cup down and pick up a piece of toast to eat a few bites dry then get off the bed to take the sheets off myself, embarrassed of what they've already seen. I bundle it inside the blanket and leave it on the foot of the bed then cross the room naked to go into the bathroom. A shower will make me feel better. And clothes. And then I'll think about what comes next.

But first, I need to see the tattoo. Standing in front of the mirror, I look at myself. No new bruises at least. Nothing fresh enough for me to notice apart from the cut on my forehead. It's small, though, and doesn't hurt much.

Will it always be that way with him? A battle?

I take off the rosary and set it on the counter to

splash water on my face and dry it, pull what's left of the pins out of my hair, releasing the last of the twist. I lift it up and turn my back to the mirror, trying to get a look at the tattoo. All I can see is that it's carefully covered in plastic.

I go through the drawers for a handheld mirror to get a look at it but find none. I'll have to ask him to show me. I hate that I have to ask him for anything. But the truth is, I know I'll have to ask for everything.

By the time I get out of the shower, the bed has been remade, the soiled bedding gone, and the lamp righted. Brand new candles have been placed inside the candleholders, a few already lit.

The large walk-in closet is filled with clothes, all new and all in my size, but hardly any of it my style. I choose the simplest sweater and pair of jeans I can find and put them on along with a pair of comfortable, thick socks. I don't bother with shoes. They mostly have high heels. I slip the rosary on although it's cumbersome but then I hear his words again.

"I think you'll do exactly as you're told."

I reach beneath my sweater, take it off and set it beside the bed. He can't seriously expect me to wear a freaking rosary around my neck 24/7.

I go to the door and try it. I expect it to be locked so I'm not surprised when I find it is. I guess he's not taking any chances that he's wrong. That I won't do as he says. With a shake of my head, I turn back into the room, trying to ignore the part of me that is relieved at least one choice to disobey him has been taken away.

My gaze lands on that mask. It's in a glass box set on a stand and I go to it, open it. It's not locked.

It's ugly and beautiful at once, the mask. Made of metal with, if I peer close, skulls and roses carved into it, the letters of the society, I.V.I, the V slightly larger than the I's on either side woven in with the skulls and roses. De La Rosa. *Of the rose.* It must be what's on the back of my neck too.

I lift the thing out and remember how that weight felt on my head. My neck could almost not bear it. But that probably had something to do with the sex. With how he took me. There's a flutter in my stomach at the memory, and I wonder how I can be turned on by something like that. By someone like him.

But I am. And I'm not going to lie to myself about it. I've not been with a man before him so I can't judge, but all I know is I've never come so hard as when he made me come. And even given the rawness between my legs, I'm aroused thinking about it.

There's another side to this too, though. He was just as turned on.

"Maybe I'm not the only weak one, Santiago."

I put the mask back on its stand and run my fingers under the small chains that dangle from it, crosses hanging off them. I remember the Hail Marys he made me say as my punishment.

"Freak," I say to the room and walk to the two windows on the far wall. I have to pull up a chair and stand on it to see outside, and I can't open either of them because they're actually bigger windows, but the wood all around the room has been carved to only let in this little bit of light. I wonder if he chose this room especially for me. I'm sure he did. Will he deprive me even of sunlight?

I step down off the chair carefully, holding onto the back when I feel myself wobble, then lower myself into the seat.

He could do that. Keep me prisoner in this room. It would be the same as holding me in a cell below ground.

I rub my face and get up. Walk around. Take in the carvings on the wooden walls. Skulls and roses. Like the posts on the bed. The one he bound me to. The whole thing is stifling.

It doesn't take me long to look through everything and then I sit, and I wait.

But he doesn't come for me as the sun begins to descend the sky. He doesn't come as I light all the candles in the room and wait. He doesn't come long after I've changed into a nightgown and even when my stomach growls so loudly, I'm sure he can hear it wherever he is in this house.

I'm only grateful for sleep when it becomes apparent he won't return to even feed me tonight.

J ust after dusk, Mercedes stirs me from my fitful sleep, waving a cup of coffee beneath my nose. She's perched on my bed in a tight black dress, looking much like a vampire herself. I knew she wouldn't be able to stay away.

"What are you doing?" I glare up at her.

"Tell me everything." Her eyes are dark, lined with kohl, and she can't contain the eagerness churning in their depths.

"There's nothing to tell." I toss the covers off me and sit up, gesturing her out of the way. "Nothing that you should hear anyway."

"Santiago." She pouts. "Don't toy with me."

I offer her a sharp look over my shoulder and catch her staring at the ink on my back. She hasn't seen this piece yet. I'm not in the business of showing the art to anyone, much less my sister. I can tell she's surprised by it.

The art on my face is my own, as is much of the work on my arm. But it wasn't within my capabilities to tattoo my own back, no matter how much I would have liked to.

"Who did that?" she asks curiously as I drape last night's shirt over my body.

"A friend."

"It's beautiful," she murmurs.

"It's a means to an end."

My ink serves one purpose, and despite what some people may believe, it isn't to scare anyone. I was capable of that on my own before I ever had a single scar on my body. I just don't like to look at the memories of that night branded into my skin, and this was the only reasonable alternative.

I walk to the closet and retrieve a white dress shirt and a pair of black slacks. Mercedes continues to annoy me by touching the things in my room, gliding her fingers over the ornate bedposts, and scanning the space with snake-like eyes. She's looking for evidence that my bride was in here last night, determined to destroy any perceived weaknesses in my plan.

"She's in her own room," I inform her. "She has been since last night."

"I know." Her lips curve into a mischievous grin.

My eyes narrow. "How long have you been back home?"

"Since this morning." She shrugs. "Presumably not long after you went to bed."

"I trust I don't need to warn you to leave her alone." My voice carries an edge to it Mercedes doesn't miss.

She eyes me speculatively. "Of course, brother. I would never dream of interfering."

Now she's toying with me.

"I have work to do," I tell her. "If you're going to lurk around The Manor, you will need to stay out of the way. And find something productive to do with your time. I can't have you sitting idle."

"No, we can't have that," she says bitterly. "The elders surely wouldn't like it."

"Mercedes." My jaw clenches.

She rolls her eyes. "I'm going to visit the chapel. I'll pray forgiveness for my many sins."

"I expect that should keep you occupied for the rest of the night," I answer dryly.

She snorts and leaves me to shower and dress. It is already later than I would like, and I have work to do. Since the incident, I have not been able to sleep through the night. I often find myself wandering the halls of The Manor or working until the sun has risen before I am exhausted enough to close my eyes and seek rest.

Typically, my day would begin in the study

downstairs. My position within IVI consists of managing the funds. I am tasked with distributing payments, investing collective earnings to amplify our wealth, managing stocks and bonds, and shuttling money into offshore accounts.

The founding families within The Society come from old money. They were wealthy to begin with. Now, they are gods among men. In no small part, thanks to me.

Since I took over Eli's position, I have elevated our status considerably. Numbers are what I'm good at. I can stare at the data all day, recognizing patterns, predicting trends, deciphering the undecipherable. I do not possess the same talent for humans.

Ivy Moreno is an abstract equation, and I feel as though I'm missing a variable required to understand her. I had so many notions about what she was, but so far, she is proving most of my theories incorrect. There is a burning need in me to analyze her until I crack her code and all of her pitiful little secrets spill out.

This desire unsettles me. And still, I can't deny it. As I walk down the corridor, I forget about going straight to my study and continue to her suite. Work will not come until I have looked at her at least once. This much, I think is a logical indulgence.

The lock unbolts, and the door creaks open, and I am greeted by only a few waning flames from the candles nearly gone. The room is silent and still, a sliver of moonlight slicing in from the window to bathe the silhouette of Ivy's body in the large bed.

I move closer to examine her, noting the way her dark hair spills across the silk pillow. She is curled into herself, and even in sleep, she appears tormented. It puzzles me exceedingly as I consider the reasons. Beyond myself, I am certain other things haunt her dreams. But I am not yet sure what they could be.

I sit down beside her on the bed. She does not stir, even as I smooth a strand of hair away from her face. She is beautiful. I will give her that much. Already, my groin is tightening in memory of the way she felt around me last night. The way her body came alive for me, despite how much she wanted to resist.

The question is why. Why did she marry me without a fight? Why did she give herself over so willingly? There must be a reason. And it will eat at me until I uncover it.

She murmurs something in her sleep and then clutches her stomach as if it pains her. My brows furrow, and I don't realize my hand is moving to touch her until it's already there. On top of hers.

The cold of my skin against hers startles her awake, and she gasps as her eyes fly open to meet mine.

"Santiago." My name falls from her lips like a curse.

She pulls herself upright, curling her knees into her chest, peering back at me with an innocence I want to despise. But when I see the gash on her forehead, an unidentified emotion rolls through me like a black cloud.

"What happened?" I reach out to touch her and she dips her head.

When my fingers fall across her skin, she does not flinch. She does not close her eyes or shudder. Instead, she seems to draw in a sharp, shaky breath as if to fortify herself. I suppose she is trying to be brave. To prove she is not frightened of me. But her silence is grating at my last nerve, and the clawing desperation to know who hurt her is poisoning me from the inside out.

"Ivy." My voice comes out so sharply, she does finally flinch. "Tell me."

"Don't act as if you care." She yanks away from my grip and glares up at me with watery eyes. "Why should it matter? You are the biggest hypocrite I've ever met. Starving me all day and then coming in here to act as if a cut matters to you."

A deep grimace settles over my features. "Starving you?"

Her lip trembles and she looks away. "You hate me. I can see it in your eyes. I don't know why you want me here. Just so you can torture me? Then go on and do your worst. Show me how terrible you truly are."

I should. Because she's right. I do hate her. I hate her more than I ever knew I could hate anything. Yet I can't bring myself to prove it at this moment. I can't allow her cutting remarks to slide as if they are of no consequence. There are so many ways I will apply my cruelty to her. But she is to carry my child, and if she thinks I would starve her while she does so, she is mistaken.

"Tell me what you ate today." I grip her chin and force her gaze back to me.

She looks at me as though I'm teasing her. "You know the answer to that."

"Tell me," I growl.

She wavers, trying desperately to hold onto her stubborn refusal, but is still tethered by the values ingrained into her. She knows she is to please her husband.

"I ate the only thing they brought me!" she hisses. "Toast and orange juice. Does that satisfy you, Lord of Darkness?"

My fingers bite into her skin under the force of my anger, and she cringes. When I realize the power of my grip, I soften it and close my eyes, trying to rein myself back in.

"They brought you only one meal today?"

She is quiet for a moment before she answers, her voice softer this time. "Yes."

"That was a mistake," I answer darkly as I release her.

MY THUNDEROUS FOOTSTEPS STARTLE THE housekeeper awake before I even reach her door. She is scrambling out of her bed, clinging to her bedsheets when the glow from the hall spills into her room. I never come to this part of The Manor, so she knows something is amiss.

"Mr. De La Rosa," the words falls helplessly from her lips. "Is everything okay?"

"Everything is not okay." I stalk toward her, and she stumbles back, nearly tripping over the sheet in her pale grasp.

"This is about the food, isn't it?" She winces. "Oh, please have mercy. I beg of you."

"Mercy?" I spit the word from my lips with such vehemence she begins to shake. "What mercy should there be for a woman who can't perform the most basic task of feeding my goddamn wife!"

Tears begin to cascade over her cheeks as she shakes her head in denial. "But it was your order, sir! And I know I fed her against your wishes, but she was feeling faint, and I simply could not..."

I draw in a sharp breath and try to calm myself.

"Master, please," Antonia sobs. "I did not mean to offend."

I turn away from her and drag a hand over my face. I hate it when she calls me that. Antonia has known me since I was a boy, and truly, it does not please me to see the old woman cry. She showed me kindness when so many others did not. She cleaned my wounds and kept me fed and never once treated me to a repulsive glance, even at my worst.

In my gut, I know this was not her doing. She is not capable of such betrayal. And for a moment, I wish I could express that sentiment to her. But the dynamic has changed so much since I returned from the hospital. My unpredictable moods and harsh demands have left the staff scurrying around the mansion like church mice, trying their best to remain unseen and unheard. They do not know what to make of the cold, reclusive man who walked out of the flames that night. And I am certain they only see me as the monster I am now.

"Tell me why my wife was only fed once today." I turn back to her slowly, watching Antonia dab her eyes with the sheet.

She takes a shuddering breath and collects herself with a nod. "Mercedes came to me with the instructions this morning," she says softly. "She told me they were your orders. I was only doing as I was told, sir."

Mercedes.

Darkness creeps into the edges of my vision as I give her a stiff nod. "Let me be clear, Antonia. My wife's health is a priority until I say otherwise. That means any orders pertaining to her will only come directly from me. She will eat when she is hungry, and should she have any other needs, I trust you will meet them accordingly."

Relief makes her shoulders sag. "Yes, master."

I grimace at her and shake my head. "And from now on, call me Santiago, for God's sakes. You have known me since I was in diapers."

Her eyebrows shoot up in surprise. "But, sir, what if the other staff hears me address you as such? It would not be proper."

"To hell with that custom." I wave my hand flippantly. "I am not my father, and you can inform them you have my permission if you must. I don't want to hear another word on the subject."

"Yes, sir." A small, kind smile crosses her lips. "If I may?"

I tilt my head to examine her. "Yes?"

"Mrs. De La Rosa is very beautiful. You have done well for yourself."

I feel my lips tilting at the corners before I dip my head curtly. "Thank you, Antonia. Now, please, attend to her."

DESPITE MERCEDES'S ASSURANCE OF FINDING USEFUL employment for her mind this evening, I find her on the computer in the library, stretching the limits of her credit card with luxury clothing.

When she hears me approaching, she nearly knocks the chair back in her haste to get up and greet me. She can tell by the look in my eye that I am not pleased.

"Santiago." She pleads with me as I stalk toward her.

I wrap my fingers around her neck, applying enough pressure to make her sputter. "What the fuck do you think you're doing?"

"I'm looking after our best interests," she chokes out. "You are letting her get to you already. Giving her that suite. The dress. The ring. This manor. She should be locked in a basement with nothing more than the shame of her family name to keep her warm."

I shove her away with a snarl. "How easily you forget your place."

"My place is beside you, as your equal." She rubs at her throat. "We are De La Rosas. Our blood is stronger than any other. That is why you survived, Santi. So you could lead. And I am here to help you."

"You are here to get in my way."

I pace the length of the floor, conflicted.

Perhaps Mercedes is right. I am letting Ivy get to me. I can see how she might draw such a conclusion, given the luxuries bestowed upon my wife already. But I have a plan, and I trust that will not alter. It is not for my sister to question me, and I must make that clear to her now.

"Betray me again, and you will not like the consequences," I say. "For now, you can accept your punishment graciously."

"Punishment?" She stares at me incredulously.

I seize her Gucci wallet and cell phone from the computer desk and pocket them.

She lunges for me, an expression of horror on her face. "No! You can't do this to me."

"You can have them back when you've shown some contrition for a change. Perhaps it will do you good."

Her jaw sets, and already I can see her plotting her revenge.

"Don't do anything stupid, Mercedes," I warn her menacingly. "You won't like the results if you test my patience further."

19

I vy is finishing up the light meal Antonia provided her when I return to her room. A fresh set of candles burns at her bedside, and it's brighter than the last time I saw her.

The gash on her head looks worse than before, and it bothers me more than I'd like.

"Tell me about the cut." I glance down at her. "How did it happen?"

She wipes her hands with a napkin and then folds it over the tray. Her eyes are cast down, and I can tell she's still trying to keep her secrets. But I will not allow it, and she should already be aware of this.

"Ivy." My voice is a warning, but my fingers are soft as they graze the back of her neck.

"I stumbled and fell."

Almost immediately, I contribute this to the faintness Antonia mentioned earlier. But then I remember the bruises on her body. And her reluctance to answer for them as well. She blamed them on the doctor, another matter I have yet to contend with. Though I suspect there is more to it than that.

"Why did you stumble and fall?"

She toys with the hem of the black silk nightgown I purchased for her. "Because I do that sometimes."

In the soft light, she looks more vulnerable than I've ever seen her. Perhaps this is the reason I find myself tilting her face up, so I can study that emotion and try to understand it.

"You can have no secrets from me." I pet her face beneath my palm, and she closes her eyes with a soft shudder. "We can do this the hard way or the easy way. The choice is yours."

"I have vestibular dysfunction," she admits reluctantly. "Sometimes, I get dizzy. Blurry vision. It can affect my balance. It's a defect I can't control."

I consider her words carefully, focusing on the term defect she chose with obvious disdain. She believes she is defective. Her eye, and now this. It brings me a strange sense of satisfaction to know this about her. The intimacy of her secret and the realization she is ashamed of it are both a balm to my own scars. But they shouldn't be.

My fingers fall away, and she peeks up at me.

"We'll have to be more careful with you then," I

answer ominously. "I didn't realize you were quite so... breakable."

Her eyes harden, and I leave her to stew in her anger as I retreat to her bathroom, gathering the supplies I need. When I return, she is still sitting at the small table, staring down at the hands tangled together in her lap.

"It's time to clean your tattoo," I inform her.

She straightens her spine and tries to glance back at me as I step beside her and drape her hair over one shoulder. She shivers, and I turn her chin away from me, forcing her gaze forward.

Slowly, I peel off the sanitary wrap. I use a wet, soapy cloth to wash over the ink, and fight the strange desire to trace over the symbol of my owner-ship with my fingers. It's my family crest. A crowned skull and crossbones flanked by roses and dueling revolvers. This image leaves no question who she belongs to. And to witness my mark upon her skin is more powerful than I expected.

Ivy sucks in a breath as I wash her with a gentle-ness I'm certain she doesn't expect. I want to inform her it isn't for her benefit, but only so I know the wound will heal properly.

When I have finished cleaning her, I apply more salve, rubbing it into her skin until she bows her head, as if to say it feels good to have a monster's hands upon her. I rub her longer than necessary and then wipe my hands.

There is still work to be done this evening, and I feel as if I am behind already. But it is no longer at the forefront of my mind when my palm skates down over her shoulder and dips into the silk nightgown, skimming over her breast.

Ivy closes her eyes and leans back into me, unaware of how much it affects me when she melts into me. I close my eyes too, hating her for tempting me this way. Hating her for her name. Her blood. Her sweetness that I want to imbibe, even as she poisons me.

My free hand grazes over her neck, reaching for the rosary, only to come up empty. Her shoulders stiffen, and our eyes collide at the same time. Mine dark and hungry, and hers, terrified.

"Santiago," she whimpers.

I grasp her jaw and squeeze it shut. She swallows audibly, and I lean down to her face, my lips a breath from hers.

"I'm beginning to think you actually like my punishments, dear wife."

He has me on my feet in an instant. All the tenderness of a moment ago has vanished almost like it hadn't happened. Like I imagined it.

"Santiago." Holding my arm at an awkward angle, he picks up the rosary from the nightstand and marches me out of my room, his footfalls sure while mine are silent. "You're hurting me."

"I'm being more than patient with you when you seem incapable of following one simple instruction."

We hurry through the house, and I try to keep up while taking it all in, all the shadowy corridors, the dimly lit spaces, richly textured carpets and curtains, intricately carved wood. It's out of an old vampire movie, this place.

"Slow down," I ask when I slip on the stairs he hurries us down.

"Keep up," he retorts, righting me before I fall.

There's no one around, and I wonder what time it is. All I can see is that it's nearly a black night apart for a sliver of moonlight.

"Where are we going?" I ask when we walk through the large kitchen, also dark and ancient looking with only the appliances seeming to be from this century.

He pulls open the door and is about to take a step but pauses and looks at my bare feet.

"Do you ever wear shoes?" he asks, but he's not waiting for my reply. I don't even think it's a real question. But in the next instant, he has me hauled over his shoulder, the flimsy nightgown riding to the tops of my thighs, the wind cool against the backs of my bare legs.

I bounce on his shoulder and look back at the house. It's even bigger than I'd realized. Four floors with spires disappearing into the low-hanging clouds and thick ivy crawling along the walls. At the center is a large arched window, the glass stained, at the head the window segments creating an ornate circle.

No. Not a circle.

A rose. The segments make up the petals.

De La Rosa. Of the rose.

A light goes on in one of the upstairs windows in a separate part of the house. Through the cast iron I see movement. A woman's figure. When she sees us, she draws the curtain wider and openly watches.

But in the next instant, I hear a heavy door creak on its hinges as its opened, the smell of church enveloping me again. I crane my neck to look around the small chapel as Santiago closes the door and sets me on my feet.

I take in the pews, six on each side. The wood simple. Kneelers in each without cushions and worn Bibles in two of the pews.

At the back left corner is the baptismal font. It's large and ornate, made of the same material as the altar. In the opposite corner is a simple confessional. In the place of doors is a deep red velvet curtain to give the penitent the impression of privacy.

Santiago walks to the altar. He doesn't stop to make the sign of the cross. Doesn't bow like the nuns taught us to. I wonder about that. About his devotion. His belief. He has a fascination for religion, I think. I don't know. But after what he did yesterday, how he did it bending me over the altar in the chapel, a sacred place, pouring wax from the altar candles onto my hips. A devout man would not do that, certainly. And then there's the rosary. Why give me a rosary on our wedding night? Why become so angry when you find I'm not wearing it?

At the altar, he doesn't raise his head to acknowledge the crucified Christ. Instead, he picks up a box of matches and lights several candles. I notice, though, that the red of the tabernacle lamp glows, and I wonder who maintains it. If there's a priest or if it's him.

I think about the woman at the window. "Does your sister live here? At the house I mean?"

He finishes lighting the candles and blows the match out.

I take in the two framed photographs on the altar. It's a strange place to keep photos, but I wonder if it isn't his father and brother. I step closer and think yes. I remember seeing them just a few times, and there is a resemblance. They died in that explosion that scarred him.

When I look at Santiago again, I find him watching me, and I take him in. His scars. The tattoo on his face. I glance at those photos again.

He walked away scarred but alive.

They died.

Something inside me feels a tenderness I can't describe in that instant. I don't know what it is. Why this matters. I don't know if it's the look in his eyes. The loneliness he wears like a coat. No, a second skin. Not something one can remove.

Is that why all this hardness?

But then he slips the rosary out of his pocket and sets it on the altar and bends to open a chest set beneath the altar.

"Strip, Ivy," he says without bothering to look at me.

My heart does a double beat. "What?"

He glances behind him as he rummages through the chest. "Strip and kneel."

"We're in church."

He pauses, turns to look at me and half-laughs then shakes his head and resumes his work.

"Strip and kneel. I won't ask you again."

I glance back at the door, but no one will come in. I turn to look up at the altar. At Christ. Apart from the wedding, I haven't been to church since I left home. I told my father I went weekly but I never did. I haven't been to confession since then, either. Do I even believe anymore? I don't know.

"Ivy."

I blink to look at Santiago's back as he sets things on the altar. He's not looking at me, but he's warning me all the same.

I pull the nightie off, shudder at my nakedness as I lay it over the back of the nearest pew. He's just turning to me when I slip off my panties and set them on top of the nightgown, and I watch his eyes as he takes me in. They've darkened. And when he meets mine, I see the hunger inside them. Something insatiable.

And it's like my body feels it. Or maybe it's that it remembers his touch. Remembers the orgasm because my nipples tighten, and there's a dampness between my thighs.

I lower myself to my knees and look beyond him

to the altar. To what he placed on it. And my stomach falls away. I know the long, innocuous-looking cane from my years at the nun's school. And the wooden paddle, although thankfully I've never felt that. The cane, though. That was Sister Mary Anthony's favorite.

There are other things too. A short leather strap. Another heavier cane. More paddles. They don't look new. In fact, they look well-worn.

I swallow, turn my gaze up to his.

He studies me for a long minute, the silence heavy around us. The air in this place weighted.

As if reading my mind, he turns back to his collection, chooses the long, wispy cane and picks up the rosary, then walks toward me. He cocks his head to the side and taps my clasped hands with the end of the cane. I hadn't realized I'd been holding them in prayer.

"Habit," he says.

I nod, but it's not so much a question.

He drops the rosary around my neck. The beads feel cold and heavy like each one is a weight.

"You don't go to church. You haven't been to a mass in the past half year."

"How do you know?"

"You think I didn't have someone watching you?" He walks a circle around me, and I turn my head to the right, then to the left to follow him.

"Why would you do that?"

"Because I knew in time, you'd be mine." He's still circling.

"Why?"

"That's for another time." He stands before me again. "Does it hurt? Kneeling there?"

I nod.

"Do you like it?"

I shake my head.

"Are you wet?"

I don't answer that one.

He grins, then begins his circling again.

"If you're going to punish me with that thing, just do it and get it over with."

I hear the swish then, and an instant later, I fall onto my hands as a strip of pure agony blazes across the bottoms of my feet. Before I can process, there's a second strike. Tears spring from my eyes, and for a moment, I can't breathe.

He crouches behind me. I'm still gasping for breath when he wraps the length of the rosary around his fist and tugs my head backward into his chest.

"You do not give the orders."

I clutch his forearm, my breathing gasps, chest heaving.

There had been a moment earlier that I'd found him tender, kind even. Almost. When he'd learned I hadn't eaten, he'd been upset. When he'd cleaned the tattoo, he'd been gentle. When he'd slipped his hand into my nightdress and grazed my breast, I'd leaned into his touch.

"Did you like that?" he asks.

I shake my head. "No!"

He brings the hand holding the cane between my legs and rudely cups me, and I think what I must look like on my knees before the altar, my body jerked backward, knees spread, on display.

"You're wet through."

I don't know if it's on purpose that he lets the cane rest against my sex.

"But this isn't about your pleasure, Ivy," he says, smearing his wet hand over my stomach as he rises.

"Please don't," I can't help but say as I reach back to cover my feet, feel the rising crisscrossed welts there. I was only caned once at school, and it wasn't anything like this.

"That's better. I like the please. But put your hands back in prayer and kneel up."

"Please." I crane my neck to look back at him.

He raises his eyebrows as if waiting for me to follow his direction.

I do, but I brace myself.

"You'll feel that with every step tomorrow."

I keep my gaze forward on the altar, tears blurring it.

"Do you know what my father expected of me?" he starts, circling again.

I shake my head, sniffle. I'm not sure what's worse, the anticipation of the cane or the cane itself.

He stops in front of me, looks me over, slides the instrument of torture between my legs.

I stiffen.

"More than I could give," he says, drawing it away. "I spent countless hours where you are now, and I can tell you I did not sob when lines criss-crossed my back. I did not so much as sniffle when the bottoms of my feet burned, the skin opening with each step."

My mouth falls open. I glance at the photo of the stern-looking man on the altar, then up at him. I try to imagine him as a little boy kneeling here. And I think of my own father who has never in my life raised a hand to me. I think about my mother's punishments, but they were never calculated. Hers were impulse. The momentary, uncontrolled rage of a dissatisfied woman.

"I'm sorry," I tell him when he's in front of me again. "I'll wear it. Like you said."

He walks behind me again.

"Please don't," I plead. It's taking everything for me to stay still, kneel up, and not cover myself.

"Lean forward and put your hands on the floor."

I glance back, then, after a moment, I do as he says. I put my hands on the floor, presenting myself to him. The pain that is surely to come overrides my humiliation.

When he slips the cane between my legs, I cry out, but he doesn't strike. Just taps for me to spread them wider.

"Like that," he says when they're as he wants them. I'm sure he can see all of me. "Don't move."

I hear him walk away, watch as he slips into a pew, setting the cane against it in the aisle. I dare a glance and find him sitting back watching me.

We stay like that for a long time, and as cold as the stone is beneath my hands and knees, sweat drips off my forehead as I wait for him to make his next move. I swear an eternity passes before he does. Before he finally rises, and I breathe a sigh of relief when he comes to me without the cane. When he kneels behind me and puts one hand on my hip and slides the other one up along my back, exerting pressure as he reaches the space between my shoulder blades, then closes his hand over the back of my neck. It's still tender from the tattoo. His fingers weave into my hair to curve around my skull, and I know what he wants, so I lower myself to my forearms and rest my forehead on the cold stone, and when I hear him unzip his trousers, I claw my fingers into the narrow crevices between the large stones and brace myself.

He takes hold of both hips and splays me open, fingers digging into skin.

I close my eyes when I feel him at my entrance, and I'm hungry for it. I feel that hunger slide down the inside of my thigh, and I know he sees it and feels it, and when he enters me, it's in one fell swoop. I can't help my cry. It takes all I have to keep my forehead on the ground as he takes me, keeping his hands firmly on my hips, not touching me where I need him to touch me. I know this is my punishment. His pleasure. He will use me for his pleasure tonight. And I'll take it.

And when our breathing is ragged and his thrusts frantic, and I feel him thicken even more inside me, I feel his fist at the back of my neck as he winds that rosary around it and draws me up, the sensation different like this.

With one hand, he chokes me with that rosary while with the other, he digs his fingers into my hip, those fingers so close to my clit, so close to my throbbing, wanting clit. And when he comes, he wraps that arm around my middle and holds me so tight that for a moment, I can't breathe. As he empties inside me, I can't breathe.

When he's finished, when he's loosened the choking rosary, when his arm isn't a steel bar crushing my ribs, he takes the shell of my ear between sharp teeth, and I still want. Even as I feel him draw out of me. Even as I feel his come slide down the insides of my legs, I still want.

And when he finally speaks, when he finally moves his hand and cups my sex to press his thumb against my hardened clit, I come. Just like that, I come. Even as he warns me not to disobey him again. I come as his seed spills out of me onto the church floor. I come as the hand that wielded that cane cups my sex and reminds me of what he told me last night.

That I belong to him.

21

Ivy is quiet as she follows me back down the corridor inside the house. She's stepping gingerly, feeling every bit of her punishment, but no complaints leave her lips.

A strange sense of turmoil roils in my gut. I am overly aware of the pain she must feel. How many times have I walked these halls with that same tenderness burning the soles of my feet? I imagined it would bring me satisfaction to watch her suffer in a way that I understand so intimately. But her lack of tears and silent resolve has brought me little of what I seem to need from her.

I want to bury myself in her again and again. Feel her warmth and her body clenching around me. The possibilities in which I could take her seem endless. Eternity doesn't seem long enough to explore them.

But she won't be here for eternity, I remind myself

as I lead her back to her room and seal us inside. She stands on the center of the rug, watching me with uncertainty that makes her seem smaller yet.

A pliable little doll.

My jaw sets as I study her, considering how long it will take for her to break. How long until she is so miserable looking at me every day, feeling my hands upon her skin, that she decides to put an end to it?

Or will I be the one to break first?

Perhaps, that would be easiest. Maybe it's what I should have done all along. I could wrap my hands around her throat and squeeze until the light dims from her eyes. There would be no question then. It would be done. And this strange new torment inside me would die with her.

But even that notion doesn't seem to satisfy me as much as it should.

I drag a hand through my hair, smoothing it back into place. The silence has stretched on for too long, and the tension thickens in the space between us. She's glancing at me like she doesn't know what to expect from me anymore.

"Sit down." I point at the same chair she vacated earlier.

She does as I request, the rosary dangling from her neck like a beautiful collar. It is heavy, and I know she feels it. I want her to think of me every time she moves. I want her to feel the weight of my ownership pulling her down.

I step behind her and smooth her hair back over her shoulders. She shivers but does not try to look at me, keeping her gaze forward. How quickly she is proving capable of abiding by my orders.

The first-aid kit is still on the table, so I reach for it and open a packet of alcohol. Gently, I press my fingers against her chin, tilting her head back until I have access to the cut on her forehead. She watches me with a curious expression as I dab the dried blood off around the edges, but when I feel her gaze burning into the scars beneath my ink, I pause to look down at her.

"Close your eyes."

She hesitates with a sigh but then does as I ask. I continue to clean her wound and then apply some salve and a bandage.

"Why do you care if it gets infected?" she asks.

"Because it would be too easy to lose you to something so simple."

Her eyes flutter open, meeting mine again. "I don't think you are as cruel as you would like everyone to believe."

"Then you are delusional." I release her with an irritated scowl and return the items to the first-aid kit.

"If you hate me so much, then why am I here?" she demands.

The wrappers crumple in my hands before I toss them into the garbage. "You know exactly why."

She glances at me as if she's trying to decipher the hidden meaning of my message, and at the same time, I'm trying to decipher her skills of deception.

Truthfully, I am uncertain if she is aware of the events that transpired. I have questioned it so many times over the years. How much does the rest of her family know about Eli and the explosion? Ivy is close to her father, so there is certainly some level of trust there. But it is difficult to say whether she knows the truth, or she really is as naïve as she pretends. Regardless, until I know for sure, I will assume that the traitorous Moreno blood running through her veins knows perfectly well why she is here.

"If I knew the reasons, then why would I bother to ask?" she challenges.

"Because you are a Moreno," I sneer. "And that makes you a traitor by default."

"And you are a De La Rosa. So, I suppose that makes you an asshole by default."

My palm slides around to the front of her throat, fingertips digging into her pulse as I force her head back until she can't bend any farther. Her fingers come up to mine, prying at my hand as she struggles to free herself from my grasp.

"You're insane," she hisses. "Do you realize that? Just let me go. Let me leave here and you will never have to see me again!"

"Let you leave?" I laugh darkly, leaning down to

let my words fan against her lips. "The only way you're getting out of this marriage is through death."

Her shoulders stiffen, and she stares up at me with unadulterated hate. "So, what then? You will see me dead? Is that truly what you wish?"

I force her head to the side, dragging my nose along her temple and into her hair, inhaling her drugging scent before I confess the truth.

"Nothing would give me greater pleasure."

THREE DAYS PASS. IVY REMAINS LOCKED IN HER ROOM, and I do not visit her. Instead, I ask Antonia for reports, a detail she finds rather curious. She provides me updates as I request, informing me of Ivy's eating and sleeping habits. She tells me that my wife has requested access to the pool, and I return my order to deny her.

I know she will have to come out soon. Certain things will be expected of her. She is to attend events with me. There will be meetings with other wives regarding their endeavors and contributions within The Society. They take turns planning events, luncheons, dinners, and ensuring the businesses run smoothly by keeping them adequately staffed. Ivy will be expected to participate at some level, although not as much as the others. She married a Sovereign Son, so many expectations are cast upon her. The way she dresses, speaks, and carries herself will all be scrutinized. But because she bears my mark, nobody will ever dare whisper their judgments in a space where she or I might hear them. It is her duty to sew herself into the fabric of our organization and truly become one of the upper echelon.

My wife will need rules. A schedule. Something to occupy her time until she is round with my child. I should be working on that now. Night and day, until I have made her mine in every sense of the word. But the longer she remains in the house, the more difficult it becomes to remember my control.

I don't know what I'm trying to prove by my absence. Is it for her benefit or mine?

I drown myself in my work, staring at the wall of monitors in my office, picking apart the data and scrutinizing it to death. Mercedes comes to me often, trying to wear me down with her questions.

Sleep doesn't come for me. Instead, I wander the halls of The Manor at night, pausing outside Ivy's door. More than once, I have stood there with my palm on the wood, considering our last conversation. I showed her my hand, and now she understands what I want.

Will she run the moment my back is turned? Will she stay and fight?

I truly don't know.

Tonight, finally, I give in and curve my fingers over the knob on her door. When I open it, I find her sitting in the chair by the fireplace, curled up into herself as she flips through the pages of a book. Upon hearing me enter, she glances up, her eyebrows pinching together when she sees me on the threshold. She's pale, dark shadows cast beneath the fringe of her lower lashes. In place of her normally smooth hair, there is an unruliness that screams of her desperation. She is already unraveling in her captivity.

It feels as though it has been an eternity since our eyes last met. Does she feel it too?

She studies me, folding the book into her lap and waiting for me to announce my purpose.

"Starting tomorrow, you have my permission to access The Manor. Everywhere except the staff quarters, my office, and my bedroom."

She sits up slightly, the strap of her black nightgown falling down over the curve of her shoulder. "And what about the pool?"

"The pool is off-limits until your tattoo is healed. Two weeks at least."

She frowns at this but nods anyway.

"You'll need to get settled in here. Soon, we will be required to attend events together. Mercedes will be here to teach you what is expected of you. She will go over your schedule with you and show you around The Manor."

Her eyes narrow. "And if I say no?"

"You know what happens if you say no." My

fingers itch to reach out and grab her, and my cock is already hardening at the mere suggestion of her defiance.

She seems to consider my words carefully before shaking her head in frustration. "And what about school?"

"That part of your life is in the past. You're my wife now. You'll spend your time doing something productive for The Society."

"Such as?"

"Such as bearing my children. Offering your assistance where it's required. And most importantly, pleasing me."

An expression of horror flashes across her face as she echoes those words. "Children?"

"Don't tell me you haven't even considered it," I mock her.

"But you said you wanted me dead."

Those words sound bitter repeated back to me. "Well, there is time for both."

She falls quiet, and I don't like it. I need her words, her thoughts.

"When can I see my sister?" she asks. "My father? When will I be able to visit my family?"

"If you behave this week, then you will be granted those privileges accordingly."

She stiffens as my unspoken threat settles over her, but after some consideration, she seems to come to a silent conclusion as determination steels her eyes.

"Fine. I'll do what you ask as long as I can see my father and Evangeline this week."

Her insistence on seeing that scum grates at me. But a deal is a deal. If she wants it, she will have to earn it.

"Come here."

She rises from the chair slowly, her legs stiff as she takes her first step. I shake my head and point at the floor.

"On your knees."

Her jaw hardens, and she hesitates, silently considering if it's worth it. Then she lowers herself to her knees and begins to crawl.

The sight of her submission is so enticing, it takes more restraint than necessary to wait until she's before me to wrap my fingers in her hair and tug her face up. I rub the erection in my slacks against her cheek, and she closes her eyes with an agonized sound in her throat.

"I hope your visit will be worth it." I slide the delicate straps of her nightgown down until it slips over her arms and bares her breasts to me.

Nothing would please me more than to watch her struggle to take my cock in her mouth. But that will have to wait for another time.

Unzipping my slacks, I tug my length free, and

she peeks up at the monstrosity bobbing in front of her face with wide eyes.

"Stroke it," I command, my fingers tightening in her hair. "Stroke it until my come covers your breasts. And if I am satisfied, then I will consider your request."

She reaches up and wraps her palm around me, and I shut my eyes, relaxing into her touch. I told her she would have to earn it, and she does. With every firm slide of her hand, she earns another piece of my shattered restraint.

Gripping and sliding, she indulges me with her palm unlike anyone ever has before. In my mind, I know women have done this for me. But I can't seem to recall another time, another face. Only hers. And when I explode across her chest, the undeniable evidence of my pleasure dripping down over her tits, the deal is done. But the humiliation does not feel adequate when she looks up at me with soft, hooded eyes. So, I drag my fingers through the liquid adorning her skin and smear it across her lips, forcing her to lick my fingers clean. Only then do I concede in granting her what she wants.

"One visit to start," I tell her as I tuck my cock back into my trousers. "The rest we will determine based on your performance."

The next morning, I'm already dressed when Antonia arrives with my breakfast. She's been the only thing keeping me from going mad in this room the past few days. I only know how long it's been because I am marking days on a piece of paper inside the desk. I started the second day when she brought me breakfast. It's silly maybe but keeping me locked up in here, even for just these three days, is taking its toll.

I need to swim. To move. I need to see sunshine. Open a window. That little square of light isn't doing it, and besides, it's been raining. I swear it feels like it always rains at this house.

But he said I'd get to see my dad today. And I feel like Santiago is a man who keeps his word.

I close the tube of salve I've been instructed to put on my tattoo and am up as soon as the door opens, the pain on the bottoms of my feet finally gone. That was two strokes. How had he taken more? What had he said when his back had been criss-crossed? When his feet opened up when he walked?

God. Is that how his father punished him? What a horrible man. Yet he has a photograph of him on the chapel altar.

I don't understand my husband. He's a complete mystery.

"Good morning, dear," Antonia says cheerily, although I always notice that little bit of concern when she comes in here in the mornings and shifts her gaze nervously around the room, looking me over. I wonder what she's looking for. A noose maybe. After only three days, I'm ready to hang myself, but I don't need rope for that. I'm pretty sure I could hang myself on the end of this rosary that's nestled against my bare skin. I've got it tucked under my sweater, and I've only taken it off to shower and sleep.

I know she doesn't like locking the door. She's said as much. But it's what the Master wants.

The Master.

I roll my eyes at his formality. His arrogance.

"Morning, Antonia. Do you know if the car is ready to take me to see my father?" I ask her anxiously. I'm not really hungry, so I ignore the tray she sets down.

"Settle down, Miss. It's early yet."

"What time is it? If I had a clock, I'd know." But my husband won't even allow me that.

"Ms. Mercedes will be the one taking you to see your father, and she doesn't rise until noon some days."

"Noon?"

"Sit down and eat. Santiago wants to be sure you're fed and so do I. I don't want you falling down again."

I sit, slouching, one elbow on the table as she pours me coffee out of a silver pot.

"I'll tell you what, though. Once you've eaten, I'll take you downstairs and show you around. I don't see the harm in you waiting for Mercedes downstairs."

I look up at her, hopeful and as excited as a kid at Christmas. It's ridiculous if I think about it, but I check myself.

"Will you get in trouble if you do that, Antonia?"

"Let me worry about that."

"Where is he?" I ask as I pick up my cup. I don't know why I ask, and I don't know why I care, but I'm surprised he won't be the one to take me today. Maybe a little disappointed too. Because as much as I hate to admit it and never will, the enigma that is my husband makes me curious. When he's with me, things feel different. They feel...more. I don't know how to describe it. I just guess I've never really felt so much before. So much anticipation, so much pain, so much pleasure, just so much. It's confusing and annoying. It should be simple. I should hate him like he hates me.

I shake my head to clear it. The thought of spending any time with Mercedes makes me anxious. I don't like her. And I don't trust her.

Antonia makes a point of rearranging the plates on the tray. "He keeps to his own schedule."

"What does that mean?"

"Oh, nothing, dear."

"Is he here? In the house?"

"Most times, yes, when he's not called away on business."

She walks away to make the bed, which I've already made, but she tucks it in tighter. I need to tell him I don't need a maid, especially this sweet old woman, to make my bed or do my laundry. It's embarrassing actually.

"I'll be back for you in twenty minutes, then I'll take you downstairs. You eat all of that now. He'll want a report after all," she mutters that last part as she closes the door behind her.

He'll want a report? Of what I ate?

Okay, am I really surprised at that? He's a control freak.

I eat my breakfast, a generous plate of eggs and bacon, fresh fruit and toast along with juice and coffee. I'm not sure I've ever eaten as well as I have here the last few days. I'm sure my mom would be shocked to hear the number of calories I consume at breakfast alone.

The thought of mom brings me to thoughts of Evangeline. Is she getting enough to eat? Should I have pushed to see her too? Or asked to see her instead of my father.

I have to stop this, though. One step at a time. I'm getting out of this room today. And out of this house. It's something.

Once I'm finished, I brush my teeth and I'm just putting on a pair of boots—one of the pairs of new shoes without heels that were delivered yesterday—when I see Antonia at the door.

It's those things that confuse me about Santiago. In one breath, he tells me he wants me dead. In his eyes, I sometimes glimpse his hate. Then he buys me shoes so I don't break my neck on the heels when he finds out about my disorder.

I shake my head.

No. He's not doing any of this for me. He just wants to be the one to torment me. To murder me maybe. It wouldn't do if I were to have an accidental fall.

"Ready?" Antonia asks, stepping aside and gesturing to the hallway.

I smile and nod and feel ridiculous. It's been three days, and I'm acting like I've been imprisoned for years and this is release day.

I follow her down the hall, taking in all the

details—the dark walls, the thick carpet, the winding staircases, two of them.

"How old is the house?"

"The Manor dates back several centuries. It was built by the first De La Rosa to settle in New Orleans. They're from Spain, did you know that?"

I shake my head, looking up at the portraits hanging along the wall as we reach the top of the stairs.

"His mother went back to Barcelona four years ago."

I turn to watch her shake her head.

"Santiago's mother?" I ask as I take hold of the banister. I pause when I look down, and a moment of vertigo overcomes me, so I quickly sit on the stair.

"Ivy?"

I squeeze my eyes, open them and focus on Antonia's kind face. "I'm all right. I just haven't had any exercise, and it's harder then. And the stairs... when I look down..."

"Maybe this wasn't a good idea. Perhaps you should lie down."

I shake my head and stand, feeling hot and clammy and not quite steady like I always do after one of these episodes but desperate not to go back into that room.

"I'm perfectly fine. Really." I smile as wide as I can, and it's not really a lie. These episodes don't last forever. You just don't want to be at the top of the stairs when they come.

Antonia studies me for a long moment then, and maybe against her better judgment, she nods, and we proceed down the stairs.

"Santiago's mom left four years ago, you said? After the accident, I guess?"

We reach the first-floor landing, and I raise my head to look around me. The ceilings' vaulted arches create a dramatic effect, especially with the dark furnishings and iron-clad windows. Several corridors lead off into different directions, and straight ahead, I see the window I'd spied the other night.

"Accident, yes," she says, but the emphasis she puts on the word accident makes me wonder what she thinks. "It killed her too, if you ask me. She passed away shortly after she returned to Barcelona. I don't doubt it was the grief, God bless the poor woman."

The official reports had said a gas leak led to the explosion.

"Lost her husband and one of her sons in one night and the remaining son, well, he was different after."

"The way he looked you mean?" Did his mother abandon him for his scars?

"No, those scars, they were terrible, certainly, but what it did to him inside. She tried, his mother, but it was too hard. You see—"

"Are you gossiping about my brother?"

We both turn, startled to find Mercedes slink out from one of those dark corridors. She looks stunning, like the last time I'd seen her. Dressed in a tight-fitting red dress that sets off her olive skin, black hair and eyes, her makeup is flawless and she's wearing five-inch heels more appropriate for evening and more jewelry than I'm pretty sure my mom, sisters, and I own all together.

"I don't think Santi would like to hear his wife was gossiping with the help." She looks from me to Antonia, who lowers her gaze and wrings her hands. "I don't recall him telling you to let her out, Antonia."

"I have permission to be out of my room today," I say, butting in, not liking Mercedes's tone but also hating what I just said. I sound like a child.

"He gave you permission, did he?" She grins, eyebrows raised.

My hands fist at my sides as my blood begins to boil.

"There was no reason to keep her locked in that room," Antonia says. I wonder if she feels my rage.

"That's not your place to say, is it?"

"Not yours either, ma'am. Your brother's made it clear I'm to look after his wife."

Mercedes turns her sour expression to me. "Hmm. Did he? Well. I'll take it from here, Antonia. You can go back to your kitchen."

"Yes, ma'am." Antonia says, voice tight.

I'm embarrassed for the older woman as she glances at me with a nod of acknowledgment before disappearing toward the kitchen.

"We weren't gossiping," I say, not wanting to get Antonia into trouble.

"No, I'm sure you weren't. Is that what you're wearing?"

I look down at my pale blue cashmere sweater and jeans. Mercedes is a bully. She reminds me of Maria Chambers. Entitled and rich and probably never been taught right from wrong. Never been told no.

"Yes, your brother bought it for me," I say. "We're going to the hospital, not a fashion show. Is that what you're wearing?"

Distaste curls her lip, and she walks past me.

I follow her into what I guess to be the formal living room with the huge rose-shaped windows. Her heels click quickly as she walks through it while I stand there, gaping at the mural on the ceiling.

"Are you coming?" Mercedes asks.

I drag my gaze away. "It's beautiful."

She glances up, shrugs one shoulder in dismissal, and raises her eyebrows. "I have things to do apart from babysitting you."

"I can take myself. I'd be happy to."

"Then you and I both would incur Santiago's wrath. This way." She turns on her heel and walks away. I quickly follow her through the house and out the front door where a man drives up in a Rolls Royce. It's James, I realize, from the other day. I'd thought he worked for Abel, but I guess it had been Santiago keeping tabs on me. It makes sense.

He opens the door for us, and I follow Mercedes in, then stare like a child out the window at the mammoth of a house and gardens that seem to go on for miles.

"Is that a maze?" I ask when I catch a glimpse of the high hedges.

"Yes."

When we finally reach the iron gates that open for us, I crane my neck until I can only see one of the house's two spires.

I remember from the wedding night that it wasn't too far from the center of town, but it's tucked away on its own not so little parcel of land, and the room I've been locked in seems even darker now.

When I turn around again, I find Mercedes studying me, her dark eyes hard but also curious. Not in an I'm interested in finding out who you are way but in a what are your weaknesses to exploit way and I'm very aware of how I look beside her. Almost like a child.

I clear my throat and shift my gaze out the window. It'll be about half an hour to the hospital. I anticipate an awkward ride, but Mercedes just gets on her phone and ignores me altogether.

James pulls the car into a parking space, and I look over at Mercedes talking to someone while studying her fingernails. He climbs out of the car and opens my door.

"You have fifteen minutes," she says just as I'm about to climb out.

"What?'"

"I'm not coming inside. It's too depressing."

"Fifteen minutes?"

"We have a lot to do. My bother has tasked me with readying you for The Society. We'll have to take care of, well, so much," she says with a look of distaste on her face as she lets her gaze sweep over me.

"Are you serious?"

She grins, makes a show of checking her thin diamond wristwatch. "You'd better hurry."

23

L awson Montgomery leans over the financial portfolio on my desk, studying it with the hawk-like eyes he is known for. He was the best man at my wedding, but Lawson is also an old friend and the one person within the New Orleans faction who I trust without question.

He is best known as Judge to those around him, given his elected position within the Louisiana court system. He is a valuable asset to IVI for obvious reasons, but he is also one of the rare few people I can speak freely with.

"Everything looks good." He shuts the folder and returns his laser focus to me. "How is newly wedded bliss treating you so far?"

The corner of my lip tilts up at his sarcasm. Judge surely has a dry sense of humor. "As well as can be expected."

"I trust your brand of justice will be swift and harsh."

When I don't respond, he arches an eyebrow at me. I pour us both a glass of scotch, allowing my gaze to drift to the ever-changing numbers on the monitors behind him for a moment.

"Is this your way of telling me you have not marked her yet?"

"She has been marked, as you well know." I swirl the glass beneath my nose, absorbing the smoky aroma of the drink.

"But not scarred," he finishes for me.

His observation unnerves me. I'm not in the habit of laying out my plans to others, but Judge is one of the harshest men I know. He has a reputation for being severe, both on the bench and within The Society. At least when the situation warrants it. He is a firm believer of the old adage of an eye for an eye. And when I was drunk one night and confessed my plans with Ivy to him, he was the who made the obvious suggestion.

What punishment could be worse for the family responsible for disfiguring me and murdering my blood? Scars, he said simply. Leave them with scars if you choose to leave them alive at all.

At the time, it seemed so simple and obvious. Of course, Ivy should have scars. Something to match my own. A permanent, unavoidable reminder of her father's sins every time she looks in the mirror.

For months, I had fantasized about all the ways I would do it. Burn her. Cut her. Etch my name into her throat. Perhaps even ink a skull onto the right side of her face to match my own. An image that would undoubtedly haunt her.

But now she is here, in my house, and I have not followed through with those plans. I am not any closer to finalizing the details, and I am not willing to admit that I hesitate to do so for reasons I don't quite understand.

"She has a pretty face." Judge swirls the drink in his glass and takes a sip. "I suppose it would be a shame to ruin it."

Something in his tone and the quirk of his brow makes me think he is amused by my admitted weakness when it comes to her.

"It is only because she is beautiful that I have hesitated."

My words aren't convincing, even to me. But I am certain with time, I will be able to fulfill this silent promise to myself. When the moment is right, I will execute the plan as intended.

"Regardless of whether she is scarred yet, I can assure you, she will suffer."

"I'm sure she is already," he muses. "Of that, I have no doubt."

His words settle over us, and we finish off our drinks in silence. I need to ask something of him, which is a part of the purpose of our meeting this afternoon. Ideally, I should have asked him before the wedding, but I was busy dealing with Abel.

"Any news on her father?" he asks.

"No. Nothing new anyway. My men are still investigating, but there has been no new information. I have a meeting with the Tribunal to discuss the progress on the investigation at the beginning of the month."

Judge is quiet and thoughtful before he glances at me with an intensity that makes him a formidable opponent to weaker men than me. "And have you considered that there may never be more information? What then?"

"I have considered it." I shrug. "But I won't accept it."

"Well, that may be the case. But it is about as useful as a man telling Mother Nature he will not accept her storm."

Ignoring his obvious point is the only option I have at this stage. I can't accept that I may never truly have one hundred percent certainty or evidence of Eli's guilt. It is something I have considered from every angle. And I only know the obvious, what I feel deep in my gut. He is responsible, and I refuse to believe otherwise until there is undeniable proof.

"There is another reason I asked you here," I tell Judge. "Apart from the philosophical musings of my revenge."

"I suspected as much." He chuckles.

"I have a request to make." I clear my throat and feel oddly out of place. "I would like to invoke the sacred pact. For my wife, I would like to grant you the customary rite should anything happen to me."

"I trust that nothing will happen to you," Judge answers quietly, "but I accept your grant of the rite to me."

Some of the tension dissolves from my shoulders, and I retrieve an additional portfolio from my drawer, sliding it over to him. "My wishes are all documented there. Every last detail of what should happen to Ivy and her family in my absence."

He nods, eyes drifting to the portrait of my sister on the wall. "I am becoming quite the collector of responsibilities. First Mercedes, and now your wife."

There's a flicker of something in his gaze I don't recognize as he studies the image of Mercedes.

"For your trouble, I believe I should also leave you the bulk of my finances for agreeing to take on Mercedes in my absence," I jest.

"That won't be necessary." Judge smirks. "It would be a pleasure to tame such a wild mare."

My eyebrow arches at his insinuation, and I find it strange that he should mention Mercedes in such a way. He has always been cold to her. Respectful, but cold.

"You would have your work cut out for you," I assure him. "She is difficult, even in the best of times.

I'm afraid she has become set in her spoiled ways, and now I'm not certain it can be undone."

"Anything can be undone, given a firm enough hand," Judge remarks dryly. "Should you require assistance, I am available to discipline. As you know, it is a specialty of mine, and in cases like these, it's not uncommon to have a third party intervene. As her brother, you have a weakness for her that I don't possess. There would be no familial affection to taint my black heart."

I consider his suggestion and find it a valid argument. Mercedes is on a path of destruction and has been for some time. With Ivy in my care and my job within The Society, I have little time to devote to keeping my sister in check. It is something I can keep in mind, should she continue to cause problems.

"How is the little hellion, anyway?" Judge asks. "Still pining for Van der Smit?"

"Van der Smit?" I laugh. "I did not realize you were so informed on the matters of Mercedes's heart."

"It is widely spread gossip." He waves his hand dismissively. "Everyone in IVI has heard how he passed over the great Mercedes De La Rosa in favor of another woman. The rumor is she was quite spurned by the events."

"Yes, I suppose she was." I frown. "But Mercedes does not seem to form attachments too deeply to anyone. I think it was merely her pride that was wounded."

Judge nods as if this perspective satisfies him. "I take it she is back at the manor then?"

"For now," I concede. "She has been tasked with mentoring Ivy in her role as an upper-echelon wife. I suppose that should keep her busy for some time at least."

"Well, that's something," Judge agrees. "Idle hands are the devil's work."

"That's what they say."

There's a tap at the door, and it opens, surprising us both when it's Mercedes herself. She moves to enter the office but pauses mid-step when she sees Judge sitting across from me.

"I didn't realize you had company." She folds her arms across her chest and glances at him curiously. "Judge, it's always a pleasure to see you."

"So you say." He dips his head in her direction, and I don't miss the way his eyes linger on her for a moment longer than what would be considered appropriate.

"How is the thrilling life of the judicial system treating you?" she asks. "Sentence any poor souls to their death over lunch today?"

"Only the ones who deserve it," he answers. "How is the life of a spoiled princess treating you? Have you left any vanity in the department stores for the other socialites?"

Storm clouds roll into her eyes, and her red lips part, speechless, for the first time in perhaps forever. She smooths a dark strand of hair from her face, attempting to gather her wits when I decide to save her from this strange interaction between them.

"What do you want, Mercedes?"

"I have returned your wife," she spits the words out venomously. "Not a hair on her head displaced, of course. And I am here to give you a full report."

Judge smiles at her obvious irritation and rises to his feet, collecting his folder from the desk. "Then I suppose I better be on my way."

AFTER MY SISTER'S FULL REPORT, SHE TAKES HER LEAVE from my study with instructions to find something productive to do with her time. I can't help noticing that she seemed flustered and irritated throughout her rendition of the day's events, and I'm not certain if it's because of Ivy or Judge's biting but accurate assessment of her.

Regardless, I push those thoughts aside and finish my work for the day before I go in search of Antonia. I find her dusting the shelves in the library and nearly startle the life from her once again when she turns to see me standing there.

"Oh!" She gasps. "I didn't hear you, Mas... I mean, Santiago. Sir."

She seems out of sorts today and a little tired. I often wonder how long I will be able to keep her on staff. Though she has been given many opportunities to leave, should she like, the woman seems determined to remain at the manor until her dying breath. I am too proud to admit that I am grateful for that because the house wouldn't be the same without her.

"Can I get you anything?" she asks.

I hesitate, uncertain how I might phrase my proposition. She waits patiently, her eyes kindly remaining on my face without any sign of revulsion.

"How is Mrs. De La Rosa this afternoon?" I ask.

"Fine." She answers with a hint of confusion. "Last I saw, she was reading. I did suggest a nap since she seemed a little tired. But other than that—"

"I would like you to inform her that she is to have dinner with me this evening."

A small hint of a smile brightens her face. "Oh, yes of course. Would you like something special? I can change the menu if you'd like."

"What you have on the menu is fine," I answer stiffly. "Thank you, Antonia. Please tell my wife she is to join me in the dining room at seven thirty."

"It would be my pleasure." She bows her head.

With that matter settled, I take my leave of the estate. I'm not in the habit of venturing out before total darkness, but another situation warrants my attention and should have been handled days ago.

My magnetic silver Aston Martin DB11 AMR Coupe handles the crowded streets with ease as I navigate to the Lakewood neighborhood. Traffic can be a nightmare this time of day, which is why Marco offered to drive me, but I find something about driving myself calms me. He is in the passenger seat beside me, silent for the duration of the ride until I pull up in front of the colonial mansion on Garden Lane.

"I will accompany you, sir." He's already unbuckling his seat belt, unwilling to accept no for an answer.

Marco is my personal guard, and he treats his position as if it is his sole purpose in life. He was assigned by IVI, as all Sovereign Sons require a guard, but his loyalty and dedication are unwavering. He's been with me since my teenage years and has offered his regrets more than once that he was not inside the meeting with me the night of the explosion. I had told him to wait outside, and he did. He was the one who ran into the building and dragged my half-dead body out as I attempted to crawl from the wreckage. Had he not, I doubt I would be here today.

"Thank you, Marco." I open my door and make my exit, walking briskly up to the front veranda.

Marco holds back behind me, checking the street and every other invisible threat he may see. I ring the bell and wait.

A moment later, Dr. Chamber's housekeeper greets me with a startled gasp.

"Oh, hello." She barely manages to get the words out before she forces her gaze downward. "Please do come in. I will call for Dr. Chambers."

We follow her inside, and she leaves us in the sitting room, scurrying off as quickly as she can. It takes several minutes, but eventually, Chambers appears with a wary expression on his face.

"Santiago." He nods at me. "I wasn't expecting you."

"Funny, considering you've been avoiding my calls." I tilt my head to examine him.

"I haven't." He dismisses the suggestion as ridiculous. "I've been very busy. In fact, I only just got back to the city from a conference. There has been little time to go through my messages, I'm afraid."

"No time like the present." I stare at him incredulously.

He shifts his weight, glancing at Marco behind me, and then forces his gaze back to me. "Can I offer you a drink?"

"No."

He takes a seat across from me, obviously uncomfortable in my presence. "What can I help you with?"

"You can help me with an explanation of the events that transpired while my wife was in your office."

A bead of sweat hovers on his forehead before trickling down over his brow. "The purity test?"

"Unless there is any other occasion I should be informed of," I answer blandly.

"I was under the impression that you requested it," he states.

"And you thought it reasonable to perform such a request without speaking to me directly?"

"It's not uncommon for a groom to make such a request," he defends. "As I'm sure you are aware, it is a standard practice within The Society. Men who are to be married often want assurances. It is also requested frequently by the bride themselves, a subtle way to alleviate any doubts, should they arise."

"Perhaps other men accept this explanation, but I do not. So, let me make my position clear, Dr. Chambers. You never should have touched my wife without my explicit consent. I don't think this is something that requires a great deal of thought. In fact, I should think it would be obvious what my feelings on the matter might be. It leaves me to wonder about your motivations for such a treasonous act."

"It was not done with ill intent." He tugs at his collar, the sheen of sweat now dripping down his neck. "I can assure you of that. If you are questioning the ethics of my practice—"

"I am questioning your very loyalty." I narrow my

eyes at him. "You are aware it is within my power to have your medical license revoked. With a single declaration from my lips, you could be banished or have the lifeblood drained from your very body. So, why would you risk it?"

"I don't know what you think happened in that exam, but—"

"That's precisely what I would like to know. How did my wife end up with bruises on her body? Was it you or someone else?"

His eyes dart to the phone as if there might be someone he could call who would save him from this conversation. But he knows very well there is not. In the hierarchy of The Society, he is barely worth mentioning. He is not a Sovereign Son, and he never will be.

"Forgive me, Santiago," he answers gruffly. "If your wife feels she was hurt in any way, please allow me to offer my deepest apologies. It was not my intention to do so. I was simply doing my job. That is all."

Something about his nervous, beady eyes makes me believe otherwise. But he has always been this way around me, so it is difficult to know for certain. Without Ivy telling me the explicit details herself, there is not much else within the realm of reason I can do at the present.

"There is nothing more I should know then? Nothing more you wish to tell me?"

He wipes his palms on his trousers and shakes his head vehemently. "No. Not that I can think of."

"Very well." I rise from the chair, glancing down at him like the scum he is. "As for my wife, you don't exist to her anymore. I don't want you to look at her. Speak to her. Or even so much as mutter her name again in passing. Do you understand?"

"Yes, of course." He bobs his head. "Whatever you wish."

I head for the door, and one last thought occurs to me. "I want the notes from her chart. Send them to me. Now."

24

My stomach growls as I make my way down the stairs at the appointed time. I feel as though I've been summoned, and I think back to that conversation with Mercedes. About how my husband gave me *permission* to leave my room. I grow angry with the memory. At the thought of it. It's been bothering me all day, and the fifteen-minute visit with my father didn't exactly fulfill his end of the bargain.

The lush carpet pads my steps, muting any sound. I'm generally quiet when I'm not knocking into something, and in this house, I'm even more careful. There's a depth to the silence here. Even when it was quiet at my house or at the apartment as I sat there alone, it wasn't like this. There was always some noise, but you don't realize it until you hear this absolute absence of sound.

My path is illuminated by the chandeliers overhead, ancient gothic things lit with candles.

I stop for a moment and take it in, wonder who is tasked with cleaning them and putting new candles into the dozens of chandeliers in this place. They must have to do it daily. I pass one of the large iron-clad windows. It filters the moonlight to a pretty, eerie silver. Shadow is layered upon shadow here. I wonder if I'll find ghosts when I start to wander the house. I won't be surprised if I do.

I walk into the living room with its rose petal windows. The mural on the ceiling is obscured. I peer up at it, then turn a circle to take it in. It's spectacular still, the art, the architecture of the house itself, all the arches, the nooks, the darkness.

I run my fingers over the closed piano lid. I wonder if anyone plays. I wish I did, but I don't have much of a talent for it.

A clock chimes. It must be seven thirty. I walk out of the living room in search of the dining room. I find it only because I hear the barest hint of sound. Music. Low and dark and so fitting for this place.

As I follow it, I wonder if the rooms form almost a circle around the large hall. I wonder if I were to have an aerial view if the house itself would be in the shape of a rose.

I touch the back of my neck lightly. I saw the tattoo today. I expected a rose, but it's not that. Or not only that. What caught my eye first was the skull. Then the roses. Then the dueling pistols.

Violence and death and beauty all at once.

I pause when I reach the entrance of the dining room. Santiago is standing at the window, drink in hand, facing away from me. He's so still I wonder what thoughts he's lost in. I take a moment to study him because I am hopelessly curious about my husband. I didn't expect to be. He's beautiful from here. No, he's beautiful period, even with his skull face. It's his pain. I see it even when he's cruel. Maybe especially then. And it does something to me.

But it's not his pain that draws me now. It's something much more primal. His height. His broad shoulders. The suit jacket that hugs his muscles. How very masculine he is.

Heat flushes through me as I remember wrapping my hands around his biceps. How strong he is. How much stronger than me. How much bigger.

Just as I take a step into the room, a wave of vertigo hits. I miss the single stair, and when I trip, I just manage to catch the sideboard to stop from falling to the floor but knock something off the other end. It clatters to the floor, and Santiago flinches like he's startled, then spins to face me, eyebrows furrowed, expression dark as if remembering himself.

"I'm sorry!" I'm embarrassed. I blink hard, keeping my hand on the sideboard to steady myself and hurry around to pick up the antique silver candelabra lying on its side on the floor, grateful nothing is broken.

He stalks toward me setting his glass down on the candlelit table to take me by one arm and the candelabra in the other. He sets it back on the side-board and turns to me, looking me over.

"Are you all right?" He studies me intently.

I nod, forcing myself to focus. "I'm fine."

"Do I need to wrap the furniture in blankets?" he asks. I think he's trying to make light of it. I wonder if he can see my embarrassment because I feel my face burning.

"That was just...I tripped." *In part because I was staring at you. Remembering your hands on me. Remembering how your touch felt.* I don't tell him that, though.

"Antonia said you weren't quite well earlier."

"I'm fine." I pull myself free. This side of him, this almost caring side, throws me off guard, and I can't let that happen with him. I can't let myself believe him. And I can't let myself take comfort from him.

"You lost your balance at the top of the stairs, Ivy."

"I didn't lose my balance. I just needed to sit down for a minute. And it hasn't happened all day." Mostly.

He studies me like he doesn't quite believe me.

"It's why I've been asking about the pool. I swim every day. Or I used to. And it helps. As soon as I'm *allowed* to swim again, I'll be fine," I start, finding my irritation again as I say it. "*Santi*," I add.

Santiago steps back with a smile. Now we're on territory we both understand.

I feel myself flush again, sweat breaking out over my forehead this time. When Mercedes had used that nickname earlier, it had grated. I didn't really register it, but I realize now as I mock call him by her nickname for him, what I felt.

Jealousy.

Because I'm an idiot.

I shift my gaze away momentarily, feeling his eyes on me, feeling that smug grin.

"Mercedes being territorial?" he asks.

I clear my throat and make myself look at him. "I just thought it was funny she had a nickname for you. I mean, *you*."

His mood darkens.

I blink, trying to calm my breathing. He can't see my heartbeat. I just need to relax.

He looks me over, taking his time. I'm wearing a knee-length close-fitting black knit dress with buttons a little lower than I'd usually wear. Not that I have much cleavage to show, but I clear my throat again and adjust the dress when I see his gaze settle there. But maybe he's just eyeing the rosary beads.

My hair's been cut but only an inch was taken

off. And it's been styled, which I admit does look nice. I don't bother blow-drying it usually. I'm also wearing makeup which, again, I rarely do, and I won't do for him. My nails have been done, and much to my dismay, I've been waxed in places I didn't know you could be waxed. Mercedes's doing. Or maybe it was at his request.

"You look beautiful," he says, walking a circle around me, letting his fingers weave through my hair but not hurting me. "But you always look beautiful."

My stomach growls loudly then, and my cheeks burn again, my hand moving automatically to my belly. He stops in front of me, and for a moment, I wonder if he meant to say that. To compliment me.

"Hungry?"

I nod.

"Please tell me my sister fed you."

"If by fed you mean some leaves and a piece of cardboard masquerading as chicken breast, then yes, she fed me. She's seriously awful. I mean, she almost makes you look nice."

He chuckles at that, then sets his hand on my lower back and guides me to the long dining table set only for two. At least she's not eating with us. He pulls out my seat. I sit down on the plush chair and drop my napkin into my lap. He takes the seat at the head of the table, and as if the staff have been waiting and watching, they appear out of a door in the wall that must be for the staff like they used to be in old days.

We're silent as the dishes are laid out, and Antonia describes what everything is. I think there's enough to feed two dozen people, but I can probably eat for at least two of those people, so I won't complain.

"Thank you, Antonia. You've outdone yourself."

"Thank you, M—sir."

After a man opens the bottle of wine and Santiago approves, they're gone, and Santiago begins to heap food on my plate. He doesn't ask what I want. He just gives me a generous serving of meat, potatoes, and vegetables along with bread and butter.

"It's a little pretentious to have them call you Master, isn't it?"

He takes a moment to set his napkin on his lap. "Just be grateful I don't require it of you."

"I wouldn't ever call anyone that."

"Would you like to test that theory?"

When I don't answer, he raises his eyebrows, waiting for me to acknowledge his win.

"No."

"Then learn when to keep your mouth shut, darling."

I grit my teeth so hard I'm pretty sure I'm going to crack a tooth.

He finally shifts his attention to the bottle of

wine and pours himself a glass. I see the ring on his hand then and recognize it for what it is. I've seen it before but hadn't had a point of reference. Now, with having seen his mark on my neck, I realize it's his family crest.

"Do you all have that?" I ask, remembering seeing a ring on Holton's finger but not on the doctor's.

He follows my gaze to his ring and nods. "Sovereign families. Males only."

"Of course. I wouldn't think a woman would be allowed such an honor." I put the accent on honor, and I'm sure he hears my sarcasm, but I don't wait for him to comment. I pick up my glass, which is already full, and take a sip as he sips his. I raise my eyebrows.

"Juice?"

He nods, then sets his wine down.

"I'm not a child, you know." Not that I drink much. It messes with my already poor balance if I do, but I'd like the option.

"You could be carrying my baby inside you. You won't be allowed alcohol, Ivy."

"Your baby? I hardly think you're that potent." He makes a face, and I think he's about to say something rude so I continue before he can. "And again, I'm not a child. I can decide for myself, and if I were pregnant, which I'm not, I, of course, wouldn't have a drink."

"It's one of your rules. No alcohol. Period. There will not be a discussion." He picks up his knife and fork and starts to cut into his meat like this is a remotely normal conversation.

I shake my head but drop it. I honestly would only have taken a sip anyway, but it's the principle. I stab a bite of meat and put it into my mouth. It's even more delicious than it smells. We eat in silence for a moment, and I watch him, wondering if he feels any discomfort in the silence. I get the feeling he doesn't.

"She only let me see my dad for fifteen minutes," I finally blurt out.

He pauses, but I can't quite read his expression.

"Was that your doing? Because I can tell you that having to endure a spa day with your sister is not worth fifteen minutes. I want to see him again. For longer. And I want to see my sister."

He smiles, studies me, then shakes his head and returns his focus to his plate.

"I mean it, Santiago. This wasn't fair, and you know it."

He puts his fork and knife down and wipes his mouth. "If I didn't know better, I'd think you were purposely trying to push my buttons."

"I'm not. I just wanted to see my dad. We had a deal."

"A little bit of respect will go a long way. I realize you're quite young, and your upbringing leaves much to be desired, but I thought you'd understood that at least."

"You want me to ask you for permission? Is that it? Do you get off on that?"

"That's one."

"One what?"

"One strike. And I'm being generous. You have two left so take care."

I open my mouth to tell him where he can shove his strike but think better of it and stuff a potato in while I think. I have a pretty good idea where strikes two and three will lead me.

"Mercedes mentioned the masquerade ball at IVI?" he asks.

"She said something about readying me for an event, but she wasn't specific, and I didn't get a chance to ask when she proceeded to remind me how lucky I am you chose to grace me with your attention. How grateful I should be to carry your last name. How I have a duty as your wife to devote myself to you and to The Society. Etcetera, etcetera."

"Well, she is thorough if not dramatic."

"Can I at least call her?"

"My sister?" he feigns confusion.

"*My* sister."

"I will personally take you to see both your sister and your father myself after the gala."

I'm surprised. "You will?"

"If you behave."

I bite my lower lip. "For more than fifteen minutes?"

He nods.

"When is it?"

"In two nights."

"Do you promise it'll be a normal visit? No tricks? Nothing stupid you can talk your way out of?"

"You're not a very trusting little thing, are you?"

"I've learned my lesson with you." I resume eating, feeling at least a little victorious.

"You're close with your sister?"

I nod. "I was close with both of them until Hazel left."

"I remember that. Have you had contact with her?"

I look up at him, study his face in the play of candles. I would give anything to see him in full light.

"If I said yes, would you report it to The Society?" I know what will happen if they ever find her. She'll be punished publicly for having turned her back on The Society. For having walked away from a Sovereign Son.

"Have you, Ivy?"

"No, Santiago, I have not. But if I did, I wouldn't tell you."

"Your father doesn't search for her."

"What?"

"He hadn't ever really."

I'm confused. I'm sure he sees it on my face, too, and maybe he's just trying to figure out if I'm lying or if I know anything. Because he doesn't fill in any blanks.

"How do you know that?" I ask a little more uncertainly.

"I know a great deal."

"That doesn't make any sense. Of course he's looking for her. She disappeared after—" I stop abruptly. Was he friends with the man she was supposed to marry? They're all like brothers, right? The Sovereign Sons. All have each other's backs.

Hazel ran away days before her wedding. She just vanished into thin air. No note, no nothing. I understand her not leaving anything for our parents because they were the ones pushing her, but she didn't even leave one for me. I have always wondered if she could because I don't believe she'd leave without a single word to me.

"They won't stop looking for her. But you probably know that," he warns.

I do. The Society does not let those who wander from the path they've laid out for them go unpunished. If they let them go at all.

Especially a woman.

Especially a woman ranked as low as we are.

"And they will find her. In time," he adds.

I shudder at the thought and slip my fork and knife diagonally on my plate. I've lost my appetite.

"It's been six years. They can't...hurt her anymore," I say. He remains silent. "Can they, Santiago?"

"They? Don't you mean we?"

I just watch him. Is he trying to scare me? Or is he trying to figure out if I truly have information on her whereabouts? I don't, and for the first time in six years, I'm glad I don't because I have a feeling my husband can detect lies.

"You've gone pale." He pushes his chair back, stands, and comes to pull my chair out. He holds his hand out to me.

I look at it, then up at him.

"Come, Ivy. I will put you to bed."

It was funny that he asked me if I was searching for which buttons to push when he knows exactly which to push for me.

He put me to bed after dinner last night, exactly as he said. Dressing me in a sexy silk slip, then taking care to rub salve into the tattoo, he tucked me in like a freaking child, knowing all along how angry it made me. He didn't touch me apart from taking care of the tattoo. When I saw the negligée, I assumed there would be something, and the fact that I'm bothered by that is even more frustrating than the rest of it.

He's a control freak. I know that. And I'm just one more thing he can and will control and that includes my pleasure too, I'm sure. And I'm also sure my defiance only makes him that much more determined.

I haven't seen Santiago all day apart from the

glimpse I caught of him getting into a little silver sports car and speeding off a few hours ago. I want to know where he went and who he's with. Is he at a fancy dinner or an evening out on the town while I sit here night after night isolated and alone? Mercedes is gone too. I heard her telling Antonia she wouldn't be back tonight. That's at least a silver lining.

Which gives me the perfect chance to do some more exploring. Maybe check out some of those off-limits rooms. Because I found something I don't think I was supposed to find today.

Antonia wishes me a good night, telling me she's off to bed, and leaves the room. It's almost ten, but I've been anxious to get going for hours.

I give it a few minutes after she's gone before I get up. I tuck the heavy rosary under the black slip. The stones of the thing are cold against my bare skin, and I pull on a sweater. I don't want to run into the staff and have them see it around my neck. It will only reaffirm his dominance over me. It's humiliating enough to submit to him, but to have them all know it? Well, I don't think I could handle that.

I searched for a phone during the day, but there doesn't seem to be one anywhere. It's not unusual not to have a landline, though. I found the pool too, and it took all I had not to just slip right in and swim. It's beautiful. Twice the size of the one at my parents' house with two-story-high glass ceilings and walls and tiny little turquoise and gold tiles as far as the eye can see.

I'd swim if I was sure I wouldn't get caught. As much as I hate to admit it, I'm afraid of what he'd do if he did catch me. I have a feeling even if no one reported back, he'd smell the chlorine on me somehow, even if I scrubbed my skin raw.

The conversation last night about Hazel still has me rattled. And his comment about my dad not really ever searching for her, is that true? Why? Or was he somehow protecting her from The Society?

And now I'm wondering if Santiago himself is looking for her. Does he care enough to bring her back to be punished? Why? He used to be like a son to my father. Does he realize that, I wonder? Surely, he wouldn't do anything to cause my father pain. Right?

I step out into the hallway and turn toward the stairs that lead down to the first floor and back to the large and well-stocked library, which just happens to be near his study. I only know that because I'd been in the library when I'd overheard Antonia tell one of the maids she wasn't allowed to be in that part of the house and to clear out.

So I make my way toward the dark corridor with the double doors at the end that lead to the library. I feel my heart race and keep glancing over my shoulder, but all is quiet.

And I'm not doing anything wrong. Yet.

If anyone asks, I'm just going to get a book and read. I'm allowed in here.

I let myself in through the double doors. The chandelier offers slightly more light than those in the living and dining rooms, and reading lamps are set beside each comfortable, plush chair of which there must be a dozen, some set up in pairs, most alone. This is where I spent most of the afternoon. I even took a nap in one of those chairs. Not on purpose but I dozed.

I pick up one of the candles in its old-fashioned holder and make my way toward the darkest part of the library. It's a little creepy in here but honestly no less so than my own bedroom, so I shake off the thoughts of ghosts and go to the cutout door similar to the one in the dining room.

I hold my candle up and have to peer close to see the outline, but there it is. The young woman had been whistling as she cleaned. It's what had woken me from my impromptu nap. I hadn't thought much of it until Antonia mentioned she wasn't to go into the Master's study.

I roll my eyes at the fact he makes them call him master.

Pretentious prick.

I search for something resembling a doorknob, but there isn't one. Setting the candle on a shelf, I feel around, and a few moments later, when I push at just the right place, I feel the spring beneath my fingers, and the door creaks open.

Feeling victorious, I grin. Then look over my shoulder to make sure I'm still alone before I step into Santiago's study.

I stand and survey the space, the light of my candle dimmer than the flashing artificial green of the half dozen monitors across from his desk. They're the only modern thing in here. It's a good-sized room with the huge antique desk at the center and a single chair across from it. A cognac-colored leather couch extends almost the length of the wall nearest me, and like the walls in my room, those here are paneled in dark wood. The far one is taken up entirely by leather-bound books and before it are two comfortable looking chairs with a small table between them.

I walk toward it, pausing at any creak in the floor, trying and failing to ignore the lingering scent of his cologne. It's subtle, like when I smell it on him, but just as in the confessional the night of our wedding, it's his scent, and I will never forget it. It's like my body has a visceral reaction to it, too, my stomach fluttering, my heart racing.

I don't know what it is about this man whose mark I wear etched in my skin. Whose ring circles my finger and whose rosary hangs heavy around my neck, but I am so highly aware of him past and present.

When I get to the wall of books, I see a glass with its remnant of amber liquid beside a book on the small table. The book itself is open and lying facedown.

I sit on the chair, and when I do, I see the pencil that must have rolled to the floor. I pick it up without even thinking and set it beside the book.

Santiago must have sat in this chair while drinking his drink.

I set my candle down and pick up the glass to inhale. Scotch. My dad had it for company at home. I bring the glass to my lips, and I'm not even sure why I do this. I'm not really thinking, and if I were, I couldn't make sense of it. But I put my lips to the glass, and I drink the last sip of his scotch.

As the liquid burns its way down my throat, I close my eyes and lean my head against the back of the chair. Leather combines with the scent of scotch and him. Keeping my eyes closed, I inhale, aware of the shudder that makes its way down my spine. I know it's not the scotch. It doesn't work that fast.

I open my eyes and set the glass down, then touch the tips of my fingers to the leather spine of the book. No title. The leather looks and feels ancient. The tome is thick and probably shouldn't be laid facedown and open like he's got it. It'll damage the binding.

Picking it up, I turn it over and peer at the page.

But it's not words at all that I see. It's a drawing that takes up the whole of the page. A skull.

I turn the page and find detailed black and white drawings on the next one. This one is a woman. She's beautiful. Older with dark hair and sad eyes and a veil that hides part of her face. I study it, something about how she seems to be peering out at me so intriguing I can't look away.

I'm so caught up in it that it's not until I hear the key turn that I realize I'm caught. I stand, hitting my knee into the table and sending the candle to the floor. I gasp as I watch melted wax spill into the fibers of the carpet before whirling to look at who has caught me, knowing there's only one person, and meeting my husband's dark eyes as they land dangerously on mine.

26

SANTIAGO

My eyes flick to the sketchbook splayed open on the table. The pages are opened to an image I sketched of my mother from the funeral. I hadn't been able to attend because I was still in the hospital, but Mercedes ensured it was videotaped for me, and I watched it more than once. That haunting image of my mother so broken burned itself into my mind. It's a memory that was never intended to be seen by anyone. Least of all a fucking Moreno.

Heat rises in my throat as I stalk toward my wife. She's already trembling, shrinking into herself as she tries to move back. But there's nowhere for her to go. Doesn't she realize it yet? She'll never escape me.

My icy fingers latch around her jaw and force her gaze up to mine. "What do you think you are doing?"

"I... I..." She stammers over the words, trying to shake her head. Wide, terrified eyes peer back at me, but it's the scent of my scotch on her breath that fuels my ire.

"Snooping through my things. Drinking my scotch. Are there any other sins you'll need to atone for this evening?"

"Santi, please."

"Don't call me that." My fingers bite into her skin, and she flinches at the menace in my tone.

I don't know what she thinks she's doing, acting so familiar to me. Trying to make me forget who I am. Who she is. As if she has a right to touch my things or stare into my darkest memories. Does she take pleasure in perfuming the halls of the manor with her scent, an ever-present reminder that the enemy is living under my roof? Even now, in my clutches, she's staring up at me with so much false innocence, it grates on my last nerve. As if she could ever make me forget why she's here. As if just by fluttering her lashes and speaking so sweetly, she could make me forget the traitorous blood running through her veins. I will never forget.

"You think I don't know what you're trying to do?" I growl.

She blinks up at me, confusion clear in her eyes. Maybe I'm a little drunk too. My visit with Judge ran longer than expected this evening, and the scotch flowed freely for the duration of it. Perhaps that's the reason the words come so uninhibited.

"I know what you are." I stare down into her strange eyes, forcing her to look at me as the monster I am. "A fucking temptress, trying to lure me in with that sweet voice and those innocent eyes. But you're a goddamned liar."

"No, I'm not." Her lip trembles.

"Shut your eyes," I command.

She doesn't obey. Her arms come up to grip mine, pleading with me as she clings to me. "Please don't be angry."

"Angry doesn't even begin to touch what I am right now." I whirl her around in my arms, and she struggles against me as I yank her head to the side, biting at her throat. "I'm your worst fucking nightmare, wife of mine. It's about time you realized it."

She sucks in a sharp breath as red blooms across her skin from the drag marks I left behind with my teeth. I'm fighting with her clothes, ripping off her sweater and trying to push her nightgown up over her hips, but the silk keeps sliding back down. In a fit of frustration, I haul her to the desk and fold her over it, opening the top drawer to retrieve the scissors.

"No!" she screams.

I force her head back down with my palm, pressing her cheek against the wooden surface with one hand while I cut with the other. It's a messy, frenzied job with her squirming beneath me, but soon, her nightgown and panties are in shreds, the remnants lying on the floor of my office.

Our heavy breaths are the only sound in the room when I yank the ruler from my drawer and slide it over the skin of her bare ass. She's craning her neck, trying to see what I'm doing, so I push her hair over her eyes.

"You lost the privilege of sight," I snarl.

The ruler cracks against her ass cheeks with a sound that echoes off the office walls, but it's soon drowned out by the force of her scream.

"Santiago!"

"That's for snooping where you don't belong."

Crack. Another shriek pierces my ears.

"That's for drinking when you know goddamn well I'm going to put a baby in you."

Crack. A soft whimper bleeds from her lips this time, her tears dripping down onto the desk.

"And that's for being a fucking Moreno."

"Stop it!" She flails under the weight of my palm, twisting her torso enough to scrape her nails down my arm.

I grunt at the sting of her endeavor on my scarred flesh. And that momentary weakness gives her the courage she needs to hurl her bare heel up into my shin.

"Motherfuck!" The word hisses from between

my teeth as I bring the ruler down against her ass once more. "You will submit to me."

"Never!" she bellows.

I smack her again and again, the force of my efforts reverberating through my palm. Ivy fights me at every turn, trying desperately to exert her will. But she is no match for me in size or strength, and eventually, even the ruler cracks under the weight of my anger.

Hot tears streak her pretty face when I toss the now useless instrument aside and stare down at her, chest heaving. I wanted her broken, but she isn't. Even as she cries into the desk, refusing to meet my eyes, I can see her resolve to withstand me, no matter what may come. As if she could.

It stokes the fire of my rage and a need for something from her I can't even identify. I don't know what it is I want as my palms skim over the red lines on her ass. They look so lovely against her flesh. In fact, I'd dare to say I've never created any art as beautiful as this. But she isn't unconsciously arching into my touch anymore. She isn't bowing under my weight, and she isn't fighting either. She's just... disconnected. Her empty gaze is focused on the wall, and she's never looked so unrepentant. There's a sudden, aching need in me to touch her softly. To coax her back to life. But that won't do.

"Beg for forgiveness," I demand.

She doesn't respond. I squeeze a handful of her

ass and repeat the order, the threat in my tone unmistakable. Again, there is no response from her. And I find that her silence irritates me more than anything else ever has, a revelation that only adds to my frustration with her.

It appears I've been too soft on my wife, and she seems to be under the illusion she actually has a choice to ignore my demands. She's lost sight of her purpose. The entire reason she's here. But after tonight, she will know it.

When I hoist her up over my shoulder and carry her down the corridor and upstairs to her room, she doesn't protest. She thinks this is the end. That her punishment is over. I can hear it in the way she's calming her breath, staring longingly at the sanctuary of her bed. When I lower her onto the decorative rug instead, her muscles become rigid once again.

I retrieve the things I need from the small dresser I keep in here. When I return with the ropes and kneel beside her, she resumes her favorite activity of trying to defy me. But she is no match, and soon, her body is bound from her wrists to her ankles. By the time I'm finished with her, she's wearing the blind mask and the collar and chain from her marking ceremony. I leave her there to silently pray for salvation while I retrieve my own cloak and mask.

Ten minutes later, we are in the back of the Rolls

with Marco behind the steering wheel. It doesn't take long to reach IVI's compound. I remove the bindings from Ivy's wrists and feet and pull her from the car, a blanket draped around her as I force her forward. Tonight, there are a few men gathered in the courtyard drinking, but they know not to look too long when they see where I'm heading.

Our identities are obscured by the masks, and when I enter the dimly lit corridor that leads to the Cat House, we will appear just like everyone else.

A guard opens the heavy door, standing aside as we enter the den. Ivy slows in hesitation as the sound of the world around her begins to flood her senses. Whips. Chains. Grunts. Feminine moans and soft, dark music fill the space.

"Santiago?" She turns her body into me, clutching at me as if I could still be her salvation. The very man who leads her to her destruction. The man she should be running from.

I can't fathom her thoughts, but it feels like a trick. Ignoring her pleas, I drag her deeper into the fray, even as she clings to my cloak. We pass by the scenes of sexual depravity at its finest. The masculine grunts of a dominant sharing his sub with another member are the sounds that produce goose bumps on Ivy's skin. When she comes to a complete standstill, my frustration wins out.

Tearing the blanket off her and discarding it, I force her onto her hands and knees, gripping the chain attached to her collar in my hand. The only identifying mark on her naked body is my tattoo, but it is obscured by her hair right now.

I can feel the eyes of others on her, but right now, my need to exert my dominance is winning out above all others.

"Crawl," I bark.

She shakes as she begins to crawl forward, struggling to hold the weight of her mask up. More than once, she has to pause to lower her head, but she never gives up. She never admits defeat. And perhaps that stubborn will is what draws me in so much. My wife wants to believe she's a fighter. Determined to handle any punishment I throw her way. But she hasn't seen the worst of me. Not yet.

When we reach an empty station, she collapses into my arms as I hoist her up onto the wooden bench, forcing her torso up over the center cushion. I make quick work of the restraints, using them to secure her in place. She's on her hands and knees, legs spread wide, arms splayed out on the wooden slats in front of her. In this position, she's forced to hold up her head, and already she is struggling.

"Hello, Sir," a feminine voice whispers from behind me. "I see you already have a playmate this evening. But would you like another?"

My eyes are on Ivy as she cranes her neck in my direction. Maybe it's my imagination, but her muscles seem more rigid than they did only a moment ago. She's frozen, listening carefully for my response.

A cruel smile crosses my face. I haven't even turned to examine the courtesan employed by IVI to work in this den. They are here for our pleasure, and she is only doing her job. But Ivy doesn't know that.

"What do you have to offer?" I ask.

The woman comes around me slowly, kneeling before me as she bows her head. "Whatever your pleasure, Dominus et Deus."

I glance at her naked form briefly. IVI has high standards for the women in their employ. They must be intoxicating. Beautiful. The loveliest sight a man has ever seen. I would be lying if I said I hadn't visited this place before and partaken in several of these women. But right now, the sight of her kneeling before me gives me no great pleasure.

I only have eyes for my wife, I find, as they drift back to her. She doesn't know it. She's still waiting anxiously for my response.

"Perhaps you can teach my playmate a lesson," I tell the woman. "Can you show her how to please a man? It seems that art is lost on her."

A wicked smile curves across the woman's face as she nods. "It would be my honor."

Ivy yanks against her restraints, the ropes chafing at her wrists.

"No." The word is a mere whisper, but it is exactly what I need from her.

She is jealous. She doesn't want to share her monster after all. That makes two occasions now I have witnessed this little beast inside her. First, when she uncovered Mercedes's affectionate nickname for me. And now, the notion that I might actually take another.

The woman before me rises slowly, reaching up for the tie of my cloak. I still her hand and shake my head, leaning in to whisper my instructions in her ear. She listens carefully and then nods, making a quick retreat.

A few silent minutes pass where I watch Ivy's trembling form. She whispers my name once, and I have to stifle the groan of pleasure her desperation produces in me. It isn't logical for her to want to possess me the way I possess her. She should know how dangerous this desire is for her. And still, I find myself questioning it. Is she trying to toy with me, even now? Playing into this fantasy that she could ever truly want me?

"Please don't do this," she begs. "You vowed to be faithful to me. It was the one vow you made."

Her head is sagging. Body quivering. And she's never looked so beautiful. I need to touch her more than I've ever needed anything. But first, I have to see how far she will go with this lie.

The woman returns as I instructed with another member in tow. He too is in a cloak and mask. He nods at me and drapes the cloak over his shoulders, unzipping his trousers as he helps the woman to her knees before him. Within moments, the sloppy sound of her sucking his dick fills the space between Ivy and me. Silent tears drip down her face under the mask, splashing onto the floor beneath her. I'm close enough to study her in a way that I never have. To watch her muscles straining, her chest heaving as she fights to hold herself upright. Even as she's being humiliated, she continues to fight, refusing to allow her body to give out.

The other member pulls the woman's mouth from his dick and pets her face. They are both silent as he clutches her hand and leads her to the small table near Ivy. He hoists her ass up on top of it and grabs her hips, sliding her toward him until she's exactly where he wants her.

A feminine moan splits the silence as he thrusts into her, skin slapping against skin. Ivy renews her fight, struggling against her restraints, chafing her wrists and ankles as she desperately tries to free herself. I keep thinking at any moment, the illusion will be shattered. She will end the charade and stop acting as if she cares who I take. But it doesn't happen. It never happens.

The sound of her mournful sobs splinter my ears as I circle around her, and it is only when my hands fall upon her back that she freezes.

"Who's there?" she murmurs.

"Who else would it be?" I lean over her body and whisper into her ear.

She sucks in a breath, tilting her head in confusion as she listens to the sounds of the man fucking the other woman not five feet away. I nip at her ear and groan as my palms slide around to her breasts, pinching her nipples between my fingers.

"How does that jealousy taste?" I tease the shell of her ear with my teeth. "I want to hear you say it."

"No," she whimpers.

"Does it make you angry?" My fingers move to the apex of her thighs, toying with her as she struggles to contain her emotions.

"I don't care what you do." Her head dips, and slowly, she forces it back up, straining against the weight.

"Liar."

She sucks in a sharp breath as the couple's fucking grows more frantic. She's squirming against me as much as her body will allow now, arching her back as I slap at her clit. When she hisses, I do it again, and then follow up with some undeserved tenderness, stroking and teasing her to the brink of her sanity.

"Nobody else will ever have you." I drag my teeth down the length of her spine and splay her pussy apart as I kneel behind her. "You'll always belong to me."

"And what about you?" she demands. "Who will you belong to?"

"That sounds like an admission of jealousy." I dip my face between her thighs, the first lash of my tongue startling her.

A strangled sound gets caught in her throat when I do it again. I want to feast on her. I want to fuck her all night until she can no longer walk without feeling me. But to do so would be weak. It would prove she has some sort of hold on me, and that can never be true.

I lick at her again, and she whines, trying to arch back into me as I pull away.

"This isn't for you. Only good wives get to come. And you haven't yet begged for forgiveness."

She groans in protest as I rise back up and unzip my trousers.

"Please," she begs. "Just take off the mask. It's so heavy. I can't—"

"I'll take it off when I feel you've learned your lesson."

I free my cock and rub the head against her sensitive bud. A shiver moves over her body, even as she's crumpling under the burden of her mask. I suspect she will come undone for me within moments, despite my declarations that she isn't allowed.

In one swift movement, I thrust into her, groaning once I'm seated fully inside. Ivy forces a startled sound from her lips and then moans when I break my own rules and reach down to tease her as my hips begin to move. I roll into her as the other man's thrusts begin to grow frenzied. The woman is moaning out her release when he slams into her and comes violently. It only reinforces my own need.

"Are you ready to ask for forgiveness?" I thrust against Ivy, making her shudder.

"No!" she shouts back. "I hate you."

"You hate me?" I laugh darkly. "Let's see if that holds true."

I start to move my fingers against her with a frantic pace as I thrust into her over and over again. From the corner of my eye, I can see the other member and the courtesan watching us with interest. Ivy is clinging to her resolve not to break, but her body is no longer under the control of her mind.

Her head sinks lower and lower as her muscles tighten and contract, only to release in a powerful orgasm that squeezes my cock so forcefully, it pushes me over the edge too. For endless seconds, my release seems to empty inside her as I dig into her hips, undoubtedly leaving finger marks behind. My eyes fall shut, and it takes a minute to catch my breath as I wonder what the hell just happened. I don't think I've ever come so hard in my life.

When I open them again, something about Ivy's head looks odd. Her hair is hanging so low the tips are skimming the floor now, and her neck is bent at a strange angle. When I pull out of her and release her hip, her entire body falls slack against the one cushion holding her up.

Panic blurs the edges of my vision as I rush to help her.

"Is she okay?" the courtesan asks.

"Untie her ankles," I order as I reach for her head. It's heavy in my hands, and I know it's the mask. I remove it with uncoordinated fingers, shielding her face against my body as I work on her hands next.

The woman manages to free her ankles, and I dismiss them both, telling them to leave us as I scoop my wife's limp body into my arms.

"Ivy." My voice has an edge of desperation I don't seem to recognize as I carry her to a padded bench and drape her over it. "Ivy, please."

After a few moments, she begins to stir, blinking slowly as she comes back around.

"Ivy." I squeeze her hands in mine as I lean over her, trying to examine her eyes. "Tell me what's wrong."

It takes her longer than I'd hoped to speak. She licks her lips and glances up at me in confusion. "I must have fainted."

She closes her eyes again, and a stray tear rolls down her cheek. Another swiftly follows, and whatever liquor was running through my veins when I decided to bring her here has quickly evaporated.

I've never felt as sober as I do when I survey the damage done to my wife. She is pale and weak, barely able to move or speak. Her hair is a tangled mess, cheeks stained with tears, and her wrists and ankles are red from the chafing of the ropes. She looks a miserable sight, and it hits me unexpectedly. I am the one who did this.

"Ivy."

"Take me home." She turns away, refusing to look at me.

I feel out of sorts as I untie my cloak and drape it over her body, securing her in a cocoon as I cradle her against my chest. She doesn't protest when I carry her into the courtyard and back to the waiting car, but she still won't look at me either.

As soon as I place her in the back seat, she slides as far away as she can get, turning away from me as silent sobs begin to wrack her body.

It bothers me more than I ever could have anticipated to see her this way. I wanted her tears but not her complete destruction. Or didn't I?

"Tell me what happened," I plead.

She barely turns to me, her jaw set, anger vibrating off her.

"What happened?" she asks incredulously. "Are you serious? You are what happened, Santiago! You pushed me past the point of what my body could handle with that display and then the mask. You knew exactly what you were doing. Don't act like you don't."

It occurs to me then that she's talking about her vestibular issues. And of course, in the back of my mind, I assumed there would be some limitations to what she could handle. But I didn't realize the severity until I saw it firsthand.

I wasn't thinking straight. But I should have been.

Dr. Chambers sent me her medical records as I requested. Not just his notes, but her entire file from all her previous visits to doctors within The Society. I read about her problems with balance and coordination. The vertigo. The stress-induced flares. Her father had taken her to the doctor, but he had done little else to help her after her diagnosis. There were things that could have been done. Things that should have been done. And now I am left to wonder why didn't they do them? Why didn't he hire the best physical therapist that money could buy to help her? Why didn't he seem to care enough about his daughter to make that minimal effort for the benefit of her health?

"Ivy." I reach for her hand, and she shoves me away.

"Don't," she warns. "I don't want to hurt you, but if you touch me right now, I will fight. I will scratch and claw until I draw blood if only to prove you are human."

Her words sting more than they should. It isn't like me to take demands from anyone, let alone my enemy. But right now, in the dim light of the car, she looks less like my enemy and more like my prisoner. I recognize that solemn expression well because I have seen it many times in my own reflection. I thought this was what I wanted, but now that I have witnessed it in her, I understand I couldn't have been more wrong.

My hand comes to rest on the seat between us. Close enough to feel the warmth of her body, but far enough away to feel the arctic chill taking over her.

Without a doubt, I have fucked up.

And I wish she could hear the thoughts so loud in my head. The words unspoken, too proud to fall from my lips.

I'm sorry for it. More so than I have ever been.

He lifts me in his arms before my bare foot even touches the ground. The cloak he wrapped me in almost falls away, but he catches that, too, keeping it huddled around me. And when I try to push away from his hard chest, when I try to free myself of his grip, he only tightens his hold on me.

"Let me go, Santiago."

"No."

Marco opens the front door, and Santiago carries me in. I'm still shivering even though it's warm in the house. The cold I feel is so deep inside me that even a raging fire wouldn't touch it.

What he did tonight, that display, another very public humiliation and his utter lack of concern for my well-being? I don't forgive him for that. And I don't believe he cares about me. No, I'd sooner believe any concern was that maybe he'd gone too far and broken me. Killed me, even. Like he's threatened to. He doesn't want me dead yet. He hasn't had his fill of torturing me just yet.

"Let me go!" I twist in his arms as he carries me past my bedroom and farther down the long corridor. I'm exhausted and weak, but I have to fight.

He doesn't budge. My struggles don't seem to impact him at all. He's stone-faced as we head up into this darker part of the house.

"I hate you," I hiss. I have to say it because I have to feel it. It's the only thing I should feel after that.

At that, he glances down at me, but it's too dark to read his eyes. It's hard enough when it's light.

He doesn't reply, though. No smart comment. No strikes against me like at dinner last night. Just him as he usually is. Cold and impassive. Inhuman.

We stop as he opens the double doors at the end of the corridor, and when we enter the large suite, I instantly know this is his bedroom.

I can't help but crane my neck to take it in. Black walls, damask paper, dark, heavy velvet curtains the color of the night sky, moonlight pale through the windows. Ironclad again. Like the rest of the house. And at the very center of the room is a high bed bigger than any I've ever seen with four hulking posts, a thick duvet, and pillows he scatters carelessly across the floor while still holding me.

"I'm not fucking you," I tell him when he

snatches his cloak away, pulls the blankets on the bed back, and lays me down. I smell him on the pillow. It's his pillow. "I won't let you touch me again. Ever! Do you hear me?"

He ignores what I'm saying, but when he lets me go, and I move to sit up, he puts a finger to my chest.

"No," he says, pushing me to lie down. "Stay."

"I'm not a dog, you bastard." I slap his hand away, but he catches my wrists.

"I said stay." I hear the nightstand drawer open, and he holds up a pair of leather cuffs. "Or I'll make you stay."

"You would, wouldn't you?"

"Your choice, Ivy." How does he sound so calm when I sound so frantic? So insane?

I look at them, then at him. He means it. So I lie back, and when he is satisfied and releases my wrists, I snatch the duvet and pull it up to my shoulders, then turn my back to him.

I hear the drawer slide closed, and he moves away. When a door opens, I turn my head and watch. Bathroom. A moment later, he comes back toward me, opening a small old-fashioned-looking bottle. Something I'd fill with sand and call fairy dust when I was little.

I sit up, needing to keep alert, to watch him. I hold the blankets tight to me. I'm still naked. Still cold. Still filled with hate for this man. My husband. I feel him between my legs still. How rough he was. How hard I came. How I passed out, my head spinning even in the blackness of that mask. All the sounds, all the people. The sex all around me. My senses heightened when he blinded me.

"I hate you," I tell him again, this time feeling the heat of tears in my eyes. "I hate you." I want him to know it. To understand that this hate is something deep inside me, rooted in the ice spreading through my veins even as a little voice inside my head reminds me that for a moment, for one undeniable moment, it wasn't hate I felt. It was jealousy.

And no, not for a single moment.

"I hate you, Santiago De La Rosa," I say with more conviction in my voice than I feel deep inside me.

Come has dried on the insides of my thighs.

I'm going to put a baby inside you.

No. No. I cannot allow that. I will not.

"Drink this," he says, holding out the strange little vial.

I look at it, then at him. I snort-laugh. "Are you insane?" I push his arm away. "You think I'll just drink your poison?"

"It's not poison. It will relax you."

"No, I guess you're not ready to kill me yet, are you? You're having too much fun." I turn my face away. "I don't want your drugs, Santiago."

"Drink it." His voice is tight, and when I don't

reply, he grabs my jaw, fingers digging into my skin as he forces me to look at him.

I want to tell him that the tear that slides down my cheek and onto his finger is just a remnant left-over from earlier. It's not from any emotion I feel now. Certainly nothing *he* has made me feel. I don't, though. Instead, I study him as he looks at me, his expression strange and hard to read. He's almost captivated. And it's then I see it. Subtle but there. He's struggling with something.

Probably his desire to kill me. To just get it over with warring with that sadistic devil inside him.

I snort, breaking the spell.

He blinks. I watch him. I sometimes catch glimpses of something akin to pain in his eyes, but those few times I've seen it, it's been there one instant and gone the next. I guess I'm searching for it now.

I shake my head. Anything I imagine I've seen is probably my mind playing tricks on me. You'd have to be human to feel pain, and Santiago De La Rosa is not human.

He is the devil.

"My mother made it for me when I was little," he says, confusing me with the admission. "For when I was agitated or upset. It won't hurt you."

I study his face. This is the closest we've been when he's allowed it. And it's the most he's shared with me ever, even given his admission in the chapel when he'd punished me. That was fact. His father beat him. This is something else. Not a mere statement of fact.

This admission carries emotion.

I don't know if it's at the mention of his mother or at what happened, but he is unnerved and almost vulnerable. I remember what Antonia told me about her. That she'd gone back to Barcelona and died there. That her grief killed her.

Is that what I see here? Is he grieving?

I shift my gaze to the vial again, remember those stories of poisonings within The Society. I always thought they were just that, stories, but now I'm not so sure.

"I don't want it," I say even though I know he can make me drink it. He can make me do anything he wants.

As if he's read my mind, he brings the strange little bottle to his lips and takes a sip, then puts it under my nose again.

He releases my jaw. "It's not poison. It will help you. I promise."

"No."

"Drink it."

"Or what? You'll make me?"

"Yes."

"What did I ever do to you to justify what you do to me?" I ask, snatching the bottle away and sniffing the contents. I smell herbs, something sweet. I tilt my head and swallow what's inside. It's only two sips. I hand it back, feeling the liquid slide down my throat almost as strong as the scotch I'd barely sipped earlier.

I exhale, lean back against the pillows when he nods, and takes the vial like he's calmed a little by my drinking it.

I don't know what I expect. Violent cramping. Vomiting. But all I feel is relaxed.

"Lie down," he says, already helping me do just that.

I don't fight him. It's no use anyway. We both know he'll win.

"What is it?" I ask when he walks around the room, lighting a few of the candles.

"Just some herbs to help you relax and sleep. You need to sleep now and regain your strength."

"So you can repeat my punishments tomorrow?"

He doesn't answer.

I look around the large suite at just a few furniture pieces I'd guess are antique. On the headboard above my head, I see the skull and roses, the dueling pistols. His family crest carved into the wood.

My eyes start to close. I try to keep them open and roll onto my side to watch him because I need to keep an eye on him. I can't let myself fall asleep in his presence. What will he do to me if I sleep? I need to watch him, but my eyelids are so heavy. My body feels so relaxed.

He lights the candles on a candelabra in the sitting area a few feet from me then sits in the large, comfortable-looking armchair.

I must drift for a while because when I look again, I find him watching me, eyes dark and intent. His hair is wet, and he's drinking from a crystal glass and wearing a close-fitting, V-neck charcoal sweater and dark slacks. Did he shower? I try to sit up. I want to go to my room.

He's at my side in an instant. Too fast. Did I nod off again? On the table beside the chair is that notebook I'd seen in his study. I recognize the leather binding.

I try to say something. Tell him I want to go to my room.

"Relax, Ivy."

I don't want to relax.

He tucks the blankets around me. "Don't fight it. You're safe."

"I'm not safe. Not with you."

"Shh. Sleep."

Okay. Yes. I take a deep breath in and let my eyes close. It's warm in his bed. And his smell is around me, and I'm safe, like he said.

I startle.

No. Not like he said.

I have to fight whatever it is he gave me. Because I'm not safe. Not in his house. Not in his bed.

I'm going to put a baby inside you.

I can't let that happen.

When I wake next, it's to a familiar humming. A familiar scent. And light.

"You're sleeping the day away, dear." I open my eyes and have to squint against the bright light.

Is that the sun?

Sitting up, I feel the silk of the nightgown against my skin. I look around my room. My room. Not his. My bed. My pillows. My room.

"What time is it?" I ask Antonia as she arranges the curtain to filter the sunlight.

"Almost noon."

I rub my eyes, look at the place where a small square had been my only source of light. It's bigger now. A rectangle. Like a panel has been removed to expose the window behind it.

"Santiago said to make sure you have lots of juice this morning, so I brought extra. And there are fresh beignets. His request. It's really not like him."

I watch her pour coffee and look at the plate piled high with the sweet, fried dough. I love beignets, but since I've been here, my breakfast has been pretty standard. Delicious but not like this. Eggs, bacon, and toast. Fruit. Today, I have a mountain of beignets covered in powdered sugar along with berries and a pitcher of fresh-squeezed orange juice.

"It's such a beautiful day. I thought you'd like to

get some sun and fresh air before Mercedes takes you to be fitted for your dress."

Mercedes again?

I swing my legs out of the bed, take a moment to let the dizziness pass, then stand. I go to the window, not sure if I'm imagining it. I push the curtain away and touch the glass, look out into the vast garden, the woods beyond, and the light mist gathered in the thicket of trees.

"I don't understand." I look at the wood paneling, and sure enough, a piece has been removed. When? He's uncovered about half the window.

"Come and eat while they're still piping hot."

I go to the table and sit down. I let Antonia put two beignets on a small plate in front of me, and I pick one up to eat it. Sugar sticks to my lips and coats my tongue as I break the pastry with my teeth, and for one moment, I just let myself feel that sweetness, taste it. I could use some sweet in my life.

"They're delicious, aren't they?" Antonia says.

I realize that moan was me. I nod and take another bite.

Powdered sugar dusts the deep purple negligée. Did he dress me? And when did he bring me back to my room?

I remember then, at least vaguely waking up last night. First, when he tucked me in. Then a few more times when he'd told me to go back to sleep. He'd been sitting there with that notebook on his lap watching me. Did he watch me sleep all night? Did he sleep at all? I don't remember him getting into the bed with me.

I remember one other thing. I saw Mercedes. Well, maybe that part was a dream because we were in the hallway. Me in Santiago's arms. Her peering at us from a dark corner.

I realize also then that I'm wearing panties too. He must have cleaned me while I was out. How did I not feel it? What exactly was in that vial he had me drink that knocked me out so thoroughly?

Heat flushes my cheeks at the thought of him cleaning me while I was passed out, and I pick up the juice glass to hide my face.

Does he feel guilty? Is all of this out of guilt for what he did?

No. That makes no sense.

Antonia pours a second glass of juice when I finish the first. I take it and drink half of it down. I'm thirsty.

"Thank you."

"You're welcome."

"When did he do that?" I ask about the window.

"I heard something quite early this morning. Had Marco do it, I think." She's smiling warmly.

"Hm." I eat another bite, and Antonia smiles kindly at me.

"I've known Santiago since he was in diapers, you know." She puts another beignet on my plate.

"His father was not an easy man, but his death and perhaps Santiago surviving it when in his mind at least he was meant to die, it changed him. You're good for him, Ivy. I see it. I feel it."

"I'm not good for him. He hates me, and I don't even know why."

"No, that's not hate. He has demons, that boy, but inside, he's good. I know it. And I think if anyone can bring it out, it'll be you."

"If I survive," I mutter under my breath, then think of something. "Why does he have everyone call him master?"

She shakes her head. "That was his father. Made sure we all called them Master even when they were children. Cold as stone, that one. But I won't speak ill of the dead."

A knock comes on the door, interrupting us then, and the maid who was here, the younger one who every time I've seen her looks like she's expecting a ghost to jump out at her at any moment stands in the doorway.

"Yes, Jenna?" Antonia asks with a note of irritation in her tone.

"Ma'am." She gestures to me but is talking to Antonia. "Her brother's here to see her."

I get to my feet. "My brother's here?"

The girl glances nervously at me but directs herself to Antonia. "I didn't know what to do, so I let him in. He's waiting downstairs."

"Oh."

"The Master is..."

Antonia clears her throat. "Well, get the man some coffee and tell him Ivy will be down in a few minutes. Surely you know how to receive a guest." She claps her hands for the girl to go, and the younger maid disappears.

I quickly get dressed and hurry down the stairs with Antonia telling me to slow down and hold on to the railing.

Abel is studying the photographs on one of the sideboards in the large living room and turns when he hears me. He's holding a framed photograph that he puts back when I enter. I notice it's one of Mercedes.

"Abel." I slow down and just catch myself before I hug him because he is still Abel. God, what a state I'm in if I think running into my brother's arms is a good place to be. This is what Santiago has reduced me to? "What are you doing here?"

"It's good to see you too, sis." His eyes fall on the rosary, which I quickly tuck under my sweater. "Find God here?"

"No, actually. Just the devil."

He snorts, looks me over. "He's not beating you, is he?"

That's complicated, and I'm about to try to explain it when I realize something. "Has something happened? To Dad? Is that why you're here?"

He inhales and exhales, then wanders deeper into the house to glance around. "No, he's the same."

"Thank goodness. Evangeline?"

"No, Ivy, everyone is fine. I just wanted to come and see how you're doing." He turns back to face me, and I know that's not it. Abel always has an agenda.

But he's also the only one who may be able to help me. "I can't stay here, Abel. You have to do something."

"What do you mean? Look around you. You live in the lap of luxury, even if it does have a Dracula vibe going. Is he too cheap to light the place?"

"No, I think he just..." I trail off because why would I explain to my brother that I think it's because of his face. I think Santiago doesn't like anyone to see him. It's strange, but it's the first time I register that myself. "Never mind. Abel, I can't stay here. I mean it. He..."

"You're married to a De La Rosa, Ivy. You're staying. There's only one way out. Well, two. He can divorce you, or he can kill you."

I shudder.

He chuckles.

Does he have any idea how close to the truth his words have come?

"Is his sister home?"

"What?"

"Mercedes. Is she home?"

"I don't know."

He shakes his head like he's disappointed and looks around, then comes closer to me. His voice is lower when he speaks. "You'll be attending the Gala, I hear."

"At the compound?"

He nods.

"Yes. Will you be there? Maybe you can bring Evange—"

"Don't be stupid, Ivy. Of course, I won't be there. Even as his brother-in-law, I'm not yet welcome. But my time is coming. And you'll do your part to make sure it comes quickly."

"I don't understand."

"Never mind. I need you to do one thing for me while you're there."

"What?"

"I want to know who Holton talks to. Do you remember him?"

"I'll never forget that man."

"Good. I'll come back here in a few days, and I'll bring Evangeline for a visit *if* you manage to get me any useful information."

"What?"

"Oh, and don't tell your husband." He checks his watch. "I have to go." He starts to head toward the front door.

"Wait!" I catch his arm. "Abel, please. I need your help. You're the only one who can help me."

He sighs like he's bored. "What, Ivy?"

"He wants...he's planning to...start a family. I don't want, no, I *can't* have that monster's baby! Please. You have to help me."

He snorts. "Is that all?"

"What do you mean is that all?"

"Don't worry. There won't be any baby. Do you think I didn't plan for that?"

"What?"

"The shot, Ivy. It was a birth control shot."

"Dr. Chambers gave me a birth control shot?"

He nods.

"But you said it was vitamins."

"Christ." He shakes his head like I'm the stupidest person he's ever met. "That was for that fat fuck Holton's sake." He steps closer, brushing my bangs forward to cover my eye. "Hide that. It's off-putting."

"You had Dr. Chambers give me a birth control shot? Then why agree to let Santiago have me in the first place if you don't like him?"

"You don't say no to a Sovereign Son, do you? Not if you want to have any standing in The Society. I have to go. You let me know who Holton talks to. I'm not asking for much so try not to fuck it up." He's almost to the front door when I think of something.

"How long?"

"How long what?" he asks, sounding exasperated.

"Birth control. How long is it good for?"

"Two or three months."

"And Dr. Chambers knew?"

"He gave you the shot, didn't he? Honestly, Ivy, some days, I wonder about your cognitive ability."

I push a hand into my hair. Why would Dr. Chambers give me a birth control shot when he knows Santiago wants sons?

"Ivy?" Abel calls out.

I look up at him.

"Do I need to tell you not to mention the birth control to your husband?"

I shake my head.

"Good. Remember, Holton. I want to know anyone he talks to."

My eyes blur in and out of focus as I try in vain to study the monitors in my office. A constant stream of numbers inundates me. Patterns emerge. Money ebbs and flows. This is the one sanctuary I have in life. The one area I know without a doubt I can find solace. Yet it seems to evade me this past twenty-four hours.

I have spent all day holed up in this room, trying not to think about my wife and what she might be doing. Antonia has entered several times to offer me anything my black heart might desire, but her menus for the day lack the sustenance I truly crave.

I reach for the bottle of scotch, twisting the cap in my hand before I think better of it. This restless energy building up inside me is unfamiliar. I don't recognize it, and I don't know what to do with it.

"Fuck!" I growl, swiping my hand across the desk and scattering the contents around the room.

The scotch bottle shatters on the floor, and papers rain down like my fragmented thoughts. I am tempted to call Antonia back for yet another report on the current status of my wife. But I fear even she is exhausted with my constant requests for information, which so far have proven fruitless.

She tells me what she thinks I want to hear. Ivy has eaten. She has showered and dressed. She has rested. But those aren't the details I need, and in my exasperation, I find I don't know how to express what I need because I can't even identify it myself.

"Feel better?" Mercedes enters the room, eyeing the evidence of my tantrum with an arched brow, her red heels crunching over the broken glass littering the floor.

"What do you want?" I snap.

She flinches at my tone but recovers quickly as she often does, squaring her shoulders and crossing her arms as she pins me with her gaze.

"What is the matter with you?" she demands. "You've been sulking around in here all day. It isn't like you."

"I'm busy," I answer shortly. "It's a concept you might understand if you had any other motivation in life besides devouring the souls of the innocent."

A dry laugh erupts from her lips as she shakes

her head in disbelief. "Really, brother? You of all people are going to lecture me on morality?"

I don't know why I'm being such an asshole to her. But it can't be helped, and I'm not in the mood for a confrontation with her, which is exactly what she came here for.

She takes a seat in the vacant chair opposite my desk and crosses her legs, cocking her head to the side as she studies me. Mercedes has always had the ability to stare at you like she can see into your very soul. It's an unnerving quality, and she has used it to bring many men to heel and plead for her attention. But hell hath no fury when it doesn't work.

"I hate to break it to you, Santi." Her lips curve into a wicked grin as she leans forward and lowers her voice to a whisper. "But you and I are exactly the same."

Had it been any other day, I would have agreed with her. We are the same. Or at least we were. But somewhere between the events of the last few days, it feels as though my thirst for revenge has taken a short leave of absence, leaving only confusion behind in its place. That's the only logical explanation that makes sense, given that I've been sitting here all day considering my wife's feelings. Trying to understand human emotion on a level I never have before. Feeling so off I can hardly sit still for more than a moment.

I want to destroy something, but for once, it isn't

her. I want to force her to be sweet to me again. What a grand delusion that is.

I must be going insane.

"She's getting to you." Mercedes mirrors my thoughts.

"No." My response is lifeless, and even I can't pretend the conviction in my voice doesn't sound contrived.

My sister narrows her eyes at me, a fire-breathing serpent from the depths of hell. If jealousy had a face, it would be hers right now. I know that's what makes her question my resolve. She has always been the baby in the family. The cherished princess who was adored by our mother and protected by her brothers at all costs. But things have been so different since the explosion. She lost half her family in one instant, and then her mother in the aftermath. We are both just ghosts, living in this house, haunted by the memories. She has been watching me slowly slip away ever since, trying with all her might to pull me back. That's what it boils down to. She fears she will lose me to Ivy like she has lost everyone else.

"I have seen it with my own eyes," she hisses. "You carrying her around the halls of the manor like a broken little doll in your arms. It's pathetic, Santiago. If you don't have the guts to go through with this, then tell me now. I will do what is necessary."

My chair crashes into the wall behind me as I

rise up and lean over the desk, breathing my own fire into Mercedes's face so there can be no doubt to my authority.

"Don't ever question my abilities," I snarl. "You will do exactly as you are told, and nothing more. If you even so much as think about pulling another stunt, I will have you shipped off so fast your head will fucking spin. Is my intention clear enough for you now?"

She shoves back her chair, lip trembling as tears cling to the edges of her eyelids. It's unlike my sister to show such a display of emotion, and for a moment, I question if she is right.

"You think you have it all under control," she sneers. "Yet you don't even realize your sweet, perfect wife has been sneaking in her brother right under your nose."

This information takes me by surprise, and Mercedes shakes her head at me when she sees it.

"She is a traitor. And you'd be wise not to forget it. Not even for a second, Santi. She will ruin you if you let her."

With those words, she disappears, leaving me to my thoughts. Within moments, I find myself scouring the cameras, checking the videotapes of the entrance until I find the undeniable proof. Abel was here. He was in my fucking house. And Ivy is going to pay for it.

I'm halfway down the corridor to her bedroom when Antonia appears in the hall up ahead with a tray in her hands. She startles when she sees me stalking toward her, her lips drawing into a frown when she recognizes the stormy expression on my face.

"Santiago?" She pauses before me. "She is sleeping, sir."

"I don't care." I move to forge on, but Antonia steps into my path, peering up at me with an expression I don't recognize.

"Perhaps, tonight you should let her rest."

My eyes dart over her head, fists clenching at my sides. "No."

It is unlike Antonia to challenge me in this way, and I don't know what to make of her strange behavior, but when she casts her eyes downward, it appears that she feels remorseful for something herself.

"It's my fault, sir."

"What is?" I demand.

"Her brother," she says softly. "That's what this is about, right?"

Her answer surprises and confuses me.

"What do you mean it's your fault?"

"I know all visitors are supposed to be approved by you," she answers, her voice choked with emotion. "But I figured, he is her family. I did not think it would be too much of an imposition."

My tempered breath leaves my lungs in a rush of hot air. "Ivy did not request for him to come here?"

"No, sir. He arrived of his own accord," she assures me.

I drag a hand through my hair and glance over her shoulder once more. I should have known Mercedes was trying to provoke me. And Abel is something I will have to deal with later. But for now, I am content to know that it was not Ivy's doing. At least, not this time.

"He is never to step foot in this manor again without my explicit permission," I inform her. "Is that understood, Antonia?"

"Yes, sir." She dips her head. "I am sorry."

"Do you know what was discussed between them on his visit today?"

"No, I am afraid I was not present, other than to escort him into the room."

It's a fact I am already aware of, given that's exactly what I saw on the camera. But still I had hoped there would be some useful scrap of information. I know Abel was not visiting his sister out of the kindness of his heart.

Antonia remains there, uncertain, waiting for me to dismiss her. But I am trying and failing to find my next words, and when I do, my voice is stiffer than usual.

"Did she request to see me at all today?"

Her eyebrows shoot up in surprise, and she shuffles her weight uncomfortably from one foot to the other. "No, sir."

"I see."

I consider turning around. That's what I should do. But try as I might, I find that I can't.

"You are dismissed, Antonia. Have a good evening."

She nods and scurries away, leaving me to a strange emptiness as my only companion when I make my way toward Ivy's door. When my palm curves around the knob, I try again to find a justification not to go in. I have no doubt she is still angry with me. There will be bitterness. There will be hatred. And for a moment, I'm not sure I want to see those emotions reflected in her eyes. Not tonight.

My forehead sags against the door as I consider what needs to be done. I'm still trying to find my anger when the knob turns from the other side, and the door opens to the sight of a startled Ivy.

She gasps when she sees me and immediately turns to flee back to the sanctuary of her bed. But the predator in me captures her around the waist before she even makes it two steps, dragging her back into my arms.

She trembles as I turn her in my grasp, my fingertips gliding over the silky material of her nightgown. Her head falls forward, hair shielding her face from my eyes as she tries to hide from me.

"And where exactly do you think you were going, Mrs. De La Rosa?" I whisper into her hair.

"Nowhere." She tries to yank away from my grasp but fails. "I heard a noise out there. I didn't realize it was you. If I had, I would have just barricaded the door."

I close my eyes and inhale the sweet scent of her shampoo. "Is that any way to greet your husband?"

"You are my husband in name only," she declares.

"So much fight in you." I stroke her hair back away from her face and clutch her jaw in my hand, forcing her gaze upward. "I am glad to see you have not been broken yet."

The words sound like too much of an admission, and I can see the confusion in her eyes when she peeks up at me from beneath her lashes. "I thought that was exactly what you wanted."

"That is the least of what I want," I threaten, guiding her body back into the room until her legs hit the bed behind her.

"I am tired." She closes her eyes and shudders as I lean into her, grazing her neck with my lips. "Please. I don't want to fight."

"Then don't." I seize the opportunity when her eyes are closed to force my lips to hers, startling her.

Her lips fall apart, and her eyes fly open as I kiss her deeply, curling my arm around her waist and bunching the fabric of her nightgown in my fist.

My other hand moves up to cover her eyes,

obscuring her vision as I tilt her head backward and give in to the temptation to devour her lips, if only for a moment.

She's breathing hard against my chest, nipples scraping against her nightgown, body arched so beautifully, I could witness her like this for an eternity and never be satisfied.

As I deepen the kiss, her hands come up to mine, nails digging into my skin. She wants me to believe she doesn't like this, but her body tells me otherwise. And when I release my grip on her waist to slide my fingers down between her thighs, she jolts at the touch.

She's breathless and gasping for air when I finally let go of her mouth and dip her head back even farther to kiss her throat, nipping at the fragile skin.

"Santiago," she croaks.

I'm teasing her, even as she tries to squeeze her thighs together around my fingers. Taking her tonight is out of the question, but I am compelled to touch her simply for her pleasure. A notion I don't want to examine too closely. It is only a momentary weakness. That's what I tell myself when I turn her around and hoist her body up onto the bed, yanking her hips up and forcing her facedown into the blankets as I kneel behind her.

"Santiago," she begins again but abruptly falls silent when my nose glides along her slit.

She nearly jolts out of her skin, sucking in a sharp breath as I hold her hips in place and really taste her for the first time. The first lash of my tongue produces a cascade of goose bumps along her skin, and the second has her fists curling into the blankets.

She bites back her sounds, trying to swallow them down as I force her legs wider apart, taking pleasure in the vulgarity of her spread wide open for me. One hand clutches the flesh of her ass, holding her in place as the other skates up beneath her, groping her breast through the silk. She is already wet for me, the faint groans of her restrained pleasure muffled into the bed as I eat her like a man starved.

It occurs to me that this isn't right. It isn't my place to provide her pleasure. But I can't seem to stop now that I've started. I want her sounds. Her weak, trembling thighs squeezing around my face. Her almost silent pleas as I bring her closer and closer to a different kind of destruction. The kind that is dangerous to us both.

She tries to fight the inevitable, even as her body tenses past the point of breaking and the first crest of pleasure starts to rumble over my tongue. Her shoulders collapse into the bed as it overtakes her completely, spasms wracking her body as I draw it out to the point when she can no longer handle it and begins to shake her head.

"Please," she begs.

I smirk against her, taking one last taste of her pleasure before I turn to her inner thigh, pressing a soft kiss against the flesh there. She shivers and then collapses into the bed entirely, glancing back at me over her shoulder.

Her face is a mixture of unfamiliar emotions as I pull the nightgown back over her hips and stroke my palms down her thighs. She knows better than to stare at me, yet it seems she can't help herself.

"I still hate you," she whispers.

I close my eyes and feel a torment unlike any I've ever known. "As you should."

The room falls silent, only the sounds of our breathing between us. Her eyes are growing heavy, and there is no reason for me to stay. But I find that I am not yet ready to go. And so, I sit there, stroking her thighs beneath my palms. Studying the curves of her body. Trying to make sense of this growing war inside me.

I want to know if she carries my child yet. I want to own her. Possess her from the inside out. I want it more than I have ever wanted anything, and it unnerves me.

I turn my thoughts toward the gala. It will be our first public appearance together since the wedding. Mercedes has been instructed to help her prepare. But I still have lingering doubts in my mind about her readiness for the occasion.

"Tomorrow is the event," I murmur. "I'm sure I don't need to tell you it's important."

She glances at me over her shoulder. "I'm well aware."

I stare into her eyes and consider telling her that Mercedes might need her as a welcome distraction, though she would never admit it. She will be seeing Van der Smit and his new wife there, and it could undoubtedly stir up some issues in her. But my sister would never forgive me for telling Ivy such an intimate detail of her life. She doesn't like to appear human to anyone.

I will need to deal with her later this evening after I've finished my conversation with Ivy. In the lingering silence, I know what it is I need to address. But I suspect as soon as I bring up her brother, she will shut down entirely.

Just as I'm about to mention it, there's a knock on the bedroom door. It's late, and my staff knows better than to interrupt me in here unless it's something important.

Ivy sits up, glancing at the door as I rise from the bed and move to answer the door. I open it enough to see Antonia standing there in her pajamas, an apologetic expression on her face.

"I'm sorry to disturb, sir," she says tiredly. "But one of your men is waiting for you in your study. He says it's urgent."

I nod and dismiss her before glancing back at my

wife. Our conversation will have to wait for another time.

"Go to sleep, Ivy."

She drags the sheet up to cover herself and meets my gaze for one lingering second before breaking it.

"Okay."

29

IVY

I sit up as I watch Santiago walk out of my room. The door closes with a soft click. I wait to hear the lock turn, but it doesn't.

I wonder who's here to see him so late at night. Wonder what could be so urgent.

Throwing the blankets off, I pull on a robe, very aware that I'm still damp between my legs. I'm trying not to think about what he just did or remember the feel of his mouth on me, his tongue inside me.

He's a monster. That's all I need to remember about my husband.

My one consolation is what my brother told me.

I walk to the door and lean my ear against it. He's quiet, though, and rarely makes a sound, so I wait, giving him time to go before I open it and peer out.

The corridor is dark and empty.

Taking a few steps, I glance over the banister

down to the first floor. I can't see more than the large hall that connects the different corridors, but I don't hear anyone, and the rooms are dark, not even the usual candles lit now.

If he has a guest, then he'd have taken him into his study, especially if he wants privacy.

I take a defiant step toward the staircase. If he or anyone sees me, I'll say I'm hungry. Or lost if I'm caught near his office. After what he did to me, I need to be smarter about things. Not so passive. Not allowing things to happen to me. I need to be more proactive about saving myself. Because I'm on my own, and I know it.

I think back to the days before the wedding. It feels like years ago. I feel like I was a different person then. To think that for a brief span of time, I'd thought I could ask Santiago to help me. I'd thought I could go to my husband for help in keeping my sister safe against my own brother. I'm an idiot, though, because I can't even keep myself safe, and the man I thought I might turn to is the devil himself.

The last step creaks, and I stop, holding my breath as I wait to see if anyone else heard. But there's no one. The servants must be asleep, and Mercedes is probably out prowling the night for fresh blood.

She never did come to take me shopping or whatever it was she was going to do to ready me for the gala. Just sent word with Antonia that something had come up, and I was free for the day.

When my heart rate settles, I take the final step down, my bare feet silent on the cold marble floors. I hurry through the hall to duck into the corridor where Santiago's office is. It's dark here, too, but the sconces that line these walls are lit and I can see light under his closed door at the far end.

I'll need to be quick. If he catches me here, I'll have hell to pay, so I move as quickly as I can and quietly open the library door. I'm not stupid enough to listen at his door. I slip inside the dark room and close the door behind me, giving my eyes a minute to adjust. Once they have, I make my way through the aisles of bookshelves to the false wall. He never did ask me how I got into his office. He doesn't know I know about this, and the thought makes me feel like I've got one win. One to his dozen.

Now that I know the cutout door exists, I can almost see a thin line of light coming from inside his office. I'm quiet as I approach, holding my breath because I'm too afraid to breathe. I press my ear to the wall.

"Why didn't they see this before?" Santiago asks, voice raised, sounding angry.

The other man's voice is muffled. Quieter. I hear mumblings and only a few words, but those words give me chills: "...Toxicology...Metabolized too quickly...Coma."

Santiago speaks again, but it's only the low timbre of his voice, not the actual words that I make out.

I think about what happened last night when he brought out the vial. How my thoughts had gone to those old stories of poisoning within The Society. How Santiago had sipped the contents to confirm it wasn't poison as if guessing my thoughts. As if that were a real thing. A possibility.

Poison.

Who uses poison? What year is this?

No, that can't be what they're talking about.

But I keep going back to that last word. Coma. I think about my father lying in a coma in that hospital bed. He'd gone into cardiac arrest. It made sense, given his lifestyle.

I shake my head. This is stupid. They're not talking about poison.

"Does anyone else know?" Santiago asks.

"No."

"Good. If you find any more information," he starts, but that's my cue. I'm sure he'll come check on me before he goes to bed, and I need to be back in my room if he does.

Without waiting to hear anything else, I hurry out of the library but knock my hip on a shelf in the dark. I don't have time to wait to see if anyone heard the sound. I keep going, pausing only briefly to listen at the library door to make sure the hall is clear before hurrying back to the main part of the house, then up the stairs, slipping into my bedroom and closing the door, my heart in my throat as I throw off my robe and hurry into my bed.

THE NEXT MORNING, I WAKE UP TO CRAMPS LOW IN MY belly.

I open my eyes to watch the soft orange glow of the rising sun coming through the sheer curtains. I left the heavier drapes open.

I push the blanket back and get up, seeing the smudge of red on the white sheets. Different than the blood on our wedding night. Abel came through. Santiago will be disappointed, though.

Good.

Walking into the bathroom, I open the cabinet beneath the sink to look for tampons. I hadn't thought to look before, but a slow panic comes over me when I don't find any. In fact, there's nothing here I can use at all.

I go into the closet to look through the drawers there. Did he really miss this detail? He doesn't seem like he'd miss any detail. I was joking about his potency, but did he really think I'd be pregnant instantly and not have the need?

Unbelievable.

I walk back into the bathroom and wad up toilet

paper to absorb the flow, then wash my hands and put on my robe to find Antonia. I'm not asking Santiago for tampons. And I'm definitely not asking Mercedes.

The house is still quiet when I walk out into the hallway, but I hear voices when I get closer to the kitchen, and I see candles are being lit in the down-stairs rooms. I'm about to push the door to the kitchen open when Antonia comes through, wiping her hands on a dish towel and giving someone instructions over her shoulder.

"Ivy. You're up early," she says, obviously surprised to see me there.

"I..." I quiet as a maid slips past Antonia into the kitchen. "This is embarrassing, but I got my period, and...um, there isn't..." I clear my throat and tell myself to grow up. It's a fucking period. "I need tampons."

After the briefest of moments, Antonia nods, but I swear I see something on her face in that split second of time that gives me pause.

"Of course. Come with me, dear."

I follow her as she walks past the kitchen and down several corridors to a door farther away from the center of the house. That door, which she uses a key to unlock, which I knew was locked because I'd tried it on one of my explorations of the house, leads to a corridor different from any in the house. For one thing, it's lit with electrical lights, and for another, it's nowhere near as ornately or beautifully deco-rated as the main part.

"What's here?" I ask, appreciating the brightness.

"Staff rooms. Three maids live on property plus security and myself, of course. These are our rooms."

"Oh," I say, remembering Santiago's rule that I not enter the servant's quarters. I roll my eyes at the memory.

"Here we are," she says, unlocking a door. When she opens it, a light automatically blinks on, and I see it's a laundry room. I smell detergent and watch one of the washing machines already spinning its load.

"This is like a hotel," I comment.

She smiles and heads to a shelf where I see several boxes of tampons. "The house is old and requires a lot of upkeep. I'm just glad your husband does it, although he has closed off some rooms since he became head of the household. With only him and Mercedes, it made sense, but now..." She trails off.

"How big is it?" I ask, watching her count out five tampons.

She holds them out, and I hear her talking, but I stop listening because I realize something.

This wasn't an oversight.

"I'll just take the box. I'm sure I'll need more than five," I say, irritated not by her but hearing my tone, nonetheless. I know she's just doing what he's told her to do.

Antonia's gaze falters, and she takes a deep breath in. "I'll give you what you need. Just ask me, Ivy, but..." She trails off.

"He wants to know," I say, feeling a little sick. Feeling my eyes fill up. Feeling powerless and hated and trapped all at once.

"He's just anxious to start a family. That's all."

I snatch the tampons out of her hand. "Then when you tell him, make sure he knows how happy I am that he'll be disappointed!" I spin around, wiping the back of my hand across my face to get rid of the idiotic tears that wet the skin around my eyes at this fresh humiliation. Because what did I expect? What did I think? That he felt bad about what he did that night he took me to the compound? The night he had me crawl naked on my hands and knees for everyone to see? I don't even know who was there. Don't know who saw me being led like a dog by my husband. Being fucked by my monster.

God.

I hate him. I hate my husband.

And the worst part, the stupidest part is that I don't want to. That I thought—

Fuck!

I find my way back to the main part of the house and have to pause at the bottom of the stairs when a dizzy spell overtakes me. It's always worse around my period. I clutch the handrail and hold on until it passes, ignoring the girl asking me if I'm okay. I squeeze my eyes shut and beg for it to pass quickly. Not to come until I'm back upstairs in my room. In my bed. Until these vultures won't see more weakness to exploit.

"Ivy!" It's Antonia.

"I'm fine!" I force myself to move, sweat making my grip on the wide handrail slippery as I concentrate on getting away. Just getting away. Not letting myself stop until I'm back in my room and in the bathroom, the only door with a lock on the inside where I drop to sit on the cold tile floor, my back against the door head between my knees, stupid tampons scattered at my feet.

30

IVY

I lie in bed most of the day, staring at the rectangle of waning light coming into my room. I flushed some of the food Antonia brought down the toilet so she would think I ate and leave me alone. He's managing that too. Probably getting daily reports. Hourly, maybe. He's just controlling enough.

I am a body to him. A body he can humiliate and fuck and ultimately use to make babies. Then what? What happens when I'm all used up?

No. I don't need to think about that. I know. He's told me.

I turn over as the door opens. No knock. Mercedes strolls into my room like she owns the place.

"Well, aren't you lazy," she says, gaze condescending.

I sit up. "What do you want, Mercedes? I'm not in the mood to deal with you."

Two women follow her in, one carrying a garment bag, the other rolling in a small suitcase.

The gala.

Shit.

"I'm not going," I tell her before she can get a word in. I get out of the bed to go to the bathroom. Although my period's lighter than it would usually be, the birth control shot has done nothing for my cramps.

"That's not up to you," she says, slipping the toe of her blood-red stilettos in the doorway so I can't close it. "Or didn't my brother mention that? You do as you're told. Period."

I stop pushing at the door, let it go and step into her face. She's taller than me with those shoes while I'm barefoot, so I have to look up at her. "You and your brother can both go fuck yourselves. I have cramps. Get the hell out."

"Cramps?"

"What? You don't get the report about my cycles too?"

"What are you talking about?"

The fight goes out of me. I'm more depressed than angry, and it's not her I'm angry with. "Nothing. Just go. You can torture me tomorrow."

"I don't think so. We only have an hour to get you ready, so do what you need to do in here," she says, walking away to return a moment later with her purse and taking out a bottle of aspirin. She sets it on the counter. "Here. I'll even give you aspirin. Not that you deserve pain relief."

That anger is back, and now it's directed precisely on her.

"What the fuck is wrong with the two of you? I barely even knew that you existed before I was forced to marry your brother. To live in this little corner of hell. What did I do to you that made you hate me so much?"

Her eyes grow darker, mouth tighter, and I see her hands fist at her sides. She's gritting her teeth, and I know she wants to say something, but she's holding back. "You're lucky my brother stands between me and you, Ivy Moreno, because I wouldn't be so gentle with you."

"Gentle? You think he's gentle?"

She snorts.

"Do you? Because you're as deluded as he is if you do!"

"Don't forget your place."

"My place? Get out. Just get the fuck out of my room!"

"You're in *my* house. Mine. You don't tell me to get out."

"It's Santiago's house. *My* husband's house!" I don't even know why I say it. Why I'm goading her.

"Oh! Your husband. That's right." She tilts her

head to the side and grins. "Do you have any idea why he made you his wife? Why a man like my brother would even look at you twice?"

"I wish I did. Get out, Mercedes. I mean it."

"He hates you."

Her words manage to hit something tender inside me. I don't know why. I don't care about her or what she thinks. And maybe it's the day or the past few days. I don't know. But before I can open my mouth to tell her to go away again, she continues.

"Please tell me you knew that," she says, that grin growing wide.

"Just go. Please."

"Aw. You didn't know?"

I feel my face crumple at her feigned concern. I'm not even sure why. I knew all of this. It's not news to me that he hates me.

"He may enjoy fucking you, but he's a man. You're a toy to him. Like so many others."

She shows all her teeth as she sneers, victorious at that last dig.

I force myself to stand up straighter and step closer to her. "What's the matter, Mercedes? You feeling threatened by someone so inconsequential as me? Because from the look of you, I'd say you're jealous."

Her face goes beet red, and she fists her hands. For a moment, I think she's going to hit me, but then she spins on her heel. "Get Nathan in here!" she snaps to someone.

I push the door closed but listen, my heart hammering. I hear a man's voice a few minutes later. I recognize it, but I hadn't known his name. Nathan is one of Mercedes's bodyguards.

"You make sure they get her dressed in the dress I brought. Make sure she sits her skinny little ass down and lets them do their work exactly as I've instructed. And you call me before she's allowed out of here. Do whatever you need to do to make sure she does as she's told, am I clear?"

"Your brother gave—"

"I will deal with my brother! You just do as I tell you, or you're finished here! Am I fucking clear?"

"Yes, ma'am."

I back away from the door and turn on the tap to wash my face, seeing how my hands are trembling.

I knew I was hated. I never doubted that. At least when it came to Mercedes. With him, there were moments—

No. I can't do that. I can't ever think about those moments. He is a monster. He is the devil. They both are. And they have me in their sights, and I don't even know why.

I'm not strong enough to fight them.

That's the one thing I know without a doubt.

I splash water on my face, then dry it. I pick up the bottle of aspirin and open it. It's almost full. I swallow two, then set the bottle back down and prepare myself to face the women gathered in the next room, ready to do as I'm told, trusting that Nathan will do exactly as Mercedes instructed, even if it means hurting me.

31

"Here you are, brother." Mercedes appears behind me in the reflection of my mirror to assist in securing the strap of the mask around my head.

It's a silver headpiece. Half skull, half minotaur, crowned with roses. Dark and sinister undertones with a hint of the De La Rosa legacy. Once it is in place, I can conclude she has chosen well for me.

"Perfect." She smiles wickedly over my shoulder. "You look positively devilish."

I cast my eyes away from my reflection and clear my throat. "Yes, well, I suppose it will do."

Mercedes follows me downstairs to the foyer, her red dress swishing as her heels tap against the old stone. She will be attending tonight's gala as well, and I suspect she hopes to capture the attention of Van der Smit and his new wife in a dress that looks as if she were sewn into it. If I wasn't so preoccupied, I would tell her to change, but the strange energy coursing through my veins won't allow my thoughts to settle on the propriety of my sister. Not when I have my wife to consider.

We wait for ten minutes in silence until finally, she appears at the top of the grand staircase, flanked by two guards. My breath catches in my throat as my eyes roam over her figure, wrapped in a sweeping black floor-length dress decorated in traditional gold filigree. Her mask consists of matching gold and black detailing, butterfly wings obscuring half of her face entirely. I cannot see her eyes in the dimly lit room, and I am glad for it. I don't doubt beneath that mask there is an expression of hatred. But for tonight, it will be as though those feelings don't exist.

Mercedes looks exceptionally pleased with herself as she crooks her finger, gesturing for my wife to come to us.

"Is it everything you wished for?" she whispers as Ivy moves forward stiffly.

"It is," I answer darkly.

Ivy takes the stairs slowly, clutching the railing as the guards follow her. When she reaches the bottom, she nearly stumbles, and I step forward to catch her in my arms, only for her to right herself and recoil from my touch.

"I'm fine," she says coolly. "There is no need for the pretense of concern."

Her biting words are a reminder that turmoil lingers in her thoughts, but by all rights, she should expect to be punished for speaking in such a tone, regardless of her feelings. However, I find that I am not in the mood to punish her right now, and I suspect that it will not improve her feelings of attending our first event together as a married couple. I need tonight to go well. The Society has expectations of their Sovereign Sons, and part of those expectations are a smooth integration of their chosen partner into the upper echelon. It is my duty to take Ivy to the masquerade gala tonight and show her off. Every man will be envious of me when they see her, and I take pleasure in knowing it. There can be no exceptions to her performance as a dutiful wife.

Mercedes glances at me questioningly, waiting for my reaction to Ivy's bitterness. I am aware it will only further her contention when I forcibly take my wife's arm and lead her to the door without another word. My sister follows behind, and we all converge at the car where Marco is waiting to drive us.

The journey to the compound is stilted with silence. Mercedes stews on one side of me, and Ivy on the other. None of us speak, but when we arrive, I tell Mercedes to go inside without us. We exit the car, and I hold back to study my wife. Her blood-red lips are tempting me beneath the streetlight. Veiled in mystery, draped in black and gold, she has never been so beautiful.

I drag her close to my body, even as she resists, my lips brushing against the shell of her ear. "You know what is expected of you this evening."

"Yes," she bites back.

Despite the harshness of her tone, I can feel the tremble in her muscles as I press my body firmly against hers. Is it a sign of her fear or her unwanted desire?

Darkness settles over me as I conclude it is of course fear. It can never be anything else.

"Be good, and you will be rewarded," I tell her. "Misbehave, and I will make you beg for mercy."

She turns her face away from me, and I release her only to settle my palm over my mark on the nape of her neck, guiding her inside the compound and down the corridor to the ballroom. Two men in suits open the doors for us, ushering us inside the space reserved for the biggest events of the year. Rich shades of crimson and black adorn the walls, and to my satisfaction, the grand chandeliers cast only a soft glow over the floor, in keeping with the mystery of the evening. The seductive notes of jazz float from the speakers, luring us into the center of the room.

Within moments, a waiter appears, offering us each a glass of champagne. Ivy reaches out for one, only to have it commandeered by my fingers with a dark look cast her way.

I swirl the glass in my hand, sniffing the alcohol before I drain it in two swallows. Once it is returned to the tray and the server disappears, Ivy peers up at me with a cold smile.

"There's no need to refuse me a drink," she says sweetly. "It seems you have not done your job and produced a child in me. Perhaps, I was wrong about your potency after all."

My fingertips dig into her arm as I glare down at her. I was already aware of her unwanted visitor this morning. Antonia informed me with a whispered voice before she shuffled away and left me to stew in my irritation. But Ivy is being purposely spiteful, and I will not have that. I am considering my reproach when another masked man appears. He is well dressed in a formal suit, and his presence here means he is a Sovereign Son. But I don't recognize who he could be until he speaks in a low greeting.

"Santiago." He dips his head in a nod. "Would you mind having a word?"

I am surprised to find it is Angelo lurking beneath the mask, still clearly in disguise. I did not expect to see him again, particularly in New Orleans, as I assumed he would be back in Seattle dealing with his own revenge plans.

I nod and look at my wife before my eyes find my sister across the room.

"Go join Mercedes," I tell her. "She can introduce you to a few people while I have a word."

"I'm going to the bathroom." She tilts her chin up at me defiantly. "And then I will join your sister. But I don't need her introductions. I'm perfectly capable of conducting myself."

I lean down to growl in her ear, gripping her arm in warning. "Then you can start by watching how you speak to me. Don't fool yourself into believing I won't punish you in public. In fact, I would take great pleasure in doing so for all my brethren to witness. Don't test me, Ivy."

She yanks herself away and gathers a handful of the fabric of her dress, treating us to a view of her exposed back as she stalks away and disappears into the crowd.

32

As soon as I am out of his line of vision, I take a flute of champagne off a passing waiter's tray. I half expect someone to stop me. My husband has eyes and ears everywhere. But no one does, and I turn to glance casually over my shoulder as I bring the crystal to my lips and sip.

I don't actually like champagne per se, but I want the slightly heady feeling I know the bubbles will bring. I don't plan on getting drunk. I know what that will do to me. But tonight, I need just this little bit.

All around me, men and women float about the rooms of The Society's main house in the center of the French Quarter talking, laughing, drinking. Some wear elaborate masks, others simple ones. The women's gowns are beautiful, each one more so than the last. I see them looking at me, too, both the men and the women. Do they know who I am?

I touch the back of my neck with my left hand, his ring heavy on my finger. Those are the only things that would give me away. The tattoo and his ring.

I glance at my hand. It's not as recognizable as his. Not like the monstrosity some of the men around me wear. The Sovereign Sons and the rings bearing their crests, their link to IVI. Like a status symbol of the elite. It's disgusting.

At least Santiago's isn't horrendous like some I see tonight. Like the one I remember Holton wearing during my exam. I scan the room, remembering my brother's request. Remembering if I get him information, he'll bring Evangeline to see me. But when I do finally find him, recognizing him through his half mask, I realize I couldn't tell my brother what he wants to know anyway because I can't see the other man's face, and even if I did, I probably wouldn't recognize him.

Still, I walk closer, keeping my head down as if I were just making my way across the room. When I get near the two men, I look at Holton's companion's hand and take in his ring. He moves his hand quickly, though, so all I can make out is what looks like two hammers, which can't be right. I'll need to figure out a way to ask Santiago tonight.

Slipping behind cover in a corner, I watch my husband. He's still talking to the same man. They're thick as thieves, and I wonder what they could be discussing. The masks they wear are among those that hide the most. Santiago, I understand. He doesn't like people looking at him. I wonder what the other man has to hide.

When Santiago raises his head to look in my direction, I quickly turn to walk away. I don't think he can see me here through all these people, but maybe I'm wrong. I can see him clearly enough, after all.

I hurry out of the elaborately decorated room and out into the courtyard. I pass the place where we had the marking ceremony. It's so different now. Not so ominous. The canopy of roses and vines is gone. The ornate chair and table nowhere in sight. No brands smoking in any fires. I look down at the ground and see the only thing that suggests anything like that ever took place here at all. The small ring between the stones he attached my leash to.

My leash.

Jerk.

But at least he didn't make me wear that rosary tonight.

The voices around me fade as I stretch my foot out to touch it with the toe of my flat sandals. I didn't wear the heels Mercedes provided knowing I'd have Santiago's support if it came to it. But I should remember it's not out of concern for me. If I trip and break my neck, his toy will be gone.

Mercedes's words sting me again, and I swallow the rest of the bubbly champagne to numb their impact. When I look up, I notice more eyes on me and hear whispers around me.

God. I'm as paranoid as Abel. They're not talking about me. They don't even know who I am under this mask. That's one thing Mercedes did well. She's hidden my face. I'm sure this privacy she's afforded me in the midst of all this wasn't intentional, even if the mask is irritating and hinders my peripheral vision.

I set my glass on the pedestal of the statue behind which the girl had hidden on our wedding night, only realizing then where I'm headed as the voices fade behind me and the corridor grows darker. I reach out my hands to touch the walls on either side of me as it narrows, and from here, I can already smell incense.

It's not a comfort. My association with the church is linked to the nuns who were rarely kind, but when I reach the doors, I don't hesitate. I push one open and slip inside and away from all those people. There is a comfort in that, at least, and in the red glow of the tabernacle lamp. A constant.

I reach back to untie the mask and slip it off as I step deeper into the chapel.

My heart skips when I look at the altar and up at the crucified Christ. As I remember what we did here. What would Sister Mary Anthony think of her Sovereign Son if she only knew?

The thought of it makes me giggle. Or maybe that's the champagne.

Someone clears their throat then, and I startle. That and movement at the back of the chapel draw my attention, and I feel instinctively guilty. But I need to remind myself that I'm not doing anything wrong. Even if Santiago were to find me here, he certainly couldn't accuse me of anything.

"I just..." a soft voice starts. She steps out of the shadows. "I was lighting a candle." She's holding a long thin white candle in her hand. She's not wearing a mask, and I recognize her instantly. She's looking at me with the same wide, almost frightened eyes.

It's the girl who'd hidden behind the statue the night of the marking ceremony.

I smile. "Sorry. I didn't know anyone was in here." I realize when she turns that she's pregnant. I hadn't noticed it before. I'd only seen her face, and even that partially, and I hadn't noticed it now, either, not when I first saw her a moment ago. She has one hand under her belly, the tight moss green dress she's wearing accentuating its roundness against her otherwise petite frame. I see how her wavy strawberry-blond hair falls to her waist down her back.

She sets the candle in the holder, mutters a prayer in Latin, and bows her head as she makes the sign of the cross, then turns to me. She's pretty. And young. My age, I guess. I watch as she walks down the center of the aisle more swiftly than I'd guess she could with her oversized belly. She stoops to pick something up from one of the pews. Her mask.

"You're Santiago De La Rosa's bride."

I nod as she comes to stand a few feet from me, mask in one hand.

"I'm Colette." She extends her free hand.

"Ivy," I say, shaking hers. It's small and hardly a handshake at all.

"It was getting a little much out there," she says and holds her mask up, then lays her hand on her belly again. She takes a seat on the edge of the closest pew and bends down a little, trying to reach for something.

That's when I notice she's barefoot and what she's reaching for are a pair of strappy golden sandals that must have a four-inch spiked heel.

"Here, let me get them." I stoop to pick them up and set them where she can slip her feet inside. "Those can't be comfortable. I mean, with..." I gesture to her belly.

She smiles wide, showing a row of perfect white

teeth. "They're not comfortable when I'm not pregnant either. But you know how they are." She gestures to the door, and I assume she means men in general.

I sit beside her and nod, wondering about her. Why would her husband make her wear those shoes when she's obviously not comfortable?

"When are you due?" I ask her.

"I still have three months to go!" She looks down at her belly. "I hope he comes sooner, honestly. I'm pretty sure he's ten pounds already."

"He?"

She nods as she squeezes her foot into the sandal. "Damn."

"What is it?"

"My feet have swollen so much. I probably shouldn't have taken them off in the first place."

"What size are you?"

"Seven and a half normally but these days, eight."

"Here," I say, slipping my feet out of my flat sandals. "We can swap. I mean, if you want. They're not as pretty as yours, but they're a size eight and probably more comfortable than those."

She looks at my sandals, then at me. "I swear mine are torture devices, Ivy," she says, trying for a laugh.

"They look it. I don't mind. These are a little big on me anyway."

"Are you sure?"

I nod, some part of me wondering how I'm going to walk in the spikey heels, but I'll make it work.

"Thank you. Really." She smiles so warmly I wonder again how much we have in common within The Society.

"I'm happy to do it."

"I have your veil," she says, surprising me.

"What?" I ask, tying the sandals. They're a little tight but not too bad.

She turns to me. "I came in here that night. When...the marking." She lets her gaze drift like she's embarrassed for me, and I wonder if she saw us in here. If she saw what he did. No, that's not possible. She was out near the courtyard, but maybe she guessed.

"Oh."

"I repaired the tear." She clears her throat as if just realizing how awkward this conversation is about to get. "I can bring it to you. I mean, if you want it."

"You repaired it?"

"I like to sew, and it was such a pretty veil. It was a shame not to."

"Thank you." I'm not sure honestly that I want it back, but I do want a friend. I could use one, and she seems nice. And a little like me, maybe.

"Should you be home, Colette? I mean," I start,

looking at her stomach, "you don't look very comfortable."

She smiles and shrugs a shoulder. "Jackson likes these gatherings, so well, I'll be fine."

"Jackson is your husband?"

"Yes. Jackson van der Smit."

"I don't know the name. I'm sorry."

"It's okay. You're not one of...I mean, Mr. De La Rosa chose..." She breaks off. "That's all coming out wrong."

"Don't worry about it," I say, realizing she means to say I'm not from one of the upper-echelon families. I guess she must be to know.

"I just meant you couldn't know. I didn't mean to sound arrogant. I mean, I hate that whole thing."

"It's okay. You didn't sound arrogant."

She does something unexpected then. She turns to squarely face me and takes my hands into hers. "Are you doing okay, Ivy?"

Her question makes me want to cry. Makes me wish I'd kept my mask on. I pull my hands away and shift my gaze down.

"I know it's hard at first," she continues when I don't answer. "All their requirements and The Society, and well, it gets easier."

"Does it? I'm not so sure for me." I can't help the tear that slips out, but she doesn't comment when I wipe it away.

She takes my hand again. "You know I don't live

too far from you. Jackson's family home is just a few miles away. I mean, if you come over, you'll have to deal with his grandmother." She makes a face, and again, I wonder how old she is. "She's a mean old witch, I swear."

I have to laugh at how she says it.

"I'll talk to Jackson if you like, and he can talk to your husband, and then maybe you can come over for a visit."

"I'd really like that." Again, I have to wipe away tears. How pathetic is your life when a stranger's kindness makes you cry? And how much more pathetic that two grown women need to ask permission of their husbands to have a visit?

A gong goes off then and Colette gasps, looking at the diamond-encrusted watch on her delicate wrist. "Shoot! That's dinner. We'd better go. They'll miss us now." She adjusts her mask and stands, a sense of urgency about her.

I stand too and put my mask to my face. She helps me to tie it.

"It really will get better." She takes my hand and squeezes it before releasing it once we get to the door. "I promise."

I smile and am grateful again for the mask.

"Colette, there you are," a man says, and Colette gives my hand one more squeeze before hurrying to him.

The moment she's gone, I hear the sound of

Mercedes's laughter coming from behind me, and I don't bother to turn around to confirm it's her. Instead, I hurry to find a bathroom because I'm sure Santiago is looking for me by now too, and I need a new place to hide away for a little while.

33

A ngelo removes a flask from his jacket pocket, taking a drink before he offers it to me. When I smell the smoked scotch, I help myself as well before returning it to him.

"I didn't expect your visit to last so long," I say. "Have you been here all this time?"

"No." He shakes his head. "I have been up North, gathering information. Which is what brings me to my visit. I have some accounts I'd like you to look over. I need to know who opened them. There is no one else I trust."

"You never have to ask," I assure him. "My loyalty is never in question. Provide me the details, and I will trace everything I can."

He nods stiffly. "I will deliver them to you personally before my flight leaves at sunrise."

"I take it you won't be staying for tonight's events then?"

He scans the room, shaking his head. "No. I just came here to see you."

"Very well. Then I will let you make your escape. I'll expect you in the early morning hours."

He dips his chin, returning to the fray just as quickly as he arrived, vanishing within moments. I take my leave after him, seeking out my sister and my wife. But before I can find them together, it appears Ivy has found me.

She approaches me with a feline smile, pushing me back into the darkness with a firm palm against my chest.

"What are you doing?" I demand.

Her response is to drag her fingertips up the nape of my neck to curl into my hair, grabbing a handful as she leans up on her toes to brush her lips against mine. The unexpected kiss renders me temporarily paralyzed, and she takes advantage of my shock, smearing her blood-red lipstick across my mouth as she forces her tongue between my lips.

It's aggressive. Violent. And strange.

I'm kissing her back without a thought and thinking of what else I'd like to do to her tonight. But something about her sudden change of mood makes me question her motives. It starts as a small irritation, and quickly evolves into full-blown paranoia. When I grab her by the hair and pull her away from my face to examine her, the room seems to tilt. I blink slowly, trying to comprehend what I'm seeing, but she is little more than a blur as my hand falls away from her. Everything around me appears to sway as I try to find balance, and before I realize what's happening, I'm grasping at my chest. My heart is a hammer against my ribs as I stumble back, attempting to catch my breath. Sweat beads on my forehead, and a piercing pain stabs through my skull as I fall onto my knees, gasping for air.

I can't breathe.

Someone screams, and then there are low murmurs as I collapse onto my back, body convulsing against the hard marble. The last conscious effort I am able to make is to force my lips apart, trying desperately to suck in air. But none comes.

My head lolls to the side, and the life begins to slip from my body with one last fleeting thought. My wife truly is a Moreno, and she just gave me the kiss of death.

34

I spend the next ten minutes sitting on the lush velvet couch in the bathroom, listening to the sound of music and laughter and people coming from beyond the door. I know I have to get back. He's definitely missing me by now, and I'm surprised no one is banging the door down.

Reluctantly I get up, look at my reflection, and reapply lipstick, a deep red that I'm sure my mother would approve of. Mercedes made sure I took the tube with me so I could freshen up. She doesn't want me looking bad. It would make people talk, and since I'm a De La Rosa now, it matters, so I smear it off with the back of my hand. A small rebellion.

I hear another gong, and with a groan, I go to the door. But just as I get there, I hear a woman's scream, the shrillness of it sending a chill through me that stops me in my tracks.

Mercedes?

I turn the lock on the door and twist the handle, but when I do, nothing happens.

Loud voices and another scream pierce the strange silence that seems to have fallen just beyond my door.

"Santiago?" I call out, a panic seizing me as I try the handle again only to find it jammed. "Is anyone there?" I cry out, banging on the door, trying the handle again and again to no avail.

Something shatters outside like a server has just dropped a tray of crystal champagne glasses.

I yank off my mask and throw it to the floor.

"Mercedes?" I call out, my purse slipping to the floor as I bang with both fists. "Santiago!"

I bang and bang, but I chose this bathroom because it was the farthest from the room where long tables were set for dinner, so maybe there's no one here.

"Someone let me out!" Just as I say the words, I turn the handle for the hundredth time, and this time, it gives, and I'm not expecting it to so when the door flies open, I stumble backward falling against the wall.

I straighten, then run through the door to where a crowd of people have gathered. Where someone is barking orders. I know the sirens I hear are coming toward us as I shove my way through, knowing I have to see. Feeling deep in my belly that whatever has just happened is very bad.

And when I get there, when I see, I can't process right at first.

Mercedes is screaming. She's on her knees, and on the floor is a man, and I know it's him. I don't even have to see the discarded mask, the strange skull he wore. Like a dead man's mask. Like the ink on his face.

"Santiago?" My eyes fill with tears as I put my hand on someone's shoulder to push them out of the way. To see.

And I do.

I see his pale skin. His dark eyes unfocused, then closed.

"Santiago?" I ask again, my voice a whisper.

He doesn't respond, but Mercedes hears me.

"You!" she accuses.

I shift my gaze to her, the venom in her eyes almost making me topple backward.

"You!" she hisses, pointing her finger at me.

I shake my head, open my mouth to speak. To explain... but explain what? The medical crew rushes in. People follow Mercedes's accusing gaze and turn to me, and then there's a sound, a thud in the distance, and in the next instant, the room is plunged into darkness, a black so solid, so thick the women around me scream, and I feel hands on me, clutching me, nails digging into me as chaos breaks out.

The dark and the noise are dizzying, the look on Mercedes's face before the lights went out terrifying. That on Santiago's indescribable.

Dead?

No. It can't be. He can't be. Not Santiago.

A beam of light illuminates the space where his body lies. I try to push through to get to him. To see for myself.

"No pulse," a man says, his voice carrying over that of the crowd.

No pulse? They can't mean that.

"...start compressions..."

I open my mouth. I don't know if it's to scream or call his name or to tell everyone to get out of my way. He can't be dead. He can't. But there are too many people. And just when I'm about to shove hard, something wraps around my middle. I'm pulled into a man's grasp, arm like a solid steel bar circling my ribs, crushing them as I'm lifted off my feet, the lights blinking once, twice coming back on just as I'm taken from that room to another, this one deserted.

The man sets me on my feet, and I stumble, then turn to face him. He's wearing a dark cloak with a deep hood that he pulls back to reveal a masked face like all the others.

My mouth goes dry. The sound from the other room background now. White noise.

No, his mask isn't like the others.

His is one of menace.

I cringe away, turning in a desperate attempt to find an exit, seeing only the door behind him as he stalks toward me, backing me into a corner.

"What do you want?" I scream when my back hits the wall.

He doesn't speak, though. Instead, his fingers come to my jaw, an iron grip. My hands claw at his forearm, but it's no use. He's too strong. And one jerk of his wrist is all it takes for the back of my head to smash against the wall.

That's when he steps backward.

When I stumble forward.

Stars dance before my eyes, and the room spins.

I reach out to steady myself, but there is nothing to hold onto, only air. He's saying something but I can't quite make out his words as my knees buckle, and I drop to the floor.

That's when I feel his hands on me. Powerful arms lifting me. The room going black around me, arms hanging limp and useless as he carries me out of the compound and into the night.

THANK YOU

Thank you for reading **Requiem of the Soul.** *We hope you loved Santiago and Ivy.*

Their story continues in **Reparation of Sin.**
One-click Reparation of Sin here.

ALSO BY NATASHA KNIGHT

To Have and To Hold

With This Ring

I Thee Take

Stolen: Dante's Vow

The Society Trilogy

Requiem of the Soul

Reparation of Sin

Resurrection of the Heart

Dark Legacy Trilogy

Taken (Dark Legacy, Book 1)

Torn (Dark Legacy, Book 2)

Twisted (Dark Legacy, Book 3)

Unholy Union Duet

Unholy Union

Unholy Intent

Collateral Damage Duet

Collateral: an Arranged Marriage Mafia Romance

Damage: an Arranged Marriage Mafia Romance

Ties that Bind Duet

Mine

His

MacLeod Brothers

Devil's Bargain

Benedetti Mafia World

Salvatore: a Dark Mafia Romance

Dominic: a Dark Mafia Romance

Sergio: a Dark Mafia Romance

The Benedetti Brothers Box Set (Contains Salvatore, Dominic and Sergio)

Killian: a Dark Mafia Romance

Giovanni: a Dark Mafia Romance

The Amado Brothers

Dishonorable

Disgraced

Unhinged

Standalone Dark Romance

Descent

Deviant

Beautiful Liar

Retribution

Theirs To Take

Captive, Mine

Alpha

Given to the Savage

Taken by the Beast

Claimed by the Beast

Captive's Desire

Protective Custody

Amy's Strict Doctor

Taming Emma

Taming Megan

Taming Naia

Reclaiming Sophie

The Firefighter's Girl

Dangerous Defiance

Her Rogue Knight

Taught To Kneel

Tamed: the Roark Brothers Trilogy

ALSO BY A. ZAVARELLI

Boston Underworld Series

CROW: Boston Underworld #1

REAPER: Boston Underworld #2

GHOST: Boston Underworld #3

SAINT: Boston Underworld #4

THIEF: Boston Underworld #5

CONOR: Boston Underworld #6

Sin City Salvation Series

Confess

Convict

Bleeding Hearts Series

Echo: A Bleeding Hearts Novel Volume One

Stutter: A Bleeding Hearts Novel Volume Two

Twisted Ever After Series

BEAST: Twisted Ever After #1

Standalones

Tap Left

Hate Crush

For a complete list of books and audios, visit http://www.azavarelli.com/books

ABOUT A. ZAVARELLI

A. Zavarelli is a USA Today and Amazon bestselling author of dark and contemporary romance.

When she's not putting her characters through hell, she can usually be found watching bizarre and twisted documentaries in the name of research.

She currently lives in the Northwest with her lumberjack and an entire brood of fur babies.

Want to stay up to date on Ashleigh and Natasha's releases? Sign up for our newsletters here: https://landing.mailerlite.com/webforms/landing/x3s0k6

ABOUT NATASHA KNIGHT

Natasha Knight is the *USA Today* Bestselling author of Romantic Suspense and Dark Romance Novels. She has sold over half a million books and is translated into six languages. She currently lives in The Netherlands with her husband and two daughters and when she's not writing, she's walking in the woods listening to a book, sitting in a corner reading or off exploring the world as often as she can get away.

Write Natasha here: natasha@natasha-knight.com

Click here to sign up for my newsletter to receive new release news and updates!

NATASHA KNIGHT

www.natasha-knight.com
natasha-knight@outlook.com

Made in United States
Orlando, FL
09 October 2022

23174014R00202